The Lost Property Office

Also by James R. Hannibal

The Fourth Ruby
(SECTION 13, BOOK 2)

— SECTION 13 · BOOK 1 —

The Lost Property Office

James R. Hannibal

Simon & Schuster Books for Young Readers

New York   London   Toronto   Sydney   New Delhi

SIMON & SCHUSTER BOOKS FOR YOUNG READERS
An imprint of Simon & Schuster Children's Publishing Division
1230 Avenue of the Americas, New York, New York 10020

This book is a work of fiction. Any references to historical events, real people, or real places are used fictitiously. Other names, characters, places, and events are products of the author's imagination, and any resemblance to actual events or places or persons, living or dead, is entirely coincidental.

SIMON & SCHUSTER BOOKS FOR YOUNG READERS
is a trademark of Simon & Schuster, Inc.
For information about special discounts for bulk purchases, please contact Simon & Schuster Special Sales at 1-866-506-1949 or business@simonandschuster.com.
The Simon & Schuster Speakers Bureau can bring authors to your live event. For more information or to book an event, contact the Simon & Schuster Speakers Bureau at 1-866-248-3049 or visit our website at www.simonspeakers.com.
Also available in a Simon & Schuster Books for Young Readers hardcover edition
Book design by Lizzy Bromley
The text for this book was set in Weiss.
Manufactured in the United States of America
0917 OFF
First Simon & Schuster Books for Young Readers paperback edition October 2017
2 4 6 8 10 9 7 5 3 1
The Library of Congress has cataloged the hardcover edition as follows:
Names: Hannibal, James R., author.
Title: The Lost Property Office / James R. Hannibal.
Description: First edition. | New York : Simon & Schuster Books for Young Readers, [2016] | Series: Section 13 ; book 1 | Summary: "An American boy travels with his family to London for his mother to find his father, but it turns out his father was involved with something nefarious . . . and now so is he"—Provided by publisher.
Identifiers: LCCN 2015045654| ISBN 9781481467094 (hardback) | ISBN 9781481467100 (paperback) | ISBN 9781481467117 (eBook)
Subjects: | CYAC: Mystery and detective stories. | Missing persons—Fiction. | Secret societies—Fiction. | Americans—England—London—Fiction. | London (England)—Fiction. | England—Fiction. | BISAC: JUVENILE FICTION / Fantasy & Magic. | JUVENILE FICTION / Mysteries & Detective Stories. | JUVENILE FICTION / Action & Adventure / General.
Classification: LCC PZ7.1.H3638 Lo 2016 | DDC [Fic]—dc23
LC record available at https://lccn.loc.gov/2015045654

This story is dedicated to

ALL THE TRACKERS OUT THERE.

You know who you are.

'Well ... perhaps you don't.

BUT YOU'LL LEARN

soon enough.

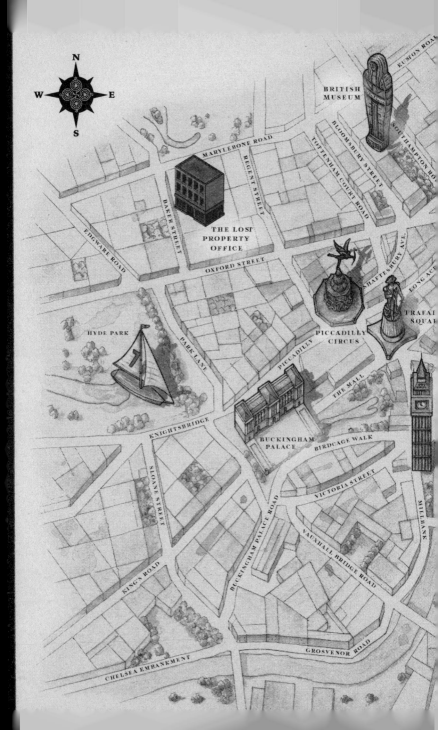

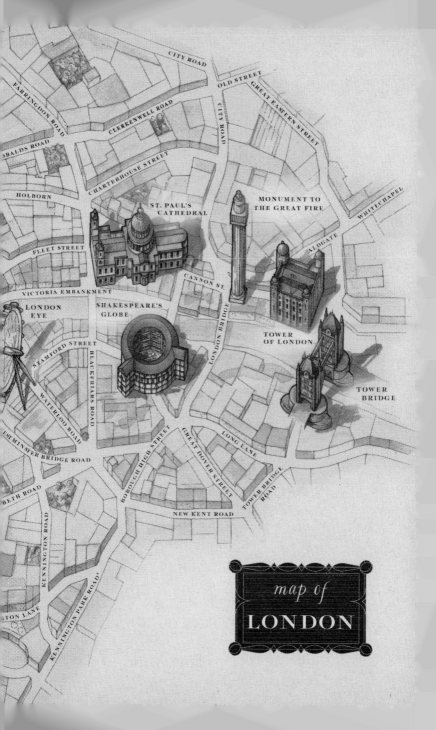

map of

LONDON

Chapter 1

A PAIR OF RATHER LARGE, blue-green beetles buzzed north over the River Thames, weaving back and forth over the water's surface in that haphazard pattern that beetles fly. Had they bothered to look, the early-morning joggers in London's Victoria Tower Gardens—wrapped up against the December cold in their leggings and winter caps—might have caught the glint of the rising sun reflecting off iridescent wings. Had they looked even closer, they might even have wondered if those wings were made of some strange metal alloy.

But they did not look. No one ever does.

The bugs did not go entirely unnoticed. A pike leaped out of the river and snatched one from the air for breakfast.

As the fish splashed down with its meal, the remaining beetle halted its progress and hovered, buzzing impatiently. The murky brown depths lit up with a muted blue flash and the pike floated lifeless to the surface, a look of dreadful shock in its round eye. The captured beetle crawled out of its gill, shook off a bit of fish goo with an indignant flutter of its clockwork wings, and rejoined its companion in flight.

The beetles left the Thames at Parliament and flew skyward, hugging the eastern wall of the House of Lords. Upon reaching the rooftop, they continued north, dodging dozens of Gothic spires and hundreds of pigeon spikes, before climbing again, this time flying up the southern wall of the Great Clock Tower—known to the world as Big Ben. They alighted on the giant minute hand, rested a moment to watch the long morning shadow of the tower recede along Bridge Street, and then, with the rapid clicking of six metal legs apiece, they crawled down to the hub and wound their way inside.

In the quiet chamber below the clock, Constable Henry Biddle sipped his morning tea. Certainly, sitting in an uncomfortable folding chair and guarding the door to an old staircase was not the post he envisioned when he had joined the Metropolitan Police the year before, but one had to start a career in law enforcement somewhere. Besides, left unguarded, the rickety iron stairs and the open-air bell platform at the top were a real danger to overcurious tourists.

A dull, metallic *clunk* interrupted Biddle midway through a long sip. He lowered his paper cup and turned in his seat to stare at the lock on the upper stairwell door. He stared, in fact, for quite some time, but the old iron lock made no other sound.

Odd. Biddle gave the door a frown to let it know who was in charge, then returned his gaze to the lower stairwell door across the chamber and raised his tea again. Once more, he was interrupted by a noise—static from his radio. He let out a dissatisfied grunt as he set the tea down next to his chair. Couldn't a man have some peace at the start of a long shift?

"Nigel, I couldn't read your last," he said, raising the radio. "If you're looking for a report, all's quiet in the upper stairwell." Even as he made the transmission, Biddle noticed movement on the radio. He held it farther from his face and saw an enormous beetle perched on the dial, beautiful, with shimmering faceted wings and silvery legs. If it hadn't

3

moved, he would have taken it for a jeweled trinket. "Oi. Bug. What're you doing there?"

The beetle's wings quivered. "All's quiet in the upper stairwell."

Biddle's eyes widened at the sound of his own voice. "What the devil—"

The bug launched itself straight at Biddle's face. A resounding *zap* and a blue-white flash filled the chamber, followed by a light *sizzle* and the lingering scent of burning hair. The constable slumped in his chair. His checkered hat fell from his head, knocking over the paper cup and sending a river of tea winding through the joints and crevices of the old stone floor.

The chamber remained silent for several seconds, with the beetles hovering patiently over their victim, until a man in a long black overcoat and a black fedora emerged from the lower stairwell. He swept past the stricken constable, through the door, and up the spiral staircase, with the two beetles heeling at his shoulder like a pair of well-trained hounds.

The man in black climbed right past the great gears and the giant, two-story clockface, all the way up to the belfry, where he stepped through one of the tall, arched windows, out onto the western balcony. There, he leaned against the iron rail, surveying St. James's Park, and his clockwork beetles hovered before his grizzled face, bobbling against the breeze in the effort to hold their position. "Wind's from the north, no?" he asked, a French accent coloring his English. He let the bugs come to rest on a gloved finger. "Not for long, *mes amis*. Papa will see to that."

The Frenchman peeled back the lapel of his overcoat, revealing a deep inner pocket that undulated with the creeping movement of whatever nested inside, and the two clockwork bugs happily fluttered over to join in. Their master then bent to scrutinize the rail posts, his eye mere inches from the black-painted iron. He fixated on the center post, holding his ear close to the knob and knocking on it with his knuckle. He tried giving it a twist, but it wouldn't budge. After a frown and another careful knock to confirm his suspicions, he tried again, this time twisting with both hands. With a great *crack*, the knob finally gave.

Once loosened, the ornament turned easily, and the man in black removed it and placed it in his outer pocket. From the opposite pocket, he withdrew a copper weather vane, green with age and formed in the silhouette of a tall ship. The instrument fit the post as if it belonged there, and he turned it to point the prow of the ship at Buckingham Palace. The northern breeze dropped to a standstill. A fraction of a second later, he felt the barest breath of wind from the west, and grinned. "*Voilà*. All is set in motion. Now, let us see about poor, lucky Jack."

Chapter 2

"WHERE IS IT? I know I had it last night."

Jack Buckles was vaguely aware of his mother bustling about their small London hotel room, checking drawers and lifting up magazines. He tried to ignore her, nose buried in his smartphone, playing a 3-D game that required him to search goblin tunnels and orc dens for wizards' gems, but when she dropped to her knees right in front of him to check under the bed, he couldn't take it anymore. He sighed, still battling a goblin with his thumbs. "What're you looking for?"

"Glove. Red leather." She reached up and flopped its twin back and forth in front of his face. "Matches this one."

Thirteen-year-old Jack and his eight-year-old sister, Sadie, sat cross-legged, side by side on one of the room's two queen-size beds. Without looking up from his game, Jack grabbed the loose fabric of Sadie's jeans and tipped her backward. Sadie did not protest. She kept both hands on her e-reader and let Jack rock her back into the pillows, uncrossing her legs and flopping them down on the comforter to form a V. Jack held his arm straight out to the side and pointed down. There, between his sister's knees, sat the missing glove.

His mom let out a little laugh—a sort of sad chuckle. "Amazing. Just like your dad."

Jack cringed. He hadn't meant to do anything that would remind her of *him*.

She kissed his head as she retrieved the glove, pausing for a few uncomfortable seconds to hover over him and smooth out his mop of deep brown hair. As soon as she turned away, Jack raised a hand to mess it up again.

His mom put an arm into her dark blue peacoat. "I have several hospitals to visit, Jack. With all the forms I'll have to fill out, it may take all day. Jack, are you listening?"

He nodded, still playing his game. "Yeah, Mom. Red tape. Gone all day." He didn't mean to sound as sarcastic as he did, but he made no effort to take it back either.

She frowned. "I know the circumstances are tough, especially after yesterday, but—"

8

"Tough?" Jack shifted his eyes up from the phone, just enough for a glare. It was the first time he had looked her in the eye since they got off the plane from Denver the morning before, and what he saw in her eyes caught him off guard. His mom didn't look like she wanted to argue—far from it. At that moment, she looked as if some merciless force was about to crush her where she stood. Tears pooled in her eyes, threatening to come pouring down. "I'm sorry, Jack. I'm so sorry about all of this."

Jack shot a sideways glance at Sadie. Her head was still back on the pillows, auburn hair—the same color as her mother's—spilling out in all directions, eyes fixed on her digital book. He dropped his eyes to his phone again. "Don't, Mom. Just . . . don't."

In the long silence that followed, Jack knew she was looking at him. He hunched his shoulders under the weight of his mother's sad gaze, willing her to hold it together. He didn't want to be this cold. He really didn't. He wanted to take her hands, tell her that none of this was her fault. He wanted to cry into her shoulder. But he couldn't. Jack knew what would happen if he looked his mother in the eye. He would lose it. And if he lost it, she would lose it too, and Sadie would start asking questions that neither of them wanted to answer. Not until they had answers to give.

So Jack kept his head down. Another goblin appeared on the screen. He slashed through it with a vengeance and it vanished in a pillar of green flame.

Jack's mom dabbed her eyes with the wayward glove, then tucked her hair into a red knitted beret and kissed both her children on their cheeks, as if she were merely heading off to the store. "Do your best to entertain each other while I'm gone. There *are* games that don't require screens, you know—games you can play together, like I Spy." She let the suggestion hang in the air, and Jack knew she wanted a response, at least a laugh or a grunt. He gave her neither.

His mom placed a hand on his knee. "If you get hungry, buy something from the café downstairs." She took him by the chin and gently lifted his face. "Something *small*, Jack."

He pulled away. "Yeah, Mom. I know. Future uncertain. Eat cheap."

"Whatever you do, *do not* leave this hotel. Got it?"

"Yeah. Got it."

She stared down at the top of his head for another second, then sighed and walked to the door. "Okay, then. I'm off to find your father."

Chapter 3

SADIE SAT UP on the bed, dropping her hands to her lap so that her e-reader hit her legs with a melodramatic *slap*. "I'm bored."

"No you're not." Jack winced as another goblin took a swipe at him with its dagger. He had searched the orc dens and found nothing but a rock telling him to go back to the goblin tunnels—a wild-goose chase. He could practically hear the guy who'd designed the game laughing at him, but Jack was in too deep to quit. If he could only find the red gem and return it to the wizard, he would level up and become a wizard's apprentice. He thumbed his character left for a dodge and chopped his enemy in half. Ice-blue flame lit up the screen. "Mom's only been gone five minutes."

"She's been gone ten minutes. And how do you know if I'm bored or not?" Sadie pushed the e-reader out of her lap and onto the comforter, then bounced herself around to face the pillows, causing Jack to sway back and forth on the mattress. After arranging and rearranging the pillows on her side, she crawled behind her brother to get at the rest, bumping into him repeatedly as she worked. He knew she was doing it on purpose, but he ignored her.

Sadie huffed, bounced, huffed again, rearranged pillows, bumped into her brother, huffed a little louder and bounced again, and then finally bumped Jack so hard that he missed an attack and got slashed by a goblin's blade. His screen flashed red. He flopped the phone down on his knee and looked hard at his sister, who was now standing directly in front of him. "Seriously?"

"Let's watch TV."

"Mom doesn't want you to watch British TV, Sadie."

"She never said that."

"She didn't have to. Besides, Americans can't understand British TV shows."

Sadie folded her arms. "I'm not stupid. London people speak the same language we do."

"Don't say stupid. And that's not what I meant."

12

In truth, Jack did not want to watch television. There was always too much going on, too much to notice, and his brain had a tendency to notice everything whether he wanted it to or not. That was why he always retreated to his smartphone. He used it as a refuge from a world that perpetually closed in around him, crowding him to the point of exhaustion. Lately he had also been using it as a refuge from his own thoughts, and Sadie's interruption was bringing them back again. He handed her the e-reader. "You have lots of games on this thing. Play one."

That seemed to placate her. Sadie plopped down on the mattress and raised the device above her head. Thirty seconds later, she dropped it onto her lap again. "I'm *sooo* hungry."

Jack dropped his forehead into his palm. "You are *not* hungry. You had a granola bar for breakfast like ten minutes before Mom left. That was only fifteen minutes ago."

"Twenty minutes. And stop telling me what I am. Mom said we could go downstairs if we got hungry."

Jack started to counter but stopped himself. Years of forced togetherness while their dad was off doing whatever international sales associates did had taught him a few things about little sisters. Arguing would get him nowhere. *Bargaining,* however, always worked. And being older and wiser meant he could skew the deal in his favor. "Fine. If I get you something to eat, you have to be quiet for at least four hours."

Sadie popped up off the bed. "Deal!"

Too easy. He should have asked for six.

The Eurotrek Lodge had little in the way of amenities. There was a buffet restaurant for dinner and a tiny café in the lobby for everything else. Jack selected a ham and cheese and let Sadie pick out a strawberry Danish. She also wanted a soda, but Jack was old enough to know that little girls and sugar highs didn't mix. "We'll take two bottled waters," he told the cashier.

"Hey, that looks like Daddy," said Sadie, glancing over her shoulder.

Jack winced, choking back the knot in his throat. "It's not Dad, Sadie." Jack didn't look, and not only because he knew she hadn't really seen their dad. There was too much going on behind him in the lobby. Hearing it was enough. Seeing it would be too much. A Frenchman at the counter was complaining about his bill. He was wrong, and he knew it. Jack could hear it in his voice. A woman near the exit was ordering a taxi by phone. She didn't want to get lost in the Tube. Jack didn't blame her. An American couple was standing by a rack of tourist brochures, planning a trip to some castle. His voice was beefy, like a bodybuilder's. Hers was small and reedlike.

The cashier dug their food out of a display case hung with green-and-red garlands that had seen too many Christmases. She was pretty, in a frumpy sort of way, with long dark hair pulled back into a bun that didn't quite contain it all, and wearing a black hotel uniform that didn't quite fit. She had seven earrings in the left ear and six in the right. What was that all about? Was it a statement or an oversight?

Jack shuddered. He didn't want to notice these things. He just . . . couldn't turn his brain off, not without a little help. He pulled out his phone and played his wizard game while he waited for Pretty-frumpy girl to wrap up the Danish.

"It *is* Daddy. Same brown coat and everything. Look, Jack!"

"Quiet, Sadie. That was the deal. I'm buying you sustenance. That means you have to zip it."

"Cash or credit?" asked Pretty-frumpy girl. Her accent sounded Polish.

Jack kept his eyes on his screen, picking a fight with a trio of goblins. "Can we charge . . . it . . . to . . . our . . . room?" He asked the question slowly so the cashier would understand.

"He doesn't see us. He's going to leave, Jack. *Look!*"

15

"*Not now*, Sadie."

"Yes, of course you can charge . . . it . . . to . . . your . . . room." Pretty-frumpy-Polish girl spoke as slowly as Jack had. Apparently she understood him fine and took offense at the implication she wouldn't. "But I will need to . . . see . . . your . . . key."

Still battling evil creatures with one thumb, Jack fished in his pocket for the key, grateful to find it there. He might just as easily have left it in the room. That kind of thing happened to him all the time—forgetting keys, wallets, homework. It was the same with simple tasks like returning library books. His mind was always grinding on something else, one of a thousand distractions. His school counselor frequently recommended he take those drugs that ADHD kids took, but his dad always forbade it. Maybe now his mom would finally let the school dose him.

Pretty-frumpy-Polish girl set the food on the counter and Jack handed over his key. "See, Sadie? Food. You have to leave me alone for *six* hours." He said it to distract her, expecting her to correct the number to four. Sadie was pretty sharp like that.

"I said *six* hours," said Jack, finally glancing down.

Sadie wasn't standing next to him anymore.

Jack scanned the lobby, squinting against the sunlight pouring in through the entrance. There wasn't much to it— the reception counter, the roped-off buffet, a few benches, and a sad phony Christmas tree. The Frenchman still argued with the clerk, and the bodybuilder and his tiny wife still stood by the tourist brochures. Jack couldn't see his little sister anywhere.

Sadie had disappeared.

Chapter 4

PANIC SET IN.

"Sadie!" Jack left the food on the counter and raced to the elevators—the only nook he couldn't see from the café. No Sadie. One car was open. The other was on the fourth floor, already coming down. She hadn't been gone long enough to make the trip all the way up there.

"Sadie!" Jack called again, eliciting worried glances from the Americans. The rest of the adults in the lobby—the Frenchman, the clerk behind the counter, and the woman who had called for a taxi—all scowled. Jack instantly took in every expression, felt them pressing against him. He wanted to jump into the open elevator car and disappear, but he couldn't, not without his sister. He squeezed his eyes shut and covered his ears.

Think!

Sadie had seen a man in a brown coat, some guy who looked like their dad. Then Jack had looked up and she was gone. No . . . She had said something else, hadn't she? *He's going to leave, Jack.* Not just leave the lobby. Leave the hotel. While Jack was playing on his phone, Sadie had followed some random guy out into the street. His mom was going to kill him.

The exit from the Eurotrek Lodge was a big, automatic revolving door that moved at the pace of a hundred-year-old tortoise. Jack tried to push it, but that only made it stop. He pushed again and it squawked at him in the excessively calm voice of a digital Englishwoman. "Caution. Door in motion. Door in motion."

Jack threw his arms in the air. "No it's not!"

Once the revolving door finally let him out, the situation did not improve. The hotel stood on one corner of a busy four-way intersection, meaning Sadie could have followed the man in the brown coat in any direction. Horns honked. Taxi drivers shouted. Bells jingled in every direction. And beneath it all was the relentless buzz of pedestrian chatter.

A man to Jack's left was calling in late for work. A woman to his right was on the phone with her bank—he heard the account number and everything. At the same time, some synapse deep in his brain informed him that the engine of the nearest double-decker bus needed tuning.

I don't care about the bus! He almost shouted it to the crowd as he covered his ears again. But covering them didn't help. The street noises were too numerous, too loud. Fighting a headache, he scanned the pedestrians, all shuffling along in one direction.

One direction. Of course. This was rush hour. Sadie had followed a random guy in a brown coat, but Random-brown-coat guy had his own, not-so-random purpose for being in London. Odds were that he was headed in the same direction as everyone else at seven thirty in the morning—downtown. Jack clenched his teeth and dove into the stream.

The shuffling pedestrians absorbed him into their amoebic train, bumping and shoving him along so that he barely kept his feet. The onslaught of chitchat and cell phone conversations hit him from every side—flashes of color in his brain that obstructed his vision.

White noise. I need white noise. His mother had suggested the solution several months ago. She had bought an MP3 for his phone—a continuous loop of rushing rivers and ocean waves that drowned out the world. He fumbled with his earbuds, struggling to plug them into his phone and constantly missing the port, thanks to the jostling of the crowd. Suddenly the phone flew from his grasp. It clattered to the pavement behind him. Above the horns and engines and the buzz of the crowd, Jack's oversensitive ears picked up a heart-wrenching *crunch*.

Chapter 5

SO MUCH for white noise.

Fighting through his frustration, Jack rose up on his tiptoes to scan the crowd ahead. He knew there was no way he would see Sadie among all those adults—she was barely four feet tall—but he might see the coat she was following.

It is Daddy, she had insisted back at the hotel. *Same brown coat and everything.*

Jack knew exactly which coat she meant. His dad hardly wore anything else when the weather at home in Colorado turned cold—a suede duster, a sharp reddish-brown overcoat like no other Jack had ever seen. "Like a red stag," his dad would always say. "A man's coat." Jack almost smiled at the memory. Then he caught sight of his quarry.

Sadie's mystery man was a good fifty feet ahead, passing a strange wall covered in shrubs, like a sideways garden. The red stag overcoat looked right at home against the vegetation. He *did* look like their dad, and it wasn't just the coat. He wore a bowler hat. What were the odds that two different guys who favored old-fashioned hats and rust-colored suede were wandering around London? *No way.* Jack's heart beat against his chest. Tears came to his eyes. He rose up on his toes and waved a hand above the crowd. "Dad! John Buckles!"

The mystery man turned with the crowd to descend a set of stairs, and Jack got a look at his face. His heart crashed within him. There *were* two men who favored bowlers and suede. The mystery man's chin was too short, hardly even there, and his face too grim and grizzled. Jack wiped his eyes with the sleeves of his T-shirt. Why had he let Sadie get his hopes up? Why had he let her draw him in to her denial? Then the implication of the stairs caught up to him.

The Tube.

"Pardon me! Excuse me!" Jack surged forward through the crowd. Amid the jumble of coats and briefcases on the stairs, he saw blue polka dots on a white background—the pattern of his sister's blouse—surfacing and submerging beneath the waves of gray and brown. It was a miracle she wasn't trampled.

"Sadie!"

Then she was gone again, out of sight beneath the street.

Jack reached the stairs a few seconds later, and the Tube station below slowly came into view—a half-dozen aluminum turnstiles at the center, ticket machines decorated with plastic holly to the left, and a guard wearing a red-and-silver reflective coat standing in a Plexiglas box to the right. A musician leaned against the right-hand wall beyond the barriers, wearing a Santa hat and playing a rhythmic riff on his guitar, but no one paid him any notice.

Another flash of blue polka dots caught Jack's eye. Sadie walked patiently behind a woman in an electric wheelchair, following her through a wide gate at the end of the turnstiles.

"Sadie, stop!"

No one prevented her from going through. If the guard even noticed her, he must have assumed she was pushing the chair. Jack reached the same spot seconds later and hesitated, hoping another wheelchair would materialize. He glanced from side to side, bouncing nervously on his toes for a couple of seconds, then planted both hands on the barrier and vaulted over.

"You! Green shirt. Stop!"

Of course.

24

Jack imagined that rebel types who routinely jumped turnstiles knew how to do it without getting caught. He was not a rebel type, and would have obeyed the Tube cop, but he needed to catch his sister before stopping to explain himself. He ducked into the crowd, turning left with the multitude down a passage marked BAKERLOO.

"The boy in the green shirt," the guard called out behind. "Stop him!"

Despite the obvious authority of the Tube cop's red, high-visibility jacket, no one heeded his command, leaving Jack free to continue squeezing his way forward through the shuffling mob. The passage arced slightly right and then straightened out so that he could see all the way to the platform. There, standing in the open doorway of a packed train, looking down to smooth out her flouncy polka-dot shirt, was Sadie.

"Sadie! Get off the train!"

She looked up as the doors closed, giving Jack an innocent little smile—glad to see that her brother had decided to join the chase. She tried to wave but had to grab the handrail instead as the train jerked into motion.

Chapter 6

"ANY OF YOU seen a kid in a green shirt?" Jack heard the Tube cop puffing behind him. He turned left along the platform, looking for a place to hide. All he found was an alcove, barely a foot deep. The gray door inside was labeled DANGER: HIGH VOLTAGE and secured with a padlock. Jack pressed himself up against it, turning his head to make sure his nose didn't stick out. His eyes fell on another teenage boy with spiked blue hair, wearing red skinny jeans and a black leather jacket with studs all over it. The boy was staring right at him. Jack gave him a pleading look. The kid snorted and turned to face the tracks.

Thirty more seconds passed with Jack trying to look as casual as possible while pressed against the high-voltage door. Another train rolled into the station, and the same voice he had heard while trapped in the hotel's revolving door said, "Mind the gap, please."

Spiky-hair kid sauntered on board.

Jack had no choice but to follow. Sadie was somewhere down the line.

Once on the train, Jack shrank into the nook at the front end of the car, trying to stay out of sight. Spiky-hair kid gave him a smirk, but he positioned himself between Jack and the window, blocking the sightline of the Tube cop on the platform. Jack offered a grateful nod.

Spiky-hair kid snorted. After that, the two boys did their best not to make eye contact.

The train was mercifully quiet. No more street noises. The passengers played with their phones instead of talking on them. Unfortunately, the enclosed environment brought with it a new threat to Jack's senses.

On the street above, the cold and the westerly breeze had removed the smell of the pedestrians, leaving only the sooty, gray smell of any street in any big city. Here, in the warm, stagnant air of the train car, Jack could smell them all. Spiky-hair kid hadn't bathed in a while, and had one arm raised to hold on to the rail. He had clearly tried to cover his personal

27

musk with cologne, but succeeded only in creating a sort of fruity, leather-onions motif.

And Smelly-spiky-hair kid's musk wasn't the worst part. An oozing, oily scent of digested fish hung in the air like a red haze. Jack guessed that at least half the people on the train had eaten herring for breakfast, and not one had brushed afterward. He scanned their faces. No one else seemed to notice. What was wrong with these people?

The train slowed and Jack bent down to look out the curved window, searching the platform for any sign of his sister or the man in the brown bowler. He didn't see either one. He didn't see any Tube cops either. It seemed the men in the red high-visibility coats weren't exactly Scotland Yard.

"This is . . . Marylebone Station," said the revolving-door-Tube voice. "Mind the gap, please."

Jack considered getting out, but he hadn't seen Sadie, or even the man in the bowler hat.

Smelly-spiky-hair kid raised one blue eyebrow.

Jack shook his head.

"This train is leaving the station."

Smelly-spiky-hair kid snorted, and the two continued avoiding each other's eyes as the train lurched off toward its next destination. Jack did his best not to breathe, trying to balance a desperate need for oxygen against the smell of fruity onions and herring.

"This is . . . Baker Street. Change here for connections to the . . . Metropolitan, Circle . . . and . . . Jubilee lines. Mind the gap, please."

Again, Jack bent down to scan the platform. The walls were covered in rust-colored tiles, painted with murals that looked like sketches from an old book. The nearest showed a huge, wolfish dog pouncing on a terrified man. Two other men raced up from the background, both carrying revolvers. One of them wore a bowler hat. Jack almost laughed.

The doors opened and Smelly-spiky-hair kid leaned out of the way.

Jack shook his head again. He didn't see Sadie.

"This train is leaving the station."

As the revolving-door-Tube voice made its announcement, the last of the disembarking passengers made their way into a tunnel labeled WAY OUT, giving Jack a clear view of the benches. There was Sadie, sitting quietly, hands folded in her lap as if waiting for the next train.

Jack shoved his right hand between the closing doors, winning a shocked look from Smelly-spiky-hair kid. It would have felt like a victory if he wasn't about to lose his sister again.

"Please step away from the doors," insisted the revolving-door-Tube voice.

"I don't think so," grunted Jack, jamming the fingers of his other hand into the crack. He pulled with everything he had. Smelly-spiky-hair kid joined in and grunted too, letting out a heavy breath. Jack winced at the smell.

The doors finally slid open. "Mind the gap, please," said the revolving-door-Tube voice, determined to have the last word. As the doors closed, Jack gave Smelly-spiky-hair kid a thumbs-up through the glass. Smelly-spiky-hair kid only snorted and turned away.

"I lost him." Sadie looked crestfallen as Jack came running up to the bench. "I lost Daddy. He got off the train and then he was just . . . gone."

Jack knelt before his sister, so grateful to be able to take her hand that he wasn't sure he would ever let go again. "It wasn't Dad, Sadie."

"Maybe we can catch him. He's not far. I can feel it."

The hope on his sister's face tore at Jack's heart. He squeezed her hand, trying to get up the courage to say what needed to be said. Even now, he couldn't. He hugged her, kissing her forehead. "We're gonna be okay, but we have to stick together from now on. Understand?"

Sadie nodded, looking up with a smile that told him she didn't understand at all.

Jack sighed. "Okay. We need to get out of here."

The sign that declared WAY OUT looked tempting, but ticket barriers and guards going in meant ticket barriers and guards going out. They couldn't go that way. Then his eyes fell on another gray door marked DANGER: HIGH VOLTAGE. The padlock was missing. Jack pulled it open and found a dark, iron staircase that wound its way up through electrical boxes, cables, and rusty pipes. There were bound to be spiders. Maybe rats, too. He wasn't sure he wanted to take Sadie into a place like that, until he leaned far enough through the door to see the platform at the very top of the staircase, where daylight streamed in through a partially open door. *Jackpot.*

Jack winced as he and Sadie stumbled out into the light, back into the noise and chaos of rush hour. He looked up and down the sidewalk, shielding his eyes, searching for a quiet place to figure out how he was going to get his sister back to the hotel.

Pedestrians poured out of the station exit to his left, flooding the sidewalk. To his right, he saw a window display, filled with all sorts of knickknacks—a rotary telephone, stacks of vinyl records in yellowed sleeves, a top hat with edges so worn that the gray felt showed through the silk. *An antique store.* Quiet, but Jack had no desire to deal with the crusty old shopkeeper that probably lurked inside. Farther up he saw a grocery—aisles and anonymity. "Come on," he said, taking Sadie's arm and pulling her along.

They didn't get very far.

A tall figure in a black overcoat came storming down the sidewalk, heading in the opposite direction. He bumped hard into Jack, spinning him back against the double doors of the antique shop. The man paused and glared down from beneath the shadow of a wide-brimmed fedora. Strangely, he had the same small chin and grizzled aspect as the man in the bowler. The look in his eyes made Jack's blood run cold.

"Excuse me," mumbled Jack, and yanked his sister backward through the wooden doors. He kept on backing up until he bumped into the counter. The doors swung closed and the man in the fedora cocked his head, peering between the antiques in the window and staring at the children for a long, uncomfortable second. Then he finally continued on.

"You can probably let go of me."

Jack glanced down at the iron grip he still maintained on

32

his sister's arm. "Sorry." He let go, flexing his stiff fingers. "You okay?"

Sadie massaged her arm and nodded.

"Good. We'll just hang . . . out . . . here . . ." Jack's voice trailed off as his eyes shifted from his sister to the long counter behind them. The two of them slowly turned. This was no antique shop. It was some sort of government office, like the Department of Motor Vehicles back in Colorado Springs, except much, much older.

Two nicked and dented counters made of dark-stained wood and lined with live evergreen garlands ran the breadth of the entire shop, with an absurdly tall podium jutting between them, its braided lip even with Jack's nose. Fading letters were carved into the faces of the counters—LOST PROPERTY to the left, ENQUIRIES to the right—and a great bronze seal hung on the podium, so dark with age that it nearly matched the wood. The emblem on the seal showed a falcon in flight, eyes focused below. The title imprinted around the edges read:

LOST PROPERTY OFFICE
BAKER STREET BRANCH

Chapter 7

"AHEM."

Jack looked up to see a tall, matronly figure leaning out from behind the podium, her salt-and-pepper hair pulled back into an impossibly tight bun. The black dress she wore could have come from the same century as the dark wooden counters, with the barest hint of pouf at the shoulders and fabric buttons that rose in two straight lines all the way up to the collar. She raised a set of stemless spectacles that hung from one of her buttons by a chain and held them against the tip of her nose to peer down at the children. "Enquiry or lost property?"

Jack had no idea how to answer.

The strange woman stood on a platform behind the

podium, giving her an intimidating height. Her accent didn't help either. She enunciated each syllable of the short question with such aristocratic distinction that Jack was tempted to believe he was facing the queen herself—or worse, the queen's English teacher.

"Kincaid!" shouted the woman, so suddenly and sharply that both of the children jumped. She let the glasses fall to the end of their chain, stern gray eyes shifting back and forth, searching the empty office. "Where is that clerk? Kincaid! We have clients!"

No one answered.

"I guess it's up to me, then, isn't it?" Her gaze settled on Jack again and she raised one pencil-thin eyebrow. "Let me elaborate on the question, child. Are you *enquiring* about something you have lost, or are you submitting *lost property* that you have found?"

Again, Jack did not answer.

"Lost," offered Sadie, covering her brother's silence. "We lost our daddy and—"

"*We're* lost." Jack finally found his tongue. He pinched his nose, trying to clear his mind. "She means *we're* lost. We only came in to get directions."

But the woman had already turned away. "*Enquiry*, then."

She pressed a knot in the wood-panel wall behind the podium and the entire section popped open like a cabinet door, revealing four columns of four cubbyholes each, all filled with papers of a different color. She held her spectacles to her nose and examined the labels. "Lost parasols . . . lost pearls. Ah, here we are. Lost persons." She placed a finger on the selected cubby and gave it a stiff push downward.

To Jack's amazement, the whole column shifted down, revealing more cubbies that were hidden in the wall above. Dozens flashed by to the sound of clicking gears. He blinked. "Um. No. You don't understand. He's—"

"Lost in a park, on public transport . . . lost in a residence, on the street?" She read more labels as the column clicked to a stop.

Sadie gave a little shrug. "We don't know."

"Quiet. You're not helping." Jack grabbed the braided lip of the podium and pulled himself up on his toes. A brass nameplate sat on the desktop amid the garlands.

MRS. HUDSON
MANAGER: BAKER STREET
1887–PRESENT

1887. Was that the year the branch was founded, or the year she started working there? Jack raised his voice to get

this Mrs. Hudson's attention. "Excuse me. Our dad is—"

"Lost in general?" she asked without turning around. "I see. That would require a form twenty-six-B-two if we're going to be as thorough as we ought." She straightened and held her finger to her chin, muttering to herself. "Which way? Which way? Where is that clerk? She's the one who files these things." She wheeled around and shouted at the empty room. "Kincaid!"

Jack lost his grip on the podium and fell flat on his rear with a pronounced "Umph!"

While Sadie helped him to his feet, Mrs. Hudson continued to stare out into the office, oblivious to the whole episode. She stood there for several seconds, hands on her hips, waiting for the invisible clerk to materialize, until she finally furrowed her brow and turned back to the cubbies. "Right, then. Still up to me. As always." She raised a long finger in the air, hooked it into a cubby, and gave it a good flick to the right. The row flew sideways, much like the column had flown down. Jack and Sadie exchanged a wide-eyed look. There seemed to be an infinite supply of cubbies behind the wall.

When the clicking slowed to a stop, Mrs. Hudson reached into the compartment directly in front of her and pulled out a large stack of green forms. These she attached to a clipboard. Then she touched a pen to her tongue and began filling out the first page.

Jack was thankful for the break in her momentum. "Please listen. All we need are directions back to our hotel."

Mrs. Hudson's eyes jerked up from the page. "*Excuse* me?"

"We . . . um . . . only need directions to our hotel."

Mrs. Hudson set the pen down and leaned forward, raising the spectacles again. Through the closely spaced lenses, her eyes looked huge and slightly crossed. "*Lost way. That* is another form entirely." Straightening, she flipped the clipboard around and tapped the top line with her spectacles. "Unfortunately, I have already initiated the twenty-six-B-two enquiry. Once initiated, all forms *must* be completed."

"But—"

"*If* you would like to terminate the twenty-six-B-two enquiry, you may *also* fill out a ninety-nine-A cancellation." Mrs. Hudson reached back into the cubbies and drew out a stack of pink pages. "After which, you may fill out a twenty-one-C request for—"

Jack held up his hands. "No! The green one is fine. That's all we need."

With a nod, Mrs. Hudson set the pink pages back in their

place. "Yes. I think that's best." She handed both the pen and the clipboard to Jack. "You and your sister are American, is that correct?"

"We . . . um—"

"Yes will suffice, child. In that case, I expect you will need a bit of help." Keeping her eyes fixed on Jack, and with no warning whatsoever, she brought her hands down on the podium with a heavy *slap*. "Kincaid!"

Jack would have fallen back onto his rear again if not for a steadying hand from his little sister. He frowned up at the old woman. When was she going to figure out that this Kincaid person did not exist?

"Yes, Mrs. Hudson?"

Jack spun around. Standing at the door was a blond, freckled girl about his own age.

Chapter 8

"KINCAID," said Mrs. Hudson, "this young man and his sister need to complete a twenty-six-B-two. See that they do it *correctly*." Her voice flattened. "They're Americans."

A door opened and closed, indicating that Mrs. Hudson had gone, but Jack's eyes were still on the once-imaginary-and-now-very-real clerk. She was far too young for government work—or maybe the smattering of freckles that dotted her pinkish cheeks made her *look* young. Either way, she didn't belong in this office from a bygone era. Unlike Mrs. Hudson, Kincaid was dressed for the present, wearing a gray wool coat that hung down to her knees, where black leggings took over. Her honey-blond hair fell down over a purple-and-black-striped scarf that bunched around her shoulders and threatened to swallow her chin. In short, she looked perfectly normal for a young girl on a December morning. Jack needed a little normal after Mrs. Hudson.

Without a word, the girl removed a purple cotton glove and held out her hand. Jack wasn't sure if he was supposed to shake it or kiss it, this being England and all. He opted for a gentle shake. "Hi . . . I'm Jack. And this is my sister, Sadie."

"Right." The girl gave him a quick, awkward smile that made the freckles on her cheeks rise and fall. "Lovely. And I'm Gwen. Gwen Kincaid. But could you . . . ?" She kept her hand extended, wiggling her fingers, indicating that she wanted the clipboard.

Jack's cheeks flushed as he handed it over.

"Very good." She turned on her heels and headed for a bench at the other end of the office. Jack and Sadie obediently followed.

A plan formed in Jack's head. This girl appeared sane, something he could not say for the old woman. If he could make a connection, maybe he could get her to dump the paperwork altogether. He sat down between the girls, leaving a respectful distance between himself and Gwen. "So . . . you're a clerk? I mean, shouldn't you be in school or something?"

41

"Apprentice clerk, actually. Age twelve." Gwen set the clipboard down between them and unraveled her scarf, one hand twirling in a circle above her head, making a purple-and-black pattern flash before her face. "The ministry identifies its recruits during *key stage three*—what you Americans call middle school. It's an advanced work-study program." She finished unraveling and turned to hang the scarf on a hook between the bench and the window.

"The ministry?" asked Sadie, leaning out from behind her brother.

Jack pushed her out of view before the clerk turned back again. A bunch of little-girl questions would only derail the conversation. "Wow. *Work-study*," he said with a sympathetic nod. "Work and study at the same time. You sound *really* busy." He reached for the forms. "You know, my sister and I don't mind skipping all this paperwork if that would help you out. All we need are some directions."

Just as Jack's fingers grazed the clipboard, Gwen snatched it away.

"Can't. Rule ninety-seven."

Normal and *sane* had left the building. They had probably never been there in the first place. Jack cringed, hardly daring to ask. "Rule ninety-seven?"

"Ministry regulations, volume three, section one, rule ninety-seven: 'All forms, once initiated, *must* be completed.'" Gwen waved the pen at Jack like a teacher's pointer. "An incomplete form is simply a mess of unanswered questions. And we can't have those, can we?"

"What ministry?" insisted Sadie, popping out from behind Jack again.

Once again, he pushed her back. "Um . . . no. I guess *we* can't."

Crazy-clerk girl scrunched up her nose. "I'll just fill in the easy boxes for you, shall I?"

As she scribbled away, Jack's eyes wandered, searching for something, anything, that would help him make sense of the situation. His gaze fell on the window displays—the old vinyl records, the top hat, a pair of brass driving goggles. All at once his brain made the connection. These weren't merely old items. They were old *unclaimed* items. They were *lost property*.

"Look," he said, adjusting his tone to take on a little more authority. "I don't see how this department . . . ministry . . . whatever . . . can help with a missing person. I mean—the Lost Property Office—you guys are really just a lost and found, aren't you?"

The pen ground to a halt and the clerk looked up, freckles dropping into a dark frown. "We are *not* a *lost* and *found*. Do you really think we sit around all day waiting for all things lost and all those who lost them to magically show up on our doorstep?"

Jack's eyes shifted from Gwen to the antiques behind her and back. "Well . . . yeah."

"Hmph. What a lazy, American concept." She returned her attention to the clipboard. "Now. *If* we might continue, why don't we start with the name of the missing person?"

"John," said Jack, letting out a defeated sigh. "His name is John."

"Full name, please."

"John Buckles." Jack lowered his voice a little. "The Second."

"John . . . Bu-ckles . . . the . . . Sec—" Gwen stopped mid-scribble, staring at the name for two full heartbeats before looking up at Jack. "And that would make you . . ."

Sadie hopped off the bench, dodging her brother's already reaching arm. "John Buckles the Third," she said, grinning proudly. "It's a family tradition."

"Of course it is." Gwen stood up, suddenly lost in a fog. Her eyes drifted over to the empty podium and remained there several seconds, as if waiting for Mrs. Hudson to appear, but she never did. When the clerk finally returned her attention to Jack, she gave him another quick, awkward smile—another bounce of her freckles. "Cold, isn't it?"

Jack had not seen that one coming. "Um . . . what?"

"Cold. You . . . Me . . . You, especially." The clerk nodded at the street outside. "You know, blustery winter day meets drafty old office." She snatched her scarf from the hook and clutched it to her chest. "Brrrr. You must be freezing. I know I am."

"Are you okay?"

"We should continue this in the back office. Much warmer back there. Much more comfortable." She winked, which really unnerved him, then circled around to the other side of the bench, backing up until she bumped into a wreath hanging on the wall next to the counter. After another quick glance at the empty podium, she locked eyes with Jack and pushed the wood panel open, wreath and all. There was nothing but darkness beyond.

"Please, Jack. I need you and your sister to come with me, right now."

Chapter 9

THE PANEL CLICKED closed, leaving the three of them in total darkness. Gwen had ushered them into a tiny, L-shaped room, no bigger than a broom closet. Sadie held tight to her brother's arm. "Jack, is this okay?"

He wasn't sure how to answer that. "Gwen?"

"Patience, please." The bureaucratic superiority in the clerk's voice had returned. "There's a light switch around here somewhere. See if it's on your end. Around the corner."

Above the sound of Gwen's hand sliding along the wall, searching for the switch, Jack thought he heard a rapid clicking, like six tiny legs skittering across a hardwood floor. But strange sounds and feelings often crept across Jack's mind when the lights went out, and he had gotten used to ignoring them. He dismissed the clicking as a trick of the dark and shuffled around the corner, reaching blindly in front of him until the tips of his fingers bumped into cold steel. The metal felt strange, almost malleable—another trick of the dark. Maybe. As Jack flattened his palm, his skin seemed to sink into the surface, like pressing an imprint into clay.

Then things got *really* weird.

Jack sensed vibrations. The individual molecules of the steel quivered against his skin, forming a uniform pattern, like Morse code but millions of times faster and infinitely more complex. And Jack could swear he was on the verge of making sense of it all.

The flood of input caused vertigo, threatening to knock him off his feet. To steady himself, he pressed even harder against the steel, and the vibrations intensified. An image snapped into his mind. Jack saw a hand pressed against a big steel door, palm flat like his. But it wasn't his hand. It was bigger, older, with a reddish-brown cuff at the wrist.

Suddenly the skittering-bug sound broke through from the edge of Jack's consciousness, accompanied by the sensation of something crawling across the back of his hand. He jerked his palm away from the metal with an involuntary cry. The image of the older hand evaporated.

"Are you all right?"

Jack blinked. Gwen stood next to him in the small, bright room, her hand on the light switch. How long had she been there? A steel door stood in front of him, exactly as it had appeared in the vision—big and heavy. It had no handle of any kind, just a black thumb pad jutting out from the right side of the frame.

"Jack, *are you all right?*" Gwen asked a second time.

"Fine . . . I guess. But something crawled across my hand. You have a bug problem."

Gwen wrinkled her nose. "Ew. Don't think so. Mrs. Hudson would never allow it."

"Agree to disagree. Why are we in this closet, anyway?"

"It's not a closet, silly." Gwen nodded at the vault door. "It's an entryway. The back office, remember? That's where we're going."

Jack stepped back, pulling Sadie with him so Gwen could reach the thumb pad. He knew a biometric scanner when he saw one. "All yours."

The clerk stared at the pad, chewing her lip, then shrugged. "Why don't *you* give it a go?"

"I can't. I mean it won't—" Before Jack could finish, Gwen took his right hand with hers, so abrupt and unexpected—so soft—that resisting never occurred to him. She guided his hand to the scanner and used her own thumb to press his down on the pad.

Jack felt a mild electric shock—though he wasn't sure if it came from the thumb pad—and a green light illuminated above the door. The familiar, revolving-door-Tube voice filled the small space. "Access granted. Welcome, John Buckles."

Chapter 10

ELECTRONIC GEARS whirred, followed by a deep *clang*, and the vault door swung wide, forcing Jack to back away. His mouth hung open. "It knew my fingerprint."

Gwen looked as surprised as he was, wearing a sort of I-can't-believe-it-actually-worked expression, but she recovered quickly. "Your genetic marker, actually. You might say it recognized your bloodline."

"But how did it—?"

The clerk stepped through the door. "This way, Jack. No dawdling."

She moved at a brisk pace, leading them onto a midlevel balcony that wrapped around a cavernous chamber the size of a train station. Everything from the floor to the thick

beams of the arched ceiling was made of rich, dark oak—
like the counters in the front office, except the wood here
was oiled and polished, the ornate carvings still sharp. An
intricate border of twisting vines ran around the ceiling. Jack
could make out tiny men and women among the curling
leaves, carrying lanterns or looking through spyglasses.

"The Lost Property Office was the first public branch ever
established by the ministry," said Gwen, keeping her voice
oddly low. "An agent named Doyle founded the branch in
1887, as a sort of catch-all for information and requests. We
call this part the Chamber."

"What ministry?" asked Sadie.

There was a heavy *clang* behind them. Both Americans
looked back and saw that the big vault door had slammed
closed, locking them in. "Um . . . Gwen?" Jack returned his
eyes to the front too late to see the clerk come to an abrupt
halt. He bumped into the back of her.

She gave him a pointed frown, then handed her clipboard to a man in a pinstriped vest and white shirt, seated
on a rolling stool in front of a high-definition screen with a
keyboard jutting out from the wall beneath it. Similar work-
stations were spaced every few yards along the balcony,
though few of them were manned. "File that, please," said

Gwen, her eyes shifting up and down the balcony. "Section Eighty-six protocol."

Pinstriped-vest man stared up at the clerk.

"Well?" She snapped her fingers impatiently. "What are you waiting for?"

He shot a furtive glance at Jack, then pulled a hidden drawer out from the wall at his knee and tossed the clipboard inside—pen, papers, and all. He shoved the drawer closed and silently swiveled back to his keyboard.

"But we didn't finish those," protested Sadie. "What happened to 'All forms *must* be completed'?"

"Did I say that?" Gwen started her march again. "How silly of me."

Jack noticed the clerk was hugging the left side of the balcony, keeping clear of the rail. Before he could ask her why, he heard a weighty *ffoomp* behind him. He stopped and looked over his shoulder to see wisps of black smoke rising from the edges of the drawer.

"Wait . . . Did he just—?"

She was already too far ahead of him to hear.

Looking down over the rail as he jogged to catch up, Jack saw rows of great mahogany desks lining the floor space, each topped with a brass lamp and a rotary phone. A few workers—not nearly enough to man them all—milled about between them, dressed in vintage, nineteenth-century clothing. Despite the antique look of the clothes and furniture, holographic images hovered over several of the desktops. One showed a woman wearing a dark blue peacoat and red beret, crossing a busy street. Jack grabbed the balcony rail. "Mom?"

"Watch out!"

Gwen was back at his side, pulling him into a crouch as a miniature drone whizzed by. The brown hardened case it carried missed his head by inches. An electric blue haze glowed within the four circular housings where the mini-drone's rotors should have been, reflecting off the desktops as it dropped below the balcony and zipped across the Chamber. It disappeared into a dark stairwell on the other side.

By the time Jack recovered, the projection of the woman had disappeared. The man who was seated at the desk glared up at the balcony, lifted the receiver of an ivory and brass rotary phone, and dialed. Whispers from the other workers drifted up to Jack's ears like vapors.

Buckles. Section Thirteen. Impossible.

"Oh dear. You *have* made a bit of a scene." Gwen tugged at his arm. "We really *must* keep moving."

Jack resisted her pull. "Why? It's warmer right here. Isn't that what you wanted?" Down below, the man with the phone followed them with his eyes, muttering into the receiver. Jack heard his last name again, and the words *Section Thirteen*.

The clerk dragged him onward until Jack finally took a long stride and stepped in front of her, blocking her path. He pulled his sister close, draping his arms protectively around her. "We're not going any farther until you tell us what's going on."

Gwen chewed her bottom lip, shooting a worried glance at the man below, who had just hung up the phone. "He called the wardens. Please, Jack. We don't have much time. There's a computer up here you should be able to access. Once wardens get here, the ministry won't—"

Sadie stomped her feet. "*What ministry?*"

The clerk gave the eight-year-old one of her quick, freckle-bounce smiles. "Your father's ministry, of course. The Ministry of Trackers."

Chapter 11

"DADDY IS A MINISTER?"

Jack rolled his eyes. "Ministry means something different here, Sadie." He frowned at Gwen. "And our dad was a salesman, an *American* salesman."

"That was his cover." Gwen motioned for them both to keep their voices down. "Your dad was a member of a secret society of detectives that has served the Crown for centuries—one of Britain's four Elder Ministries. He was looking for an important artifact when—"

Sadie couldn't be bothered with such details. Her face lit up. "You *know* our daddy?"

"She doesn't know anything. She's making it all up." Jack needed to get his sister away from this person, back to the hotel, where he could calm her down and keep her distracted until his mom got back. "Show us the way out, Gwen. Right now."

"No." Sadie wriggled free of her brother's grasp and turned to face him. "Gwen knows our dad. She knows how to find him." The eight-year-old folded her arms and raised her voice. "I'm not going home without Daddy!"

If any eyes in the Chamber had not been fixed on the three children, they were now. Jack clenched his teeth. He couldn't take any more of his sister's clueless denial. He couldn't take any more of his mom's sad, fake smiles. He wanted everything out in the open. "Dad *isn't* lost, Sadie. Grown men don't just disappear." He raised his voice so all the crazies looking on could hear. "Not in this century."

"But . . . we came here to find him. We came to find Daddy and bring him home."

"Jack," said Gwen in a warning tone. "Don't do this—not right now."

The dam was already broken.

Jack shot a look at the clerk that said, *Stay out of this*, and squatted down to his sister's level. "*Try* to understand. There was an accident. The London police found Dad's wallet at the scene. By the time we flew in and Mom got to the hospital, the body was gone—a mix-up with all their ridiculous British forms and British procedures." He closed his eyes, took a deep breath, and let the wrecking ball fly. "Sadie, Mom is out searching the morgues right now. Dad is *dead*."

"No." Sadie backed into Gwen, tears welling up in her eyes. "You're lying. He's alive. I know he is. I'm going to find him."

"Sadie . . ." Jack reached for his sister, but she shrank away from his grasp and ran around him. Halfway down the balcony, she took a left and vanished through a set of double doors.

Gwen scowled at Jack as the doors swung closed. "That was well handled."

"What's in that room?" he asked, scowling right back.

The clerk's expression softened. "Sadie's going to be okay, Jack. She's strong. I can see that."

She hadn't answered his question. She *never* answered his questions. "*What* is in that room?"

Gwen bit her lip. "We call it the Graveyard."

"The *Graveyard*?"

"Not a real graveyard. I mean, it's not like we keep any bodies back there." Her eyes drifted to the double doors. "Not that many bodies, anyway."

"You're nuts. All of you. I'm going to get her."

Gwen's eyes shifted past him. "Too late."

Jack turned and came nose-to-chest with a big teen wearing a tweed jacket and sporting a blond crew cut. "You're not s'posed to be 'ere," he said, poking a thick finger into Jack's chest. He was huge, with abnormally broad shoulders, though the blemishes on his plump cheeks told Jack he couldn't be more than sixteen.

"Um . . . Excuse me. I—"

Big-pimply-tweed guy scowled down at him. "Shut it, you."

"Jack, meet Shaw," said Gwen with a sigh. "He's a warden—a journeyman warden, to be exact—kind of like a museum guard in training. He's here to collect us. Aren't you, Shaw?"

Shaw's scowl shifted to the clerk. "You 'ad no right to bring him into the Chamber on your own. Why din'tcha call Mrs. 'udson?"

"I was only trying to help . . . sort of. And why shouldn't he know who he really is?"

Shaw let out a scathing guffaw. "Not for you to decide, is it? You're a first-year 'prentice clerk—barely got clearance to enter the broom closet, let alone the Chamber."

Apparently that was enough to shame the clerk. Her eyes

dropped to the floor as Shaw put a meaty hand on each of their shoulders. "Right. Both of you wi' me, now. Off we go."

Jack felt little pinpricks on his back. He craned his neck to look and saw a huge, blue-green beetle. Was it . . . made of metal? It twitched its wings and Jack could swear he saw tiny copper gears poking out beneath. The bug looked back at him with unexpected intelligence, focusing eyes made of miniature camera lenses, then twitched its antennae and crawled over his shoulder, right onto the big guy's hand.

Chapter 12

SHAW YANKED his hand away with a cry worthy of a ten-year-old girl, flinging the beetle into the air. It stabilized with its iridescent wings beating at breakneck speed, hovering directly in front of Shaw's bulbous nose and making his eyes cross. He swatted at it, but the bug darted to an empty workstation. As soon as it landed on the keyboard, the display embedded in the wall above came to life. Lines of raw computer code cascaded down the screen.

The big guy growled, attempting to grab the clockwork pest, but a purple arc of electricity flashed out and zapped his hand. He yelped and clutched his paw, eliciting a giggle from Gwen. Even Jack had to suppress a laugh, but the levity was short-lived.

Aaaht! Aaaht! Aaaht! Aaaht!

A blaring alarm echoed through the Chamber. The lights went out and every screen at every workstation flashed red, strobing in the dark. The revolving-door-Tube voice added to the chaos. "System breach. System breach."

The room swirled in Jack's vision. Nausea gathered in his stomach. Shaw glared down at him with a scowl worthy of a Gothic gargoyle, terrifying in the flashing, blood-red light. "Wot's it doin', you?"

"I don't know!" Jack covered his ears with his hands. "Not my bug. I swear!"

The big guy hauled back with an open palm, and Jack thought he was going to hit him, but then he turned and swatted the bug, gritting his teeth through a second purple flash of electricity and making contact with an ugly *crunch*. The beetle sailed through the balcony rail, wobbling off over the desks in a zigzagging, wounded-bug flight path. Shaw lumbered after it, heading for the stairs. "Oi! Stop that bug!"

Aaaht! Aaaht! Aaaht! Aaaht!

"System breach. System breach," continued the revolving-door-Tube voice with obnoxious calm. Then her message changed. "Unauthorized access in class five storage . . . Lockdown initiated . . . Mind the doors, please."

Clang. Somewhere in the Chamber, a vault door closed. *Clang.* Another one. The computer was sealing them in.

A mini-drone zipped out from the same dark stairwell where the first one had disappeared, carrying in its pincers a hardened case the size of a basketball. A worker in a waistcoat leaped up to grab it, but the drone evaded him and continued its climb, heading for the far end of the balcony, where another vault door was already swinging closed.

"The bug hacked into a drone," gasped Gwen, taking off to intercept it.

Jack fought back his nausea and ran too, not to chase the drone, but to get to his sister. He skidded to a stop at the Graveyard and pushed open the double doors. Inside was a kind of warehouse, a huge room filled with row after row of tall oak shelving units, crammed with odds and ends. Those closest to him were packed from top to bottom with worn-out dolls, all staring back at him with glassy, dead eyes.

She must be terrified in there. "Sadie!"

The eight-year-old stepped out of the shadows, one of the dolls dangling from her hand. "What's with all the noise?"

Jack dropped to one knee and pulled her into a hug.

"Ow. Quit it! What's wrong with you?"

"You're not upset?"

"Not anymore." Sadie pushed away, holding him at arm's length. "You didn't mean it. You're just confused."

"No. Sadie, you—"

Clang. The vault door at the end of the balcony slammed closed. Gwen sprinted toward them. "The drone got out! We can still catch it. There's one more exit!"

The clerk grabbed Jack's hand, yanking him into the Graveyard. He, in turn, pulled his sister with him, and her glassy-eyed doll brought up the rear. On the other side, across a hundred feet of shelves and plush red carpet, a pair of huge sliding doors slowly converged.

One more exit. Gwen's words finally sank in. Those doors were about to block their only way out—the only way to get Sadie back to the safety of the hotel. Jack stopped letting Gwen pull him along and committed to the race.

Strange images registered in his addled brain as he ran— busts of historic figures topped with ill-fitting wigs, old tin toys, dozens of umbrellas protruding from brass cylinders like bouquets of flowers. Seated at the end of the last shelf before the doors was a creepy clown, a pocked and scarred ventriloquist's dummy with sneering red lips and eyes that followed him as he passed.

"Come on!" The doors were almost closed. Gwen let go for the final sprint.

Jack sped up as well, but Sadie's legs were too short to match. She stumbled and fell, her tiny hand slipping out of his. He looked back, something he did not have the coordination to get away with. Jack tripped over his own feet, smacked his head against one of the closing doors, and stumbled through into the loading bay. The last thing he heard before darkness fell was the echoing *bang* of the doors coming together, leaving his little sister trapped on the other side with the glassy-eyed dolls and the creepy clown.

Chapter 13

JACK KEPT HIS EYES closed, hoping it was all a bad dream. Sure, his head throbbed with pain. But he got headaches all the time, and they were never the result of intruder alarms or injuries sustained in narrow escapes. Maybe he was still lying in the hotel room. Maybe this whole, crazy morning had been a nightmare. Isn't that what nightmares were, all gargoyles and creepy clowns and running for your life without knowing why? All strangeness and no answers?

"Jack?"

No such luck. He opened one eye to see Gwen standing over him, offering him a hand. He groaned. "Go away."

"Get up. We have to catch the drone."

Jack struggled to his feet without accepting her help, and saw that they had escaped into a loading bay of sorts, filled with racks of old winter clothing. Daylight seeped in around the edges of a corrugated steel garage door. He clapped a hand to his pounding head. "Sadie."

"She's fine."

"She's *not* fine. She's trapped in there with the alarm and Big-pimply-gargoyle guy."

"You mean Shaw?" Gwen scrunched up her nose. "Don't be so melodramatic. Shaw is harmless . . . sort of. And Mrs. Hudson is with them. She's wonderful with children."

Before Jack could argue the Mrs.-Hudson-is-great-with-kids point, Gwen yanked down on a chain, hauling up the door and blinding him with daylight. By the time his eyes adjusted, she was rummaging through the racks. She pulled a midnight-blue racing jacket from a hanger and shoved it into his chest. "Put this on. It's cold outside."

"I'm not going anywhere without my sister," he argued, but he *was* cold, so he donned the coat anyway. As he looked up from the zipper, he got hit in the face with a wool cap.

"That too. Stiff breeze today. No need to catch a sniffle."

"I'm not going."

"Yes, you are."

He pulled the cap down over his ears. "Why on earth would I want to help you?"

The clerk stormed across the bay, rising up on her toes to get into his face. "*You can't possibly be this dense!*" she shouted, really shouted, for the first time since he had met her. "Intruder alarms, beetles that hack into computers—you think it's a coincidence that it all happened the moment you walked into the Lost Property Office? It all happened *because* you walked in." She stayed there, nostrils flaring for another long second, then finally backed down and looked away. "You're not even supposed to be here."

"Yeah. I know. I heard Shaw."

Gwen shook her head. "You don't understand. When the ministry loses an agent, they put up a smokescreen, shuffle things around for a week or two until they've built a proper cover story. Your mum should never have heard from the police. You and your sister should never have set foot in London. Jack, all of this—the bug, the drone—all of it has something to do with your dad's last mission." She shrugged. "Don't you want to know what happened to him?"

A cold feeling churned in Jack's stomach. His eyes fell to his shoes. "I . . . I mean . . ."

"Oh. You really *don't* want to know." Gwen had clearly not considered that possibility. "Well, I don't think you have a choice anymore. That mission is what brought you here, Jack. You're involved whether you want to be or not."

"Fine." He sighed. "Whatever. So what am I supposed to do about it?"

The clerk put on a set of purple earmuffs and walked outside, pausing to look back from the bay door. "It's better if I show you."

The light but unmistakable scent of mothballs hung over Jack like a cloud as he followed Gwen up the sidewalk. "Hey!" he said to the clerk's back. "I know where this coat came from. And this hat, and your earmuffs, and all the rest of that stuff back there. It's obvious. This stuff is used—*lost.* So what does your secret Ministry of Trackers have to do with a lost and found?"

Gwen's shoulders hunched at the words *lost and found*, but she did not break stride. She reached back and grabbed his arm, pulling him up beside her. "We are *not* a lost and found. Stop saying that. The Lost Property Office is the public intersect of a much larger, secret organization. Think of it as the tip of an iceberg that innocently bobs above the surface, concealing the much larger bit below."

They stopped at the edge of a short brick alley. There, lying on a pile of rubble at the back, was the drone. It had crashed through a false brick wall from the other side—a secret panel, now broken to pieces to expose the vault door behind it. Apparently the runaway drone had made it all of four feet after it escaped the Chamber.

Gwen hurried to the crash site and knelt down to poke through the remains. "Someone has already recovered the crate. We have to move fast." She stood and manhandled Jack, positioning him at the center of the alley. "Okay. Tell me what you see."

"I see a wrecked drone on a pile of bricks . . ." He glanced at her sideways. "And a crazy person."

The clerk was not amused. She grabbed his face in her hands, pulling it down so that his eyes were level with hers. "I *thought* you decided to help."

"Yeah, I did," he said, pulling himself free. "But I don't know what you want from me."

"You know that you're special, Jack. You've always known it. You can see and hear things that others can't, just like your dad. Now, tell me what you see."

Jack sighed. He did know, even if he didn't want to admit it. As Gwen moved out of the way, he narrowed his eyes, straining to see what he was missing. Street noises echoed off the alley walls, hitting his brain in spikes of color. He covered his ears to block them out, but Gwen immediately pulled his hands away. "No. Not like that. Stop trying to see like everyone else does." She let go of his wrists and stepped back. "See things *your* way, Jack. Open your senses—all your senses. Let the world in."

"Who *are* you?"

"Just do as I say, please."

The flood of data washed over him. Asphalt, bricks, honking horns, shadows, scent of oil, scent of dust, bits of white wreckage, mothballs—all coming too fast. That had always been the problem. Too much, too quickly. He tried to compress the information into a narrow stream and winced as pain crept in from the edges of his mind.

"Stop fighting it." Gwen paced behind him. "Pressure puts the barriers *up*. Relax. Let them *fall*."

"How do you know all this?"

"I read a lot. Trust me, Jack."

He let go of his annoyance with the clerk and committed to her words. He stopped trying to control the data coming

70

in. And, for the first time that he could remember, Jack *saw*.

All at once, the fast-moving stream burst into a wide, three-dimensional field of data, every piece slowing to a crawl. Jack saw more than brick walls—he saw the bricks themselves, a hundred shades of red and brown fitting together in rectangular jigsaw puzzles. At his feet, the asphalt separated into whorls and blotches in a dozen shades of black. The sounds from the street that had so distracted him before became part of the picture as well. He watched, literally watched, the honks of multiple car horns echo off the walls in shimmering bronze waves—some thick and palpable, others thin and fading. The gray murmur of engine noises drifted around his ankles like ground fog.

As he marveled at the bronze ripples, Jack realized he was isolating a piece of the picture, without the pain of blocking out the rest. He could turn his mind's eye to one detail or another at will. He examined the wreckage of the drone, picking out the broken pieces and turning them over in his head, fitting them together again. He let out a short laugh. "How am I doing this?"

Gwen's whispered voice joined the vision, a translucent wisp of winter gray. "You're a tracker, Jack Buckles, like your father, and your father's father. This is a hereditary skill. But,

71

Jack, I don't have it. I come from a ministry family. I've studied all my life to work with trackers, read everything there is to read about your kind, but I still can't see what you see. You have to describe it to me so I can help you make sense of it."

"Kerosene," he said without hesitation. He smelled—saw, really—the deep, iridescent green scent of fuel. "I see a boot print made of kerosene. No. I see half a dozen prints from the same pair of boots, on the asphalt next to the rubble. There." He pointed, then quickly shifted his hand. "I see a thread, too, small and black, caught in a crack in one of the broken bricks."

Gwen pulled a magnifying glass out of her pocket and delicately picked up the thread to examine it. She glanced up at Jack. "Wool canvas, like the kind used in an overcoat."

"Really?" He blinked, letting all of the data fall. "A magnifying glass? Is that standard issue for a Ministry of Trackers clerk?"

"You think I intend to be a clerk forever? Hmm? Focus, Jack. I can't find the prints. Can you follow the kerosene?"

He nodded, opening up his senses again, but he no longer saw the field of data. He was back to the chaos, the pain. He started to panic, instinctively reaching for his ears.

"Breathe, Jack. It will take time for you to develop control, but you *can* do it."

It took him several seconds to regain control, but soon

he saw the iridescent green trail again. He did not find the strongest concentration on the ground as he expected. He found it on the wall to his left, drifting vapors that formed definite patterns on the brick.

"No way."

"What?"

Jack was too enthralled by what he saw to answer. Stepping closer, he found a match sticking out of a crack in the mortar at the very center of the wall, as if someone had placed it there for him to find. "Stand back." He yanked the match free, hesitated for half a second, then struck it against the brick.

The ignition nearly took his eyebrows off.

Lines of blue flame raced outward in all directions, branching off into curling, zigzag patterns to form a blazing message on the bricks.

If you want him back

XIII

Bring me the Ember

"'Thirteen,'" said Jack, reading the Roman numerals. "'The Ember.' What does it mean?"

Gwen stepped up to the wall, raising a hand to touch the already dying flames. "It means your sister may have been right, Jack. It means your father may still be alive."

Chapter 14

"WHY THIRTEEN?" asked Jack. "What does that have to do with Dad?"

"Later." Gwen tugged him out of the alley, back to the sidewalk. "Whoever left that message stepped in his own kerosene. If we move fast, you can track him, bypass whatever game he's playing, and go straight to the source. Can you see any more footprints?"

Jack nodded, half in a daze. The implication that his father might still be alive—held captive by some pyromaniac-drone-stealing-computer-hacking nutcase—left him dizzy. "Here," he said, crouching down on the sidewalk. "And here. And another one there, on the street."

Pedestrians sidestepped around the children as they

passed, hardly giving their strange behavior a second look. Gwen took two unnaturally long steps, measuring her own stride against the prints Jack indicated. "Six feet tall, at least. Heading straight into traffic." She pointed to a line of joined houses across the street. "Over there, perhaps."

The two rushed across, Gwen gripping Jack's arm and alternately halting and pushing him to keep him clear of cars as he followed the fading trail across the street. He found the last trace of kerosene on a cast-iron knob at the center of a blue door—the only door on the block of houses without a Christmas wreath. Staring at the peeling blue paint of the door, Jack suddenly realized his dad might be somewhere on the other side.

He grabbed the cast-iron knob, preparing to thrust a shoulder into the door, and instantly felt his fingers sink into the ice-cold metal, the same way they had at the vault door. Another vision flashed in his mind—a black glove, right where his bare hand was. A man in a black overcoat and fedora pushed his way through the blue door with a large crate tucked under his arm. Inside, Jack saw the rotting planks of a wood floor, flies buzzing in and out of a rusty sink. The man with the crate took a right toward an old set of stairs, and the door slammed closed. Jack was staring down at his own hand again.

He let go and backed away. "The man in black."

"What?"

"Um . . . nothing." Jack glanced down at the offending hand and quickly slipped it into the pocket of his coat. "I mean . . . it's locked."

"Mm-hmm." Gwen eyed him for a long second, then tried the door herself, giving it a hard bump with her shoulder. The door fell open with an ugly squeak. "Stuck but not locked. Welcome to England. Doorknobs at the center have nothing to do with the latch. Come on."

Dust hung heavy in the light spilling through the open door. A familiar buzzing sound pulsated on the edge of Jack's senses, though it was not the sound of the flies swooping in and out of the sink. The carpet had been ripped up, exposing rotting wood planks stained with glue and mold. To his right, a set of rickety stairs with a broken rail led up to another floor.

"That way," he whispered, tilting his head toward the stairs.

"You see tracks?"

"Yeah, something like that."

Each step let out an agonizing *creak* as the two of them picked their way around three long rolls of old, smelly carpet lying on the stairs. At the top, they found a single room with nothing but a small bed and an old desk and chair. The blue stench of ammonia hit Jack like a sledgehammer, coming from the stained mattress on the bed. He could hear some creature gnawing on the fabric inside.

The buzz had grown louder with every step up the stairs. Within a half second of reaching the top, Jack identified the source—bugs hovering behind the black curtains covering the window, probably attracted to the daylight. He walked over to let the light into the room, but his hands never reached the fabric. Four giant, blue-green beetles dove at him through the crack in the curtains, forcing him to duck. Then they climbed up to hover at the ceiling, flying in a perfectly square formation.

"They're organized," muttered Gwen, staring up at the beetles. She blinked and looked to Jack. "Same kind, you think?"

"Yeah, but there are no computers or drones to hack here. So what are they doing?"

Beams of light erupted from the bugs, each one projecting an image on the wall ahead of it. All four projections were the same—a life-size image of the man in black.

The clarity of the projections left no doubt in Jack's mind. This was the man from his vision at the blue door, and the same man had scared Jack and Sadie into the Lost Property Office. Not only that, but his grizzled features and small chin matched those of the man in the reddish-brown coat that Sadie had followed from the hotel. The strange events of Jack's morning had merely been stages in an elaborate trap—one that ended right there in that room.

The four projections tilted their heads back and laughed.

Chapter 15

WHEN THE LAUGHING started, the beams from the beetles shifted. The four images tracked down the walls and across the floor, converging to form a holographic projection at the center of the room, flickering in the hanging dust. The man in black clapped his hands and chuckled. "Bravo, Lucky Jack," he said in a distinctively French accent. "You found me. Excellent."

"Who are you?" Jack took a step toward the image. "And where's my dad?"

The Frenchman gave a short bow. "I am called *le Pendulier*. In your clumsy language, you would say, the Clockmaker. But that is of little relevance. You have an urgent assignment to attend to, Lucky Jack. That is why I brought you here."

"What about the drone?" asked Gwen, stepping up beside Jack. "You stole an artifact from the ministry. We want it back."

"I stole nothing!" The Clockmaker glared right at her, as if he could see her. "I merely recovered what was stolen from me"—he pointed to Jack—"by *his* father." Then he dropped his hand and gave Jack a congenial, if not unsettling, smile. "Though I could not have done it without you, Lucky Jack. And for that, I thank you. Now, I really must insist we discuss your assignment."

"I saw your message. You want something called the Ember. So what? I want my father back."

"Ah, but the *Ember* is the key to saving your father. Bring me my prize and I will return him to you alive."

Jack clenched his fists. "What if I don't feel like running your errands for you? How about I hunt you down instead?"

"Ooh. How frightening." The Clockmaker raised his palms, laughing. "No need to track me down. I am in the Great Clock Tower, what you might call Big Ben. There, you see? I am so helpful." His grin flattened. "And if you so much as knock on the door without the Ember, your father dies. Bring it up to the Great Clock by the stroke of midnight,

Lucky Jack, and you can have him. Fail me by just one second and I will give you *ashes* instead."

The hologram began to fade.

"Wait!" shouted Gwen. "We don't know what the Ember is. How do you expect us to find it?"

"That you must find out for yourself." The Clockmaker faded back into view. "I suggest you ask the Boy at Pye. And while you're at it, warn him that his mockery is at an end." His lips spread into a dreadful grin. "Now, here is a final hint to speed you on your way."

The projection flickered out and the beetles shot to the four corners of the room, bouncing off the walls with sickening cracks. One landed on the old mattress, sizzling with electricity. Purple flashes arced around its broken body with increasing intensity until it exploded, spreading flames across the mattress. The animal inside screamed. The other three repeated the first bug's performance. Within seconds, the desk, the floor, and the rolls of carpet on the stairs were all on fire.

Gwen threw open the curtains. "There's a fire escape here." She yanked up on the window. It didn't budge.

Blinding, choking smoke filled the room. Jack couldn't focus. He couldn't even think. Then his subconscious dredged up a single, important lesson left over from hundreds of elementary school fire drills. *Drop*.

He fell to his hands and knees, pulling Gwen with him, and his mind began to clear.

Flames were everywhere, blocking the stairs, eating the cheap paper on the walls. Jack reached up and pounded desperately on the window. Nothing. The glass wouldn't break.

Gwen leaned her back against the wall. "Impact-resistant . . . panes!" she shouted between coughs. "Building Safety Code . . . Section K . . . Gotta hit it dead center with a hammer!"

Blue and yellow flames crept across the ceiling, living jewels so beautiful that Jack almost forgot they threatened to bring burning rafters down on top of him.

"Jack?" coughed Gwen. "Did you hear me?"

"What? A hammer. Right!" He tore his eyes away from the flames and opened his senses, trying to pick out details through the haze. He didn't see any hammers.

Chair: burning.

Broken posts at the top of the stairs: also burning.

Aluminum bed frame: unreachable beneath the melting mattress.

A broken drawer underneath the desk: full of old office supplies.

He kicked the burning chair out of the way and used the toe of his sneaker to pull the drawer closer. Red-hot cinders dropped from the desk onto his jeans. Gwen smothered them out with the arm of her coat. She lifted a brass letter opener from the supplies. "Perfect! I'll hold it against the window. You hit it with the drawer." She had another coughing fit, then gave him a weak freckle bounce. "*Do* try not to hit my fingers."

Gwen pressed the tip of the blade against the pane, breathing through her scarf, while Jack dumped out the rest of the drawer and smashed it on the floor. He wielded the remaining plank like a club, hammering at the round handle of the letter opener. On the first strike, spidery cracks spread out from the point of the knife. On the second, the glass shattered.

The escape ladder let them down onto a cobblestone courtyard behind the old buildings. Black smoke poured from the broken window above. Jack went straight to one knee, coughing out the bad air and sucking in deep drafts of the good. "Why . . . would he do that?"

Gwen remained standing, looking around the courtyard. "A final test, perhaps—to see if you're good enough to find this Ember." She glanced down at him and frowned. "Or perhaps he's *stark raving mad*."

Jack finally caught his breath and stood up, and the two stared up at the burning house. The only sounds in the courtyard were the crackle of the fire and the incoming sirens.

"Jack, the Clockmaker never . . ." Gwen trailed off.

"He never what?"

"Forget it."

She turned abruptly and headed for the exit to the street. Jack stared up at the fire a moment longer and then hurried after her. "Where are you going?" he called. "Like you said, we don't even know what the Ember is."

"No," she called back. "But now we know where to start." Gwen crossed the street and turned right at the sidewalk, lowering her voice as Jack pulled up next to her. "The Clockmaker gave us hints—the Boy at Pye, the fire itself—clues that leave nothing to chance." A grim expression fell over her sooty face. "I don't know what the Ember is, Jack, but I know where, or rather *when*, it came from. And I can assure you, it was not a pleasant time."

Chapter 16

IT AMAZED JACK that he had to work so hard to keep up with a girl Gwen's size. Beneath the gray coat, her legs moved at the speed of one of those Westminster Dog Show terriers. Pedestrians ran past in the opposite direction, trying to get a closer look at the fire.

Gwen fished in her coat pocket and pulled out a flimsy blue packet of wet wipes. "Here," she said, drawing several and handing them over. "Wipe yourself down. You can't run around London all covered in soot. This isn't a West End production of *Mary Poppins*, is it?"

"The Boy at Pye, who is he?" asked Jack, rubbing his face and hands until the white cloths were completely black.

The clerk used a few on her own face. "Not really *who*. He's more of a *what*—a statue put up to mock the Great Fire for its gluttony."

Jack furrowed his brow, trying to follow the explanation. "Which Great Fire?"

"*The* Great Fire." Gwen grabbed the dirty wipes from his hand and tossed them into a wastebasket without breaking stride. "The Great Fire of 1666."

"So . . . we're going to wherever this statue is kept?"

"No. Of course not."

The clerk made a sudden turn, leaving Jack behind at an intersection. He started to jog after her but slowed, sensing a strange presence on his left—three pairs of evil eyes. He turned and saw Dracula glaring back at him, standing between the Wolf Man and Frankenstein's Monster. And they were dressed as the Three Wise Men. The sign above read MERRY CHRISTMAS FROM MADAME TUSSAUDS WAX MUSEUM.

Disturbing.

Gwen kept going, undaunted by the tacky holiday figures in the line of window displays beside them. "The Boy at Pye is nothing more than a gilded statue of a fat, naked little boy—kind of awkward, actually. Our French nutter mentioned him to give us a clue as to the Ember's history, and it was the only clue we needed, really. The fire was a bit of overkill."

"You think?" Jack caught up as she came to a halt at the next intersection. "I thought . . ." A boy band dressed as Santa's elves in the window next to him crimped his focus. He rolled his eyes and turned his back to the display. "I thought the Great Fire of London was caused by an accident and high winds. You know, like the Great Fire of Chicago."

"That's the tale every kid in England hears whenever the fire brigade comes to visit: fire in a bakery, wooden houses, and all that." She shook her finger. "Don't forget to turn off the oven, and don't play with matches. But that's just a children's story, isn't it?" The orange hand across the street changed to a green man and Gwen set off at the same quick pace as before.

"The *real* story isn't quite so simple," she continued as Jack stutter-stepped to match her pace. "The king's baker denied causing the fire to his dying day. A different man—a French immigrant named Robert Hubert—was hung for it, as a matter of arson and conspiracy. Many of the buildings, including the bakery, were built of brick and stone instead of wood, yet the fire moved at *unbelievable* speed. And then there's the death toll."

"Thousands?"

Gwen glanced up, raising an eyebrow. "Six. Yet nearly a hundred thousand Londoners were missing in the next census. Where did they all go? Historians take the royal account of the fire as gospel, but the king's own brother, the Duke of York, may have been collaborating with French arsonists. In fact, the same man would invade England years later with a French army. So royalist testimony is suspect, to say the least."

The sidewalk they had come to led them along a tall limestone wall. Gwen finally slowed to a stop next to a wrought-iron gate at the center of the block. The winter skeletons of leafless trees rose up behind it. From somewhere out of sight, muted tones of jazz touched Jack's ears.

"A cloud of unsolved mysteries surrounds that fire," said Gwen, turning to face him. "Perhaps the Ember is the key to solving them all."

"And the key to getting my father back, right?"

"Right. Of course." Her eyes drifted away and she chewed her lower lip.

Jack folded his arms. "What aren't you telling me? What was it you wouldn't say back there in the courtyard?"

She took a deep breath and met his eyes again. "All right, Jack. You were right before."

"About what?"

"About your dad—what you told Sadie, I mean. Your suspicions were correct. As far as the ministry is concerned, John Buckles died three days ago. His quartermaster was found at the Tower of London in a bad state, cuts and burns all over his body. The ministry has him in the medical ward at headquarters, but he hasn't woken up yet."

Jack tried to absorb what she was saying, but her words didn't fit together. Pieces of the puzzle were still missing. "Quartermaster?"

"Right. Sorry. Each tracker is assigned a quartermaster, a Watson to his Holmes. Your dad's man was found brutalized and alone at the Tower, but there were ashes all around him. They found . . ." She swallowed. "They found the charred remains of a bowler hat."

"But the Clockmaker—"

"The Clockmaker never gave us proof of life, did he? What if this hunt for the Ember is all for naught?"

"No." Jack turned and wrapped his hands around the bars of the iron gate. "You're wrong. The ministry is wrong."

"I know this is hard to hear, but—"

He shook the gate hard. "I said no! You really want me to give up based on a half-burned hat? My dad is alive. We're going to find the Ember and we're going to get him back."

"You're right. Of course. It was a silly thought."

Her agreement came too easily. It was not enough for Jack. "How do you know what happened to my dad, anyway? You're only a clerk, right?"

Gwen lowered her head, settling back against the limestone wall. "Apprentice clerk. That's right."

"Then how?"

"Remember your father's quartermaster, the one who hasn't regained consciousness?"

"Yeah, what about him?"

Gwen refused to look at him, studying the sidewalk instead. "His name is Percy Kincaid. He's the one who taught me all about trackers—he's been preparing me for the ministry ever since I can remember. He's my uncle."

"Oh." It hadn't occurred to Jack that other families besides his were suffering at the hands of the Clockmaker, especially not Gwen's. The suppressed sadness, the worry on her face, somehow reminded him of his mother. He softened his voice. "We're going to find the Ember, Gwen. We're going to free my dad and we're going to make the Clockmaker pay for everything he's done."

She nodded silently and pushed off the wall. "Right. Come on, then."

The clerk led Jack across the street to a fenced stairwell in the middle of the opposite sidewalk, and the mellow ribbon of jazz grew louder, twisting around him. They descended into a long, sloped tunnel, with walls covered in glossy green tiles, reminding Jack of a hotel swimming pool. Letters among the tiles read REGENT'S PARK STATION.

"We're taking the Tube?" he asked, a little frustrated. "Couldn't we have found a station closer to the Lost Property Office?"

Gwen didn't answer, not at first. Halfway down the tunnel, a man in dark glasses leaned against the ivory handrail that ran along the wall, pouring a syncopated tune from a tarnished saxophone. The clerk glanced up and down the empty passage and tossed four coins into the black case at his feet, making them land in the rhythm of "Rule, Britannia."

At the *plink . . . plink, plink, plink* of the coins, the musician straightened. With one hand, he played an answering bar of

91

the song. With the other, he pulled on the ivory rail behind him. A wide section of tiles swung outward.

Gwen nudged Jack toward the hidden portal. "Not the Tube, Jack. We're taking the Ministry Express."

Chapter 17

THE FIRST THING Jack noticed about the Ministry Express station was the black decor. Glossy, six-inch tiles lined the walls, like in the tunnel outside but jet-black—changing the feel from hotel swimming pool to mausoleum. The next thing he noticed was the silence. Other than a constant, low hum and the nearly imperceptible *flip* of newspaper pages periodically turning, his ears did not pick up a sound.

A Plexiglas box stood to one side of a bronze, old-school turnstile. Inside, an attendant flipped lazily through a newspaper, wearing a three-piece suit instead of a high-visibility jacket. A wide band on his right biceps bore the circular London Transportation symbol, all black, with the words

Ministry Express stitched in silver thread across the middle.

"My friend needs a new card," said Gwen, almost in a whisper.

The man raised one eye from his paper, staring at the girl for a half second before thrusting his chin toward a thumb pad on the wall. It looked exactly like the pad next to the vault door in the Lost Property Office. Jack cringed. No good had come from his last encounter with one of those pads.

When he didn't move, Gwen whispered in his ear, "Do I really have to hold your hand again?"

He frowned at her, hesitated another second, then placed his thumb on the pad, receiving the expected shock. A green light illuminated above a little slot and a platinum card shot halfway out with a light *ping*.

Gwen took the card and pressed it into his palm, flashing a quick smile of thanks at the attendant, who only shrugged and returned to his paper. "Good," she whispered, pulling Jack away from the turnstile. "Now, there's one more thing you need to know before we go in. Joint regulations, volume one, section seven, rule five: 'No agent, guest, or otherwise of any one of the four Elder Ministries shall, at any time except in an emergency, cause *any* sound—by utterance, instrument, body part, or any combination thereof—on or about a Ministry Express platform.'"

"Wait . . . what?" Jack's voice echoed off the black tile walls.

The attendant let out a pointed cough.

Gwen gave Jack the same look that his mom always gave him when he accidentally burped in church. "These trains run exclusively between stations that belong to the four most secretive agencies in Britain. We do not speak on the platforms. The risk of crosstalk and leaks is too great."

Again, Jack gave her a blank stare.

The clerk widened her eyes. "It means *be quiet*, you *wally*. Now come on."

Without further explanation, Gwen led him to the turnstiles, producing a small card much like his own, except hers was dark green. She held it up to a circular pad on the turnstile and a green arrow flashed. A moment later, she was through.

Jack stepped up to follow, holding his card up to the pad and getting a good look at it for the first time. It was not simply platinum in color. It *was* platinum, weighty and cold. As he stepped through the turnstile, he flipped it over and saw that one side was engraved with his given name, John Buckles. There were no other markings.

Ahead lay the most incredible subway platform Jack had ever seen. There were no tracks. Instead, great bronze rings lined the tunnel like ribs. The interior of each one glowed with bright, purple light, and this was the source of the low, electric hum.

He and Gwen were not the only patrons. Two men in long black coats and top hats shifted position as the teens entered the platform, making a point of turning their faces away. As they turned, Jack noted a hint of color from their coats, reflecting when the light hit them just right.

Farther down, he saw a striking woman in an opulent burgundy dress and tiny matching hat, seated on a bench next to a man in a black suit and bowler. These two each held a palm up in their laps, fingers moving rapidly in a sort of sign language. Jack opened his mouth to ask Gwen if that was cheating—given the big rule about no communication—but the clerk gave him a sharp look that shut him up.

The low hum increased in volume. All the patrons moved closer to the edge, toeing up to a line of silver tiles that kept them clear of the glowing bronze rings. Jack leaned forward to look down the tunnel and Gwen yanked him back by the collar as a completely cylindrical train—all black steel and bronze trim—whipped into the station, so fast it could have taken his head off. It made no sound other than a light *whump* as it jerked to a stop, followed by a long *hiss* as four doors rose up and outward. Red words flashed silently in the line of silver tiles at their feet. MIND THE GAP.

Each pair of patrons had their own car, and Jack and Gwen entered theirs, taking a seat on a long couch of plum-colored leather. Quilted blue padding covered the walls, and large, half-globe lamps were centered on the round walls at either end, filling the car with yellow light. MIND THE DOORS flashed in the line of silver tiles, and all the doors slowly lowered into place. Jack felt his ears fill with pressure.

Through the small rectangular window in the door, he saw a late-coming patron enter the platform. This one wore a gray overcoat and trilby hat, with a bright red scarf snugly tucked into his lapels. Jack drew in a sharp breath at the sight of his face. The man's right eye had no white or pupil to speak of. The whole of it was red, with a thick burn scar above and below, running from his forehead to his chin. The one good eye shifted and locked on Jack, making his blood run cold.

"You can speak now," said Gwen, her shoulder bumping into Jack's as the car lurched into motion.

Jack's eyes remained fixed on the man in the red scarf until the purple lights of the maglev rings obscured him from view. "Who was that?" he breathed.

"You mean the guy on the platform?"

"Yeah."

"It's best to keep clear of his kind. *Death* tends to follow them."

The worst part of the clerk's habit of not answering questions was raising new ones and then leaving them hanging in the air. Jack turned in his seat to face her. "And *why* would *death* follow his kind?"

"Hmm? Oh. The red scarf is the symbol of the eldest of the four Elder Ministries. The man you saw was a drago, Jack—an agent of the Ministry of Dragons."

Chapter 18

"DRAGONS?" Jack stared at Gwen. "As in, fire-breathing, flying serpents?"

She rolled her eyes and settled back into her seat. "Not *all* of them fly."

"But dragons? If dragons are real, how come I've never seen one?"

"Because the dragos are exceptional at what they do."

The cylindrical car picked up speed, so that the glowing purple ribs flashing by the window slowly merged into one faint light.

"Dragons."

"Don't repeat yourself, Jack. It's juvenile." Gwen bent at the waist, leaning down between their legs to pull a drawer out from the bench. Inside there was a rack of green bottles and a porcelain bowl of food bars in gold wrappings. "The dragos have managed to stay hidden for more than a thousand years. And the other ministries have done just as well for centuries, although the younger three each have public fronts that help. MI6, for instance"—she lifted a green glass bottle from the drawer and pressed it into Jack's hands—"is the tip of the iceberg for the Ministry of Secrets, the way the Lost Property Office is the tip of the iceberg for the Ministry of Trackers . . . sort of."

Jack eyed the bottle suspiciously.

"It's water, genius. You look dehydrated. You look hungry, too. Here, take one of these." She tossed one of the bars at him, and he fumbled it back and forth between his hands before finally getting a solid grip. He tore open the wrapper and found a plain brown bar that smelled vaguely like chocolate and a few other things, not all of them pleasant. "Is it safe?"

"Are you allergic to chestnuts, ginseng, or shellfish?"

He shook his head.

Gwen took a bite of her own bar and ground it down, one freckled cheek puffing out. "Then you'll be all right."

"What about the couple doing that weird sign language on the platform?"

"Ministry of Secrets." Gwen frowned with disgust as she chewed. "Spooks, we call them. Always cheating, that lot. The snobbish men in the black hats were toppers from the Ministry of Guilds, and you got a good look at the drago. Or, rather, he got a good look at you. None of the other agencies likes us very much. Sometimes tracker investigations have crossed paths with operations of theirs that fell into"—she paused to swallow, bobbling her head back and forth—"gray areas. They consider us a nuisance, a bunch of nosy commoners."

Jack nodded, as if what she said made perfect sense. He watched her eat in silence for a while, still not ready to try his own bar. Too much new information ripped through his mind to deal with the potential of chocolate, chestnuts, and shellfish combined.

"Gwen?" he asked presently.

"Mm-hmm?"

"What am I?"

"You're a tracker." She took a swig of water and wiped her mouth with her sleeve. "All the firstborn men in your family are."

"Yeah, I get that, I can track things because I see everything, even if I don't want to. But *why* do I see so much? What *am* I? Some kind of psychic?"

The clerk giggled. "You mean, are you magic?" She waved her hands from side to side. "Are you a wizard, Jack? Not likely. Magic is for mystic runes and men in funny hats, card games and con men in Piccadilly. What you experienced in that alley was pure neuroscience."

"Brain science?"

Gwen swallowed the last bite of her choco-nutty-shellfish bar. "You're wired differently from 99.9 percent of humanity, Jack Buckles. That doesn't make you magic, but it does make you special." She tossed her wrapper into a brass can in the drawer and set her empty bottle back in the rack. Then she pushed the drawer closed and faced him, sitting cross-legged on the bench. "Short answer: You're hyper-observant. Your brain processes sensory information in a sort of matrix, instead of in single channels like the rest of us."

Jack did his best not to show his confusion, but he failed.

Gwen raised her eyebrows. "Short answer not good enough? Okay. Try this: When you smell herring, what happens in your head?"

"Ugh. The Tube car was full of it this morning, like reddish-gray slime running down the windows. Made me want to gag."

"Yeah, well, the rest of us just smell *fish*. In our heads we

102

might see a drawing of a fish or a square can with the top rolled back. That's called association. What you experience is more real than that. The signal from your nose goes straight to a portion of the brain that most people don't use—a synaptic juncture where all your senses meet. Sights and sounds have color and texture for you. Smells and temperatures can be bright or loud, gold or gray."

Jack nodded slowly. What she said made sense, but none of it explained the hand he had seen when he touched the vault door, or the accuracy of his vision of the abandoned house *before* he had gone inside. Then again, had the vision really been so accurate, or did he just remember it that way?

The train bumped to a stop. When the door hissed open, Jack started to get up, but Gwen threw out a hand, knocking him back into his seat. "No," she whispered. "Not this one."

The door rose to reveal a half-dozen men and women in gray coats and red scarves, some in trilbies, others in newsboy caps. Five of them had burns on their faces, none so severe as the burn on the man in the last station, but disturbing nonetheless. All six fixated on Jack as they walked to the car next door.

Their stares made his skin crawl, as if he might get burns of his own from the exposure. With so many to watch, however, he noticed something new. When one of their coats flared, Jack caught a glimpse of shimmering red, as if the liner were bedazzled with jewels. Shiny fashion seemed out of place with the rest of the austere drago persona.

Once the door closed again, Jack realized he'd been holding the same breath since the moment the door opened. He let it all out in one great huff. "What was *that* place?"

"The ministry side of Temple Station," said Gwen, leaning forward to watch the platform disappear behind them. "HQ for the dragos."

Jack settled back into his seat. "So, are we going to tracker headquarters? I mean, the Ministry of Trackers?"

Something flashed in the clerk's eyes—another unanswered question. "We call it the Keep. But no. That won't be necessary. If we're tracking something from the history of the Great Fire, we should start where it all began. We're heading for Pudding Lane."

Chapter 19

THE NEXT STOP came up quickly, and Jack peered
through the window to see a station much different from
the previous two. Instead of a single line of glowing
bronze rings, there were several, some intersecting others. Instead of concrete structures laid with glossy tile,
the platforms appeared to have been cut straight into a
cave of heavy black granite. Dozens of people waited on
them, rather than the few he had seen before. Jack was
able to identify pairs of spooks with their telltale sign language, huddles of toppers from the Ministry of Guilds,
and a few isolated dragos with their red scarves. "Where
are our people?" he asked. "You know, from the Ministry
of Trackers?"

"*Crumbs*, you mean. That's what the other ministries call us." Gwen's freckles flattened. "According to them, we're the ministry of lowborn commoners. Anyway, there're not many of us around. The trackers are in a bit of a slowdown—minimum manning and all."

"But why—?"

Gwen put a hand over his mouth as the door hissed open.

Once they were out on the platform, the oddity of the place hit Jack full force. Here was a hub of sorts, a station with maybe a dozen lines. Yet the only noises were the hiss of the doors and the shuffling of feet. There were no echoing announcements of delays and track changes, no murmur of the masses. Jack felt like someone had pressed the mute button. He liked it.

Granite stairs throughout the station led up to two more platform levels, with the second supported by thick, octagonal pillars, and the third suspended from the ceiling. A train had just pulled in to one of the third-level platforms and hung there, suspended in its rings directly above Jack's head.

Jack used his platinum card to exit through the turnstiles and followed Gwen to a solitary elevator—a *lift*, he reminded himself—in an empty corner of the station. Instead of pressing a button, the clerk dropped twenty pence into a coin slot. The door slid open to reveal an ordinary restroom stall.

"Mind the loo," whispered Gwen, forcing him to squeeze between the paper dispenser and the bowl as she pushed him inside. Before Jack could ask any of the several questions running through his mind, she locked the stall door and the whole thing started upward.

The lift-loo rose into a minute public restroom, complete with a little sink and mirror. Gwen pushed Jack out of the stall, pressing a large red button mounted above the sink, and a narrow door slid open behind him. "Give me a minute to freshen up, would you?" she said, and shoved him backward into brilliant sunlight. The door slid closed between them. A red OCCUPIED sign lit up with a discreet *ding*.

Jack had emerged from a square, cinder-block structure encased in blue-tinted glass—as if colored glass could make a cinder-block toilet double as municipal art. He frowned at his own reflection, and his eyes were drawn to a real piece of art above his shoulder.

He turned and shielded his eyes to stare up at a giant column, at least two hundred feet high and topped with a spiky gold ball. A mural carved into the square base depicted a fainting woman, lying atop the ruins of a city, with flames raging behind her. Several figures—angels, workers, and a king—came to the woman's aid, but they all wore snobbish, disinterested expressions. Jack found the most compelling figure to be a diminutive dragon, half-hidden beneath the rubble. He seemed intelligent and resolute, trying desperately to lift the crumbling walls back into place.

A toilet flushed and water poured into a sink. Jack turned to see Gwen, standing in the narrow doorway, drying her hands with a paper towel.

"The secret entrance to your big station is a *loo*?" Jack held up two fingers of each hand to make quotation marks as he said the funny British word.

"It's quite convenient." Gwen crumpled up the paper towel and tossed it into a bin as she stepped outside. The door slid closed behind her, the red LED sign changing to a blue one that read OUT OF ORDER. "Why do you think you can never get into a public lavatory in London?"

He gave her a blank stare.

"Right. You've probably never tried."

"What are we doing here, Gwen? How is this helping me get my dad back?"

Instead of answering, she walked a short distance to the north, out of the square surrounding the monument. Jack followed her down off the raised, granite paving stones onto a short, cobblestone street, hidden in the shadows between an apartment building and a bank.

Gwen reached the center of the road and turned, spreading her hands. "This is Pudding Lane."

Jack shrugged. "Okay . . ."

"This is the epicenter, Jack, the place where it all began."

"You mean the fire."

She widened her eyes and nodded, clearly wanting him to come to some sort of conclusion on his own.

"And this . . . Ember . . . is here somewhere?"

"No, Jack." Gwen dropped her hands and sighed. "Don't be such a wally."

He frowned at her. "That's the second time you've called me that—as if I even know what it means."

"*Wally*, Jack. Lost in the crowd. Out of your depth. What else would you call it?" Gwen shook her head. "You're getting off topic. The Ember *was* here, and that's the point. The ministry hunts for objects like this *all* the time. Weird artifacts are sort of our bread and butter. These things often have unusual qualities that are linked to catastrophes and events that changed the course of history."

Jack stepped deeper into the shadow of the buildings. The stones at his feet looked ancient, worn and darkened by centuries of use. "So you're telling me this Ember may be the thing that caused the Great Fire."

"Either that or it was created by the fire. We can't be certain which until we know more. But we *can* be certain the Ember was here, at the epicenter."

"And what am I supposed to do? Track it? Find clues left here hundreds of years ago?"

She nodded. "Three hundred and fifty, to be exact."

Jack couldn't believe how serious she looked, how matter-of-fact—as if she had merely asked him to go and get her a soda. "You're nuts."

"For your father, Jack. For my uncle. You can do this. It's who you are."

He let out a long breath, trying to quiet his mind again. "Yeah, that's what you keep telling me." Seeing came easier this time. Soon the jumble of inputs from the lane rose into a slow-moving field of data.

Cobblestones: blackened with age, some worn nearly to nubs.

Ancient grout: white, weathered away to form deep chasms between the stones.

Lots of cigarettes and old gum: smokers and gum chewers the world over were habitual litterbugs—nothing new.

Then Jack noticed a clicking, slow and syncopated—each almost imperceptible sound a faint, silver speck floating into his mind's eye from somewhere to the right. There was a repeating pattern of six, one he had heard before.

He wheeled to his right and swatted at a clockwork beetle that crept along the aluminum frame of the bank windows. It dodged his attack, leaping into the air with a grating buzz.

Gwen groaned. "Not this again. Jack, leave it be."

"Go away!" he shouted, taking another futile swing. "We're doing what you asked!" But the beetle turned the tables, diving at him, forcing him back into the lane.

"Look out!"

Jack realized too late that Gwen was not talking about the bug. Another buzzing sound, louder and much deeper, came in fast from the left. He saw the motorcycle in his head even before he shifted his gaze to look. The biker braked and swerved. Jack stumbled forward and tripped, falling palms first to the stones.

The vision came hard and fast—not like the others, in which his fingers seemed to gradually sink into the cold metal. The instant Jack's hands smacked down on the cobblestones, reams of data shot up his arms. Suddenly he was in another place, or maybe another time.

Voices—ghostly, unintelligible echoes—bounced off stone block walls that were nothing like the apartments and the bank that had been there a moment before. The shadows around him came alive, separating into ragged, amorphous shapes that drifted past, trailing vapors of darkness. At first, he was afraid to look. Then he forced himself to focus on one approaching form and it quickly sharpened, splitting into the silhouettes of a man and a woman. Jack could swear the faceless man stared right at him as he passed, shouting something he could not understand. In the back of his mind a constant, undulating wail grew. It had the shape and flow of an air raid siren.

The shadow couple stopped at a doorway. As the faceless man pushed the woman through, he pointed up the lane. Jack looked in time to see a monstrous black flash rise up against the white sky, accompanied by a horrendous crash. The street fell away beneath him.

He was falling again, through the street, only to slam face-down into the cobblestones once more. He pushed himself up to his hands and knees and saw that the rushing shadows were gone. So were the echoing voices and the stone buildings, leaving him with only the wailing and the old street, and a gray-white mist hovering over the stones.

It wasn't mist. The stabbing scent of smoke hit his nostrils, the same scent that had nearly choked him to death in the abandoned house. The wailing became more insistent, no longer the drone of a siren. Now it sounded like voices—hundreds, maybe thousands, of miserable voices crying out in anguish.

Jack didn't want to be here anymore. He closed his eyes, trying to escape, but the vision of the stones and the smoke remained. He didn't know how these things worked, how to turn them off. He tried to call out for Gwen and discovered that he had no voice. His mouth wouldn't even open. Then he felt something cold snaking across his fingers. Black tendrils of shadow drifted up from the white grit between the cobblestones, twisting around his wrists and crawling up his arms, forming dozens of long skeletal hands with icy grips. He tried to pull his hands away from the cobblestones, but the wraiths held him fast, pulling him down. He couldn't move, couldn't even scream. Then the wailing coalesced, finally forming words he could understand. "Help us, Jack. Release us!"

Chapter 20

"JACK!" The ghostly hands evaporated in a breath of cold wind as Gwen helped Jack up from the pavement. "Are you okay? Did that biker hit you?"

"I'm fine." Jack was relieved to hear his own voice. He could speak again. "At least, I think I am. How long was I out?"

"What do you mean, 'How long'? I rushed over as soon as you fell."

Sure enough, he could still hear the motorcycle fading into the distance. The accident couldn't have happened more than a few seconds before, but the vision seemed much longer. "The beetle," he said, still trying to clear his mind. "Was the Clockmaker here?"

"Only his little emissary. Buzzed off for the moment." She

steadied him, brushing the dust off his shoulders. "Jack, what happened when you fell?"

He sat down on the curb, taking great care to avoid touching the street with his bare hands. "Um . . . do trackers see things? Not like finding kerosene boot prints or visualizing fish smells, but . . . things." He looked up at her. "You know, hallucinations?"

Gwen's eyes went wide. "You *sparked*."

"Whoa." Jack held up his hands. "I did no such . . . Wait. What?"

"You sparked." She sat down beside him. "You got a spark of vision by touching an object. You saw something from the past—recent, distant, either one. Is that what happened?"

He nodded dumbly.

She nodded with him, gaze falling to the cobblestones. *"Brilliant."* She was silent for several seconds.

"Gwen?"

"Yes?"

He shrugged and raised his hands.

"Oh. Right. Explanation." Her freckles bounced and she waved a hand, gesturing at nothing in particular. "The world around us is full of memories, Jack. Light and sound get trapped in rigid materials like stone and steel—recorded like data on a disk drive. *You* can access that data. Your unique sensory matrix allows you to sort of . . . download the memories."

"You're saying I can see movies of the past by touching random stuff."

"Eh . . ." The clerk wiggled a hand. "Let's not oversimplify. Trackers can only spark on *minerals*, and each type yields a different result. The memory of stone runs deep, going back hundreds, sometimes thousands of years. But the sounds and images are dull—mere echoes and shadows. Steel and iron are the opposite. They retain greater detail, but the data remains shallow, near the surface. It gets overwritten quickly, like RAM on a computer."

"So . . . I either get shadows of the distant past, or clear images of something that just happened."

A nod and another freckle bounce, with a hint of slyness to it. "Unless you spark on a gemstone, a big one, like the giants of the Crown Jewels. Light penetrates deep into gemstones, and their hard, crystalline structures hold sights and sounds practically forever. Trackers have solved centuries-old murders and located the tombs of pharaohs simply by holding a famous jewel in their hands."

Jack slowly stood, taking a step back. He needed space to

breathe, to think. "Why didn't you tell me about this back at the Lost Property Office?"

"It shouldn't have come up at all. Sparking takes years of training. Even with instruction, no tracker under the age of eighteen has ever managed it." Gwen popped up to join him. "Until you, Jack. Isn't that *brilliant*!"

He did not share her excitement. The idea of seeing the past recorded in everyday objects explained the vision of the hand at the Chamber and the vision of the Clockmaker entering the house with the blue door, but it certainly didn't cover specters trying to drag him down through the cobblestones. That was no memory. It felt more like crossing over into another world.

"Look." Gwen led him to the center of the lane again. "We have to keep at this if we expect to get anywhere. What did you see when you fell?"

"Shapes. Darkness. Nothing useful." Jack wasn't ready to tell her about the ghosts. He would never find his father if the only person helping him thought he was crazy.

The freckles sank with disappointment. "That's all right, being your first time and all. Cobblestones are rubbish for sparking anyway. Cheap rock. All that traffic. Next time we'll find you some proper stone."

"Wait a second." Her efforts to lower his expectations made Jack defensive. "I *did* see shadows that looked like people running . . . and a big explosion. I thought I heard an air raid siren, too."

"Well, why didn't you say so?" Gwen scrunched up her brow, processing the information. Then she slapped her forehead. "World War Two. Very common for new trackers. The first memory you see in stone will always be the most traumatic—until you learn to focus your sparks, that is. Here in London that's often a World War Two bombing raid. The stones didn't like those one bit."

"What about the Great Fire? Wouldn't that qualify as traumatic?"

"Yes, but what if *these* stones never saw the fire? I'll bet they were laid during the reconstruction, right in the ashes of old Pudding Lane."

"Ashes?" Jack gazed down at the unusual whiteness of the grout. "What kind of ashes?"

"All kinds. There was a great, deep field of it after the fire, and the king and his architects rebuilt London right on top of it all. The ashes became the foundation of the new city."

"Sure. *All* kinds." As he stared down at the disturbing ash-grout, Jack picked up a hint of red—a tiny, triangular rock deep in a crack between the stones. It wasn't lying on top of the grout like the gum or the cigarettes. It was *part* of the grout, worked into it from the beginning. Once he isolated the first fragment, others started popping up all around him, floating above the stones in his mind's eye. The distribution of the pieces formed a half circle in the lane, twenty feet long. "I see something."

"I can tell," said Gwen, a hint of exasperation in her voice. "Would you mind telling me what it is?"

Jack squatted down to pick up the largest piece, barely the size of a dime, but he curled his fingers back as they neared the cobblestone. "Um . . . why don't you get it? Your fingers are smaller. They'll fit between the stones."

She shrugged and knelt beside him, sticking a delicate pinkie down into the gap and rubbing the fragment. "It's rough. Like brick. And look how deep it is. I bet this was recently exposed, after the grout above it eroded in the rain."

Jack showed her the half-circle pattern and watched her smile widen the whole time. "This is it," she said, walking the perimeter of the brick fragments. "*This* is the epicenter."

"How can you be so sure?"

"My uncle, remember?" Gwen pointed to Jack's eyes with two fingers. "The tracker observes." Then she tapped her head.

"The quartermaster deduces. Detective teamwork at its finest. Uncle Percy taught me everything there is to know about the art of deduction."

"And you deduced from a few slivers of red brick that this is the epicenter?"

"It's simple—*elementary*, you might say—if you take a moment to think about it. The brick is *in the grout*. The grout comes from the period *right after the Great Fire*. And at the time of the fire, only one building on Pudding Lane was *made of brick*." She cocked her head toward Jack. "And that building was . . ."

"The bakery."

Gwen punched his arm. "Brilliant! And the bakery is where it all began."

"Great. Good work. So where is the Ember?"

Her smile flattened. "Don't know. Haven't gotten that far, I'm afraid."

Jack leaned back against the apartment building that stood in the place of the burned bakery. He sighed. "Maybe we're going about this all wrong. My dad used to say that *where* is a wasted question—"

"If you don't start with *who*, first." Gwen punched him again. "Of course John Buckles said that. It's an old tracker saying." She pressed her lips together, looking off into space for several seconds. Finally, she nodded. "And it tells us we should have started with the *baker* instead of the bakery."

Jack was beginning to develop a bruise where she kept hitting him. He frowned, rubbing his arm. "Except the baker's been gone for three hundred fifty years."

"Perhaps." The freckles rose into another smile. "But I know where to find him."

Chapter 21

APPARENTLY THE BAKER had not gone far. Gwen led Jack less than a hundred yards down Pudding Lane, across Lower Thames Street to an old stone chapel next to the river.

"So the baker went to church?"

Gwen glanced over at him, raising an eyebrow as they stopped before an ancient wooden door. "Lots of people go to church after they die, Jack." An old marquee informed them that the chapel was closed. She ignored it, reaching for the handle.

"Gwen, we can't."

"Sure we can." The great iron hinges creaked as she leaned back into her pull, and the door cracked open. She brushed her hands together. "If they wanted to keep us out, they would have locked it."

Plaques and commemorations of all shapes and sizes covered the plaster walls of the foyer. A hundred names, dates, and in-memoriams flashed across Jack's brain. The murmurs of a telephone conversation drifted down from the vicar's chamber above. Gwen put a finger to her lips and inclined her head toward the pews.

They crossed a raised stone threshold into a narrow sanctuary, where sunlight streamed through rows of stained glass windows, painting whitewashed columns with color. At the front, gold sculptures and rich purple cloth adorned a tall mahogany altar. All of it was beautiful, but Jack couldn't take his eyes off the drab, dreadfully disturbing floor.

Every square inch of floor space in the sanctuary was taken up with grave markers, most so old and worn that the names and dates had faded. Jack's eyes tracked down the center aisle from the altar to his feet. He gasped and hopped backward over the threshold. Even at the very back, he had been standing on a grave.

"The baker's name was Thomas Farriner." Gwen slowly advanced up the aisle, examining each marker as she passed.

"*Allegedly*, he left an oven burning overnight, right next to an open window. The wind picked up and you know the rest. According to the story, Farriner was never punished, but the guilt and shame killed him, and he was buried beneath the center aisle of *this* church." She reached the front and shook her head. "I didn't see any Farriners, but the letters are all worn. See if you fare better."

Jack had no intention whatsoever of stepping on a floor made entirely of gravestones, not after the wraiths on Pudding Lane. "I think I'll stay over here and check out the plaques."

"We're not *looking* for a plaque. Whether he started the fire or not, Farriner was there at the epicenter. He had to have known *something*. Perhaps he left us a clue."

Jack didn't move. He would rather deal with the chaos of names and dates from the foyer plaques than venture out onto the big-creepy-floor-of-the-dead.

"Hey! Do you want to rescue your father or not? I need your tracker senses out here. We're looking for a grave from 1670, but the oldest with letters I could read was from 1676."

1676. All the names and dates pressing in on Jack from the plaques and in-memoriams faded—everything except that one year.

... DONATED BY JOHN HUCKERBY, 1676 ...

... RAISED IN SEPTEMBER, 1676 ...

... DEDICATED IN 1676 ...

It popped up everywhere. "1676," he said, repeating it out loud.

"What?"

"That year. The same year you saw. It's all over this room, at the top of donor lists and lists of dedications on almost every plaque. There are only a couple without it."

Gwen came back to join him. "You can see all these engravings at once?"

He glared at her.

"Right. Tracker. *Hello-ooo*. Introduced you to the concept." She held up her hands. "I only meant you're picking up your new skills rather quickly." She punched his arm. "Well done, you. Now, exceptions are often the best clues. Show me a plaque where 1676 does *not* appear."

Jack silently indicated a small round plaque, and they both leaned in to read it.

THIS CHURCH WAS DESIGNED BY

SIR CHRISTOPHER WREN,

ROYAL ARCHITECT OF

THE RECONSTRUCTION.

WORK BEGAN IN 1671,

TAKING FIVE YEARS TO COMPLETE.

"Bad news, then." Gwen shook her head. "The stories are wrong. The baker's not here."

He stepped back, furrowing his brow. "How did you jump to that conclusion?"

"*Finding* a clue is a job only half-done, Jack. You have to *think* about the clue as well." She waited for him to connect whatever dots had come to her, but Jack only folded his arms and leaned back against a short, arched door at the edge of the foyer, which he assumed was the entrance to the world's oldest broom closet.

Gwen rolled her eyes and tapped the plaque. "Look. The church burned down in 1666. Reconstruction started in 1671. And Farriner died in 1670, one year before the first stones were laid. Jack, the baker couldn't have been buried beneath the center aisle. There *was* no aisle." She let out a little huff. "I should have known. Ministry regulations, volume two, section four, rule twenty: The written words of history rarely tell the whole—'"

The door Jack leaned against gave way with a loud *squeak*, and he fell backward, grasping wildly at the air in front of him. He bounced down the first few steps of a winding staircase and came to rest on his back.

Gwen's face popped into view between his sneakers. "Oh, Jack, you've solved it."

"Solved what?" he groaned, glowering up at her.

She jogged down the steps and pulled him to his feet. "Don't you see? The baker was buried *beneath* the center aisle. Not in the center aisle, Jack, *beneath* the aisle"—she gestured at the darkness below—"downstairs in the *crypt*."

Gwen removed a penlight—although she called it a torch—from her coat pocket, and the two descended into a rocky chamber. From the darkness beyond the beam, Jack heard the single *ploop* of a water droplet falling into a puddle.

"A bit leaky down here, isn't it?" asked the clerk. "Probably why they haven't wired it for lights." She shined her light along the walls, revealing rows of body-length niches. All were empty, making them look sort of pointless, like empty shelves in a library.

"The bodies were moved to the big cemetery at Brookwood in the 1800s," said Gwen, even though Jack had not asked. "Along with thousands of others from the city crypts. Built a whole railway for it. London Necropolis Line. Very macabre."

Necropolis. Now he couldn't stop himself from asking. "They *moved* all the bodies?"

Gwen nodded, letting her light drift along the empty niches as they crept deeper into the long chamber. "Londoners feared a plague might leach into the groundwater from the piles of bodies beneath their feet. And they had good reason for their paranoia. The bubonic plague had killed thousands. In fact, it was the Great Fire itself that finally put an end to the disease."

"Wait." Jack stopped, grabbing Gwen's arm to stop her, too. "That means Farriner's body isn't here either, and you knew it all along. What are we doing down here?"

"We were never looking for Farriner's *body*, Jack." She smiled. Her beam had come to rest on a solitary stone sarcophagus near the back of the chamber. "We're looking for his grave."

Chapter 22

THE SCULPTURE lying in repose atop the sarcophagus bore the deathly pallor of a body. Its face, once young and peaceful, was made aged and grotesque by purple mold growing in the lines and crevices. Jack had the feeling that it might sit up and greet them as they approached.

They split and walked up either side, examining the artwork. "Marble," said Gwen, running her light along the flowing stone robes. "Much better than cobblestone."

Jack bent cautiously over the middle of the effigy, scrutinizing what appeared to be a pastry crust filled with cherries, sculpted to look as if the dead man were holding it on his stomach. "He's got a pie," he said flatly.

"That's a tart, actually. And what were you expecting, a sword?"

Gwen shined the penlight in Jack's face, making him squint. "The man was a baker, not a knight." She paused and chewed her lip. "Which begs the question: How does a *baker* merit a sarcophagus like this?"

"He was the king's baker, wasn't he?"

"High marks, Jack," Gwen replied with a smile. "You were paying attention. But the king had a lot of bakers. Why did he buy this one a sculpted casket? This is the kind of work reserved for royalty, and we're talking about the man who allegedly burned London to the ground." She sighed. "I don't see any writing at all. If you want answers, you're going to have to spark."

Jack had suspected as much. He didn't relish the thought of sparking on a grave, not after the spectral hands and the voices on Pudding Lane. "Are you sure he's not in there?"

"Why should that matter?"

"Uh . . . no reason." Jack held his hands out, a hair's breadth above the stone.

Gwen folded her arms. "Go on, then."

He swallowed his fear and lowered his hands just enough to touch the cold, wet marble. It felt slippery, slimy even. But nothing happened. Jack let out a relieved sigh. "Huh. Maybe I lost the power."

"Sparking is not a *power*. It's brain chemistry. And you haven't lost it. You simply don't know how to control it yet."

"Whatever. It's not working." As he spoke, Jack let his palms rest fully on the stone. The clerk vanished in a puff of black vapor. With a disorienting, sideways rush, the room shifted from deep darkness to shades of gray. The shift gave him vertigo, yet, at the same time, he couldn't fall over if he tried. Jack's body no longer belonged to him. He had sparked after all.

Gwen was right. Marble *was* better than cobblestone. Jack could see the whole room, even make out the nose and the lips on the baker's effigy. But the niches on the walls were still empty. If the spark had taken him back into the crypt's past, it had not taken him far enough. He sensed a presence standing near him. Jack was not alone.

A dark figure materialized near the foot of the sarcophagus, the silhouette of a man in a long coat and bowler hat. *Dad?* Jack's voice would not come. Still, the silhouette began to move toward him as soon as he had the thought, shadowy hands sliding over the surface of the sculpture. Had it heard him? Jack moved as well, though he had not commanded his body to do any such thing. He shifted sideways into the silhouette, and the two merged into one.

Jack dropped through the rocky floor and landed right back where he'd started, standing in the crypt with his hands laid on the marble effigy. New silhouettes filled the chamber, a dozen shadows in bulky clothes. There were coffins now too, filling the niches on the walls.

The silhouettes gathered around him, faceless heads bowed in prayer, and the one at the front spread its hands, uttering groans and murmurs that Jack could not understand. After a long time, almost longer than Jack could bear, the murmurs stopped and the shadows drifted away. Finally, only the one at the head of the sarcophagus remained—the murmuring silhouette that Jack had decided must be the priest.

The shadow-priest lowered its arms and released another round of groans. Then it did something truly odd. It withdrew a slender object from its dark robes and stuffed it into the effigy's mouth. The moment Jack thought about reaching for it, he felt an upward rush, leaving the shadow-priest and his clue below. "No! Wait!"

"Hey!" hissed Gwen. "Keep your voice down."

Jack yanked his hands from the effigy and patted his

chest and sides, relieved to have full control of his limbs again. "I'm . . . I'm back."

"I'll take that to mean you sparked." Gwen's freckles flattened. "And you're not 'back,' because you didn't go anywhere. Sparks are *visions*, Jack, not journeys."

He nodded but said nothing. His brain was still catching up to the present.

She rolled her eyes. "Soooo, *what did you see?*"

"Oh . . . um . . . he stuffed something in the effigy's mouth."

"He? He who?"

"The priest." Regaining his temporal bearings, Jack took the light from Gwen and moved to the head of the sarcophagus. "Right here. I saw—" He stopped. The baker's lips were closed, not open. They looked as if they had been sculpted that way. Jack shook his head. "That can't be right. I saw him put an object in the effigy's mouth."

"Are you certain that's what you saw?"

He stared down at the baker's face. "Absolutely."

Without any further argument, Gwen reclaimed the penlight and began inspecting the effigy, running her beam along the side. "Then there must be some sort of actuator, a lever or something."

The immediacy of her faith astounded him. "So . . . you believe me?"

"You saw what you saw, Jack." She squatted down beside the sarcophagus, still searching. "Section four, rule three: 'Sparks don't lie.' They may require interpretation, but they don't"—Gwen cocked her head to one side, shining the light at the edge of the baker's pastry—"lie. And here's your proof. There's a gap beneath the tart, hidden by the curve of Farriner's hands."

"You mean the pie?"

"No. I mean the *tart*. Small in size. Nearly vertical crust. I don't see any room for argument here." Her eyes narrowed. "*Anyway*, there's a gap. Give us a hand, will you?" She grabbed the edges of the pastry and grunted, trying to turn it like a wheel. Jack joined her, and the pie-tart gave way to their efforts. It made a slow quarter turn, accompanied by a grinding noise from Farriner's head.

The two exchanged a glance and Gwen shifted her light. The baker's lips had parted a fraction of an inch. "It's working." She let out a little laugh that told Jack she hadn't been quite as confident in his spark as she had claimed. "It's actually working."

"Hey. What happened to 'Sparks don't lie'?"

"Oh, don't be so sensitive. Come on. Let's get it open."

They returned to their work, doubling their efforts and turning the pie-tart quarter by quarter until the baker's mouth gaped open. Gwen hurried to the head and shined the light down inside, illuminating a tiny roll of parchment.

Chapter 23

"EASY, TIGER," cautioned Gwen as Jack reached for the paper. "If that turns to dust in your hands, we're sunk."

He cast her a scowl that said *duh*, but he slowed down all the same. The roll of paper made a cringe-worthy scraping sound as he pulled it from the confines of the baker's mouth, but it came out in one piece, and the two unrolled it together, laying it out on the effigy's chest.

Jack groaned. The parchment, barely the width of a grocery receipt, appeared to have once held three full paragraphs of tiny writing. Time had faded the script into the uniform brown of the paper. He could only read the top two lines. "The Last Confession of Thomas Farriner, Conduct of the King's Bake-house." Jack shrugged. "Doesn't tell us much, does it?"

Gwen nodded, chewing her bottom lip. "Perhaps you should—"

"Spark?" His eyes shifted from the clerk to the parchment and back again. "It's paper."

She shook her head. "I was going to say you should run your fingers over the remains of the writing."

"And why would I do that?"

"You're a tracker, silly. Your senses overlap—*all* of them." Gwen wiggled her fingers at him. "Did you think your sense of touch got left out of the deal? Try it. You may be surprised."

Doing his best not to shake with the worry of destroying their only clue, Jack laid his fingertips on the writing. As soon as his skin touched the paper, black markings appeared in his mind like bumps on a gray wall. He almost jumped at the sensation. Still, they were only fragments of letters. "I see shapes, but . . . Wait. I've got something." As Jack's fingers slid down the page, a few of the fragments came together, enough that he could form them into words. " 'What . . . Pep-ys . . . saw . . . but . . . never wrote in . . . his . . . infernal book." He pulled his hand back. "Pep-ys? Is that right?"

"*Peeps*," said Gwen. "That's how you say it. Farriner must be talking about Samuel Pepys, a well-known figure of the Great Fire. Historians call him the Great Diarist." She snorted. "I call him the Great Busybody. Pepys minded everyone's business but his own, and he wrote *all* of it down in his diary, including a detailed account of the Great Fire."

Jack nodded. "Something this . . . *Peeps* . . . saw was important to the baker's confession."

"*Saw* but never *wrote*," Gwen corrected him, raising a finger. "Can you read any more?"

Jack tried again, slowly moving his fingertips down the text. Nothing else made sense until he reached the final line. Farriner must have pressed harder with his final words. Jack could read them easily. "The mayor betrayed us, the cobbler saved us, and the ravens keep their secret." He took his hands away. "Sounds like a nursery rhyme. All we're missing are the butcher and the candlestick maker. What does it mean?"

"Haven't the foggiest." The clerk handed him the light, then carefully rolled up the parchment and placed it back in the effigy's mouth.

"Wait. Don't we need that?"

"Section four, rule twenty-two: 'Leave history the way you find it.' The confession told us where to look next. It's of no other use to us." Gwen moved to the baker's midsection. "I'll need your help with the tart."

"Pie," said Jack, if only to annoy her. He helped her turn the pastry in the opposite direction, slowly closing Farriner's mouth. "The confession told us where to look? You mean the line about Pepys?"

"Even better." The baker's lips ground closed once more, and Gwen stepped back, dusting off her hands. "I know where Pepys stood when he wrote it."

To Jack's great relief, Gwen did not take Pudding Lane when they left the church. She led him up the hill one block west of it, to the great column monument he had seen reflected in the blue glass at the artsy-loo—the monument with the dragon hidden in its mural.

"In case you hadn't guessed, this is the Monument to the Great Fire," said Gwen, coming to a halt at the edge of the small square surrounding the edifice.

Jack shielded his eyes to gaze up at the column. "Shouldn't we have started here?"

"It's a monument *about* the fire," said the clerk with a shrug, "raised years after the event by aristocrats who used the king's money to build a hobby science lab rather than a real memorial." She strolled ahead of him and turned, pointing up at a Latin inscription. "According to this, Christopher Wren and

Robert Hooke built this tower two hundred two feet high so its shadow would fall on the fated bakery. But why two hundred two feet, exactly?"

Jack shrugged.

Gwen gave him what he decided must be her know-it-all grin. "They wanted to hang a two-hundred-foot pendulum string inside. That's why." She backed toward the east end of the pedestal. "Come on. This isn't really our destination."

Jack didn't move. He couldn't take his eyes off the Monument. Between the pedestal and the column, the mason had carved a layer of debris, as if the column were rising from the rubble of the ruined city. But the rubble had come to life before Jack's eyes, shifting and grinding together. He could see bones amid the debris—legs and forearms, rib cages interlocked with one another. Round pieces Jack had mistaken for stones slowly turned in place, revealing empty eye sockets and broken jaws. A host of skulls stared down at him.

Release us.

Jack blinked. The sculpture returned to its benign, weathered appearance.

Gwen stared back at him with concern. "Jack? Are you coming?"

He hadn't touched a thing—no stone, no metal, not one

140

thing. Even if he had, weren't sparks supposed to show him real events? Gwen had never said anything about artwork coming to life. "Yeah," he said, hardly able to get the word out for the dryness in his throat. He swallowed hard. "I'm coming."

Jack followed Gwen around to the east side of the pedestal, where she directed him to a doorway that led to the interior of the Monument. He balked. "I thought you said this wasn't our destination."

"Patience, Jack," she replied, and pushed him through.

A spiral staircase wound its way up within the shell of the column, all the way to the top. Jack imagined Hooke's pendulum hanging down through the middle. Then he heard a light cough. A young woman stood in the doorway of a small office to the right of the entrance, next to a sign that said ADMISSION: £5. She raised her eyebrows, waiting expectantly. Jack bent close to Gwen's ear. "I don't have any money."

The clerk slipped a hand into his jacket pocket and withdrew the platinum card, holding it up for the girl to see. Immediately she stepped aside, staring straight ahead as if she no longer saw them. Gwen nudged Jack into the office.

"We're not going up the stairs?" Jack watched the office

girl as he passed. She continued to pretend he wasn't there, like she had suddenly become one of those perfectly rigid soldiers that guard Buckingham Palace.

"Not up," said Gwen, lifting a loose rug with her toe to reveal a trapdoor. "Down."

Chapter 24

GWEN SWITCHED ON her penlight as the two descended a short staircase into a perfectly round chamber, as wide as the great column above. "I wasn't exaggerating when I told you that Wren and Hooke built this place as a laboratory," she said, shining the light along the walls. Shelves carved into the stone still held the dusty remnants of experiments from another age—a set of bronze weights, a wooden microscope, a few decaying creatures encased in yellowed jars.

The clerk walked across the room, directing her beam at a floor carved with equations and celestial patterns. She patted a brass telescope fixed to the ceiling at the center of the chamber. "They put a lens in the fireball at the very top, turning the whole column into one big telescope. Even the stairs have an ulterior purpose. Each step is exactly six inches tall, making the staircase a huge ruler. Hooke used it to measure atmospheric pressure at specific altitudes." Upon reaching the opposite wall, she pushed open a low iron door that creaked noisily on its hinges. "No time for the grand tour, though. I told you this wasn't our destination."

An endless line of weak fluorescents illuminated the tunnel beyond the door, providing just enough cold blue light to see by. "This tunnel is one of several that date back to the late 1600s," said Gwen, setting off at her usual pace. "The Royal Society—Wren and Hooke's people—used them to travel between various observation points throughout London. Some of their experiments required speed, and they couldn't be bothered to fight their way through the riffraff at the center of the city. Now the tunnels serve as utility lines. This one will take us straight to All Hallows Barking."

Jack waited for further explanation. "Which is . . ."

"The church where Pepys stood to watch the fire, of course." Gwen nodded skyward, up into the fluorescents. "Up in the bell tower."

The two fell silent, leaving Jack to listen to the textured hum of the lights and the white echo of their footfalls.

"Gwen," he said once he had built up the courage, "do trackers ever . . ." He faltered, searching for a better way to ask. He couldn't find one. Finally, he let out a short breath and asked, "Do they ever go crazy? From sparking, or maybe from seeing too much?"

She laughed. "Don't be ridiculous."

He laughed as well, trying to play it off. "Right. Dumb question."

After another long silence, the clerk bobbled her head. "I mean, sure, a few trackers have been a little eccentric— what you might call socially awkward. And, yes, one or two have gone *absolutely bonkers*." She made quotation marks with her fingers as she said the words. "But no more than you'd expect."

Jack slowly turned his head to glare down at her. But he forgot his frustration when he picked up a light buzzing sound mixing in with the hum of the lights. His eyes narrowed. "We're being followed . . . again."

He reversed course, swatting the air with the flat of his hand and missing the Clockmaker's beetle by nanometers. It retaliated with a dive, but this time Jack held his ground. He had grown tired of these pests. He swatted again, and connected.

The impact of the metal stung Jack's hand, but the bug tumbled back a good six feet through the air. It hovered there, near the fluorescents, crackling with electricity. Jack took a step forward.

"Stop!" The voice of the Clockmaker emanated from the metal bug, stopping Jack in his tracks. "Oh, Lucky Jack," taunted the Frenchman. "You are wasting time again. My little friends are happy to play, but I must warn you, their gears produce enough voltage to bring down a grown man." The voice turned threatening. "As the girl's uncle knows all too well."

"Call off your beetle," warned Jack. "I'll find your Ember, but not with your bugs hovering over me the whole way."

The Clockmaker laughed. "I am afraid you have no choice. I must be sure of your progress. The presence of my little friends is—how would you Americans say it? *Bien sûr*. A necessary evil."

"No it isn't." Gwen spoke quietly, talking to the floor. Her eyes slowly rose to the beetle and her hands absently tugged at her scarf, loosening the coils around her shoulders. "It isn't necessary at all, is it? Not unless you actually have nothing to trade."

The beetle banked and slid to her side of the tunnel,

crackling ominously. "Quiet, girl. No one was talking to you."

Gwen shifted her gaze to Jack, still unraveling her scarf. "He's only following us so he can swoop in and snatch away the Ember at the end of the hunt. And he wouldn't need to do that if he really had your father, would he?" She put a hand on Jack's arm. "I'm sorry, Jack, but that's the way I see it."

Jack kept his eyes on the clockwork bug, holding back his tears. He didn't want to believe what Gwen was telling him. He couldn't. Barely an hour before, Jack had gotten his dad back, at least the idea of him. He wasn't letting go again without a fight. "Please," he begged the Clockmaker. "Show me proof he's alive and I'll let your bugs tag along."

"You do *not* make demands," growled the Clockmaker. "My beetles will watch you whether you like it or not."

Gwen had the scarf completely off, wringing it in her hands. "I don't think so." Without warning, she lashed out, snapping the scarf like a whip. The beetle took the full impact and smacked into the light above, falling to the ground amid a shower of sparks. Blue and purple arcs danced around its body until it exploded in a ball of flame.

"Well, that was easier than expected," breathed the clerk, lowering her winter-wear weapon.

Jack couldn't believe it. "How did you . . . ?"

"Tibetan yak's wool." She gave the scarf two quick stretches and threw it around her neck. "Strong as they come. A gift from Uncle Percy. He—"

"You should not have done that." The Clockmaker's voice returned—in stereo. Two more beetles emerged from behind the rusty pipes on either side of the tunnel and hopped into the air, converging on Gwen. "I cannot promise you will survive this, *ma petite fille*. My little friends, they get so . . . excited. And, to be quite honest, I only need the tracker."

A blue bolt of electricity shot out from each clockwork beetle, converging with a *snap* right in front of Gwen's nose. She let out a cry and staggered back.

"No!" Jack rushed at the bugs, but another bolt shot out from the nearest one, catching him full in the chest. He fell, convulsing, fingers curling into rigid claws he could not control.

By the time Jack's vision cleared, Gwen was in a fight for her life, scarf alternately curling above her head and lashing out, beetles swarming around her. She would not last much longer. Then Jack noticed a big, red monkey wrench lying on the floor, partially concealed by the pipes that ran along the base of the wall.

The first beetle never saw him coming. He smashed it out of the air so hard it flew twenty feet down the tunnel, exploding where it landed. The second bug was not so easy. It backed away, dodging both wrench and scarf, darting in to shoot a bolt at Jack whenever it got the chance. Jack took a swing and it zapped the wrench. He yelped, dropping the weapon to the floor.

"Focus, Jack!" Gwen shouted through labored breaths. "Remember who you are. Use your senses."

Use your senses, thought Jack. *Easier said than done.* The beetle pressed its advantage, moving in to strike again, and Jack jerked his head back, barely avoiding a blue flash. Everything slowed. Gwen's scarf rippled. A foot-long wave traveled down the fabric toward an inevitable snap. The beetle's antennae twitched. Its wings shifted, iridescent streaks aligning to a new plane. Jack heard the bronze, tonal beat of its micro-thin wings changing pitch and frequency. *It's going up*, he thought. An instant later, the bug did exactly that. *It's going left.* An instant later, the bug did that, too. Jack knew exactly where the beetle was going before it ever moved.

He dove for the wrench, rolled as he picked it up, and came up swinging, knowing from the sound alone that the beetle had followed him. The wrench clipped the bug and smashed into one of the rusty pipes. Vapor gushed from the hole, filling the tunnel with the yellow-green smell of rotten eggs.

"Jack, no!" cried Gwen, but he had already committed to the next attack. Limping on a wing and a half, the beetle stood no chance. Jack hit it square, knocking the blue-green bug straight across the tunnel, where it hit another pipe with a heavy *pong* and crashed to the floor, six silver legs curling tight to its abdomen.

The first purple flash arced around the beetle's body.

Gwen pulled at Jack's arm.

"Run, Jack! Run!"

Chapter 25

JACK HAD NEVER heard the birth of fire before, not so much of it, so fast like this. It was beautiful and terrifying at the same time. He knew the moment the cloud of gas found the sparking beetle, the exact moment of ignition, even though it happened behind him. In his mind he saw a tiny white flash, then the emergence of an impossible, blue-gold blossom. A rippling formation of crystals flashed out from the center in a million curving points—every one of them reaching out to kill him.

Gwen reached the exit a few steps ahead, shouldering the iron door so hard it flew open and bounced off the wall. She pivoted left, out of sight for a fraction of a second before Jack's momentum carried him through after her, out onto the narrow brickwork bank of an underground canal. He thought he would fly headlong into the rushing water, but Gwen yanked him sideways, pressing him back against the wall.

The fire hit an instant later, at the moment the swinging door hit home. The blast blew it clean off its hinges with a brain-shattering *boom*. Flames shot out across the water to scorch the bricks on the other side. Then it was over, leaving a cloud of black smoke, the quiet gurgle of the iron door as it sank below the water's surface, and the lingering pain in Jack's head. "What is this place," he mumbled, blinking to make his eyes focus again.

"Sewer," said Gwen, as if any girl would be so content to make such a proclamation.

Sewer? Jack reached for his nose. A sewer could very well be a tracker's kryptonite, but he smelled nothing worse than the burned bricks and the gray musty scent he associated with caves. "Really?" he said, lowering his hand again. "It doesn't smell like a sewer."

"It's pre-Victorian. These days, lines like this one keep the city from flooding, rather than carry waste. London has a massive underground river system, both natural and manmade. In fact, the Ministry Express used to take advantage of it." Gwen pushed off the wall and touched her head. "Oh dear. I've lost my earmuffs, haven't I?" She leaned to the side, looking past Jack and taking in the blackened remains of the tunnel entrance. "I must say, that was exhilarating."

"Exhilarating?" Jack marveled at her capacity for understatement. "We almost died, Gwen. We need help."

She threw her scarf over her shoulders, curling it around her neck as she walked upstream, leaving him behind again. "Help is near, Jack," she called over her shoulder. "Off we go. There's a ladder up here that takes us right into Barking Tower. I'm certain we'll find the clues we need to—"

"That's *not* what I meant by 'help,' and you know it."

Gwen cringed at the sharpness of his voice. She slowly turned around. "Um . . . of course it was."

"Don't do that." He walked toward her, pointing. "You always do that. You always pretend you don't understand, answer the wrong question. I'm sick of it."

"Jack, you—"

He cut her off. She couldn't talk her way out of this one. "Since I met you, I've chased a mini-drone, used secret doors and hidden passages, and ridden a high-tech maglev train that predates the automobile. You have this all-mighty *ministry*, with trackers and quartermasters, wardens and"—he thrust both hands at Gwen—"clerks. *Why*, Gwen? *Why* aren't we going to tracker headquarters? Why aren't we going to this Keep of yours for help? We're just kids."

"We don't have to be *just kids*, you know." She tugged at the ends of her scarf, avoiding his eyes. "We can do this on our own, find the Ember and finish what your father and my uncle started. You're learning so fast, and I know everything a quartermaster—"

Jack lost it. "But you're *not* a quartermaster!" The outburst made Gwen shudder, but she still wouldn't look at him. He sighed. "I don't want to finish any hunt or mission. I don't need to prove that I'm more than a kid. I am a kid. I *want* to be a kid. And I want my dad back, whether you believe he's still out there or not. From what I've seen, the Ministry of Trackers can help me find him. Why haven't we gone to them? Why, Gwen?"

"Jack, if you'd only—"

"*Why!*"

She cringed, dropping the ends of the scarf and balling up her fists. "We *can't*, all right?" She finally looked up at him, blue eyes on the edge of tears. "*You* . . . can't . . . actually. That's the rule. That's Section Thirteen."

Jack threw his hands up in exasperation. "All right. I get it.

The ministry is a big secret. I'm not *read-in* or whatever. I caused a Section Thirteen as soon as I entered the Chamber. But I think we're kind of past that now, don't you? So what are we waiting for? Let's go."

"You don't know what you're asking." Gwen let out a quick, nervous laugh. "You don't know anything, really. You don't even know your real name."

He rolled his eyes. "I'm not an idiot, Gwen. My name is John Buckles the Third. I knew that long before I met you. I just don't like it, that's all. It sounds nerdy."

"That's the thing, isn't it? You're *not* John Buckles the Third, or the fourth or even the fifth." Gwen gave him the saddest freckle bounce he had yet seen. "You're the thirteenth, Jack—the thirteenth Buckles. You didn't cause the Section Thirteen. You *are* the Section Thirteen."

Chapter 26

"THE BUCKLES FAMILY has been with the Ministry of Trackers far longer than two generations." Gwen sat on the edge of the bank, boots dangling over the water. "They were there when the ministry was founded, Jack—*twelve* generations ago."

He paced the bricks behind her, arms folded. "Okay. I get it. I'm John Buckles the Thirteenth. My whole life is a lie. So, things are worse now than they were before and you *still* haven't explained why we can't go to tracker headquarters for help."

"Perhaps you'd like to dial down the hostility and let me finish." The clerk gave him a stern look that reminded him unnervingly of Mrs. Hudson.

Jack stopped pacing and let his arms fall to his sides. "Sorry."

"That's better." Gwen looked out over the water, lightly swinging her feet. "As I was about to say, the Ministry of Trackers learned early on that there are forces in this world we do not fully understand. People might call these forces magic or luck"—she glanced up at him—"or bad luck . . . but only because they have no other explanation."

"Bad luck," said Jack, taking a seat beside her. "Like the number thirteen. You're telling me we can't go to the ministry because they're superstitious?"

"They're cautious. And that's a very big distinction." She leaned back on her hands. "Why do you think it's considered bad luck to walk under a ladder or break a mirror?"

"You'd make the guy on the ladder fall or cut yourself on the broken glass."

Gwen gave him a definitive nod. "And your bad day snowballs from there. Add that to a heartfelt belief that your soul is trapped in the mirror or the ladder represents the gallows, and suddenly you're experiencing a curse. That's not *entirely* superstition, Jack. There are the natural forces of the breaking glass and the falling ladder, and there are also the natural forces of emotion and psychology at work. The number thirteen isn't any different."

"I don't see the number thirteen breaking any bones."

"Really? The order to capture and torture the Knights Templar went out on a Friday the Thirteenth. There are thirteen steps in an English gallows." Gwen raised both eyebrows. "Whether or not thirteen was unlucky to start with, a real and unpredictable force had grown up around it by the time the Ministry of Trackers was founded. And the ministry fathers knew that such a force could never be combined with tracker skills."

"So they banned a whole generation."

She shrugged, making the scarf bunch up around her ears. "Modern hotels and airlines use the same logic—no thirteenth floor, no thirteenth row. In 1726, the ministry created Section Thirteen. No tracker of the thirteenth generation would ever be trained, or even learn of the existence of the ministry. Your generation was split up, sent away to the four corners of the earth, where you could do no harm."

Jack closed his eyes. "*That's* why I grew up in America."

"And that's why you can't go to the Ministry of Trackers, not now. If you go to the Keep, they'll contain you, Jack.

They'll lock you up. You're far too dangerous."

"Wait. What about the Ministry Express? Nobody bothered us in there."

"Apples and oranges, Jack. The Elder Ministries sometimes share knowledge in their service to the Crown in defense of the Realm, but for the most part they keep out of one another's affairs. Section Thirteen is a *tracker* regulation. The spooks, dragos, and toppers couldn't care less which John Buckles you are. The same goes for the employees in the common areas, like the Ministry Express stations."

"Then why did the dragos stare at me like that?"

Gwen stood up from the bank and brushed off her coat. "Perhaps they simply don't like your face," she said, walking past him. "Your constant look of confusion absolutely screams *wally*."

Moments later, Jack was on a ladder, pushing with all his strength to lift one end of an iron grate out of its housing. The grate made a terrible *screech* as he slid it out of the way.

"Shhh!" Gwen scowled up from the rungs below. "That's a church up there. It's a safe bet the vicar heard that gas explosion. Don't you think he'll put two and two together if he catches us climbing out of his sewer? We'll spend the rest of the day explaining ourselves."

"Something you *hate* to do, right?"

"Ha-ha. Get on with it."

Jack climbed up onto the stone floor at the bottom of a square brick tower and helped Gwen up after him. As he slid the grate back into place, it slipped from his fingers and dropped into its housing with a pronounced *clang*. He cringed.

Gwen shook her head. "It's like you're not even trying." She turned to the rickety wooden staircase that wound its way up through the tower and started to climb.

The bells gradually increased in size, from softball-size chimes at the first level to a single bronze giant at the top. Gwen paused at the beach-ball-size bell level, next to a stained glass window. "Have you ever heard of Great Fire glass?" she asked as she caught her breath.

Jack shook his head. "I don't think we have that in Colorado."

"No. Probably not." She gave him her know-it-all grin and nodded at the window. "The Great Fire melted all the glass in five-sixths of London into little green globs. The window makers reformed many of them into decorative panels to commemorate the fire, but most of those were destroyed three centuries later, in the bombings of World War Two." She gestured to a pair of colored panes at the center of the window. "Only these two remain."

Jack had to admit the stained glass panes she showed him were pretty cool—rare pieces of history mounted in a church, rather than being locked up in a museum. He could make out the streaks left by the minerals that colored the glass, and the bubbles and imperfections. He stretched out a hand to feel the texture.

"Wait. I didn't mean you should—"

Chaos. More than chaos. Total bedlam. Jack saw a collage of sights and sounds, all trapped in a two-dimensional plane like the very pane of glass he had touched. Flashes, shadows, horns, murmurs—the same relentless cacophony he experienced that morning, but multiplied a hundredfold and twisted together. The pain threatened to rip his head apart. He tried to pull his hand away, to make it stop, but he couldn't. Instinctively he pushed instead.

The two-dimensional plane shattered, falling away in a hundred glistening shards to reveal the awful scene behind.

London burned. Pillars of living fire rose fifty, sixty, a hundred feet in the air, roaring like freight trains. Men and women ran back and forth, some carrying litters with groaning bodies, searching for a route of escape, but there were none. A few gave up and stood gazing upward, hypnotized by the flames. They would bake there. Jack knew it because he could feel the heat on his face and chest, growing more intense by the second.

An orange ball of flame arced through the sky and landed on a brick building not far away, burning through the masonry like it was thatch. Nothing was safe. One of the hypnotized throng turned to look in Jack's direction, staring at him with an empty, blackened face. He stretched out a hand, looking as if he was about to speak, and then his whole form changed from sooty peasant to shadowed wraith. The specter let out a silent cry and sank into the cobblestones, revealing the incoming fireball behind it. Jack couldn't run. He couldn't step out of the way of the incoming missile. He couldn't even scream.

"Jack. I said don't touch it."

The fireball was gone, and Jack was staring at the innocuous pane of colored glass again, bubbles, streaks, and all. Gwen had him by the wrist. It was she who had pulled his hand away, not him. He tried to tell her that he had somehow sparked on the glass, but his lips wouldn't part. No sound came out, not even a grunt.

The vision was over, but Jack still had no voice.

Chapter 27

JACK TRIED AND TRIED to part his lips, but he couldn't. All he could do was grunt. He seized Gwen's wrist and held it tight, eyes wide with panic.

"Ow. That hurts!" cried the clerk in a harsh whisper. She wrenched her arm free and grabbed him by the shoulders. "*Calm down*, Jack. You need to breathe and clear your mind."

How could she possibly expect him to calm down? He let go of her wrist and glowered, mustering up a growl, which sort of felt like progress.

"I warned you not to touch it."

"You did not!" Caught unaware by the sudden, and rather loud, return of his voice, Jack clapped a hand over his mouth.

Gwen gently pulled it away again. "Deep breaths. You're

all right now." She leaned back and folded her arms. "So, what have we learned from this experience?"

"That you're still hiding things from me."

"There it is." Gwen threw her hands in the air. "It's always *my* fault, isn't it? You're just like Mrs. Hudson." She marched past him, starting up the stairs again. "What we've learned is that trackers do not spark off glass—*ever*."

"Yeah? And how was I supposed to know that?" The old wooden steps creaked under Jack's weight as he followed after her. "I didn't know I could spark off glass. It's not even a mineral." He paused for a step, thinking about what he had said. "Wait . . . is it?"

"Of course it is. What do they teach you in those American schools?" Gwen glanced over her shoulder. "Glass is made of minerals that have been . . . altered. The silicates are corrupted, melted into an amorphous mess, so it doesn't record, it reflects. Glass feeds a tracker a reflection of whatever the world is throwing at it, only amplified and confused, jumbled into choas."

Gwen fell quiet as they climbed the last two flights, past the largest of the bells. Jack was stymied by her rebuke. Why was she being so hard on him? "It wasn't random noise," he began, trying to tell her what he really saw, but she lit into him again before he could finish.

"Of course it was noise—it was a loud, higgledy-piggledy barrage that muddled your delicate tracker brain. You know, more than one tracker has fallen into a coma sparking off fake gems or obsidian." The stairs terminated at the base of a ladder, beneath a wooden hatch. As Jack came up next to Gwen, she waggled a finger at him. "Don't ever try that again."

"I saw the fire, Gwen."

"You don't know what you saw." She pushed up the hatch to reveal a copper dome, green with age. "Now put it behind you and let's get to work."

A stiff breeze blew from west to east across the domed cupola that topped the bell tower, enough that Jack felt the need to pull his cap down over his ears. Balconies opened to the four cardinal directions, offering commanding views of the city, and each one had a line of etched panels attached to its rail. Jack's brain immediately registered the heading DAY ONE OF THE GREAT FIRE on the southern display. He walked over to inspect it.

September 1666
2nd (Lord's Day). Jane called us up about three in the morning, to tell us of a great fire.... I thought it far enough off; and so went to bed again and to

166

sleep. . . . By and by Jane comes and tells me that she hears that above 300 houses have been burned down . . . that it is now burning down all Fish-street, by London Bridge.

"Is this Pepys's diary?"

Gwen stepped up beside him. "Well, it's not the Magna Carta. Keep reading. These displays tell the story of the fire and add other eyewitness accounts to the excerpts from Pepys's diary. Perhaps the extra bits will tell us what Pepys *saw but never wrote.*"

Jack returned his attention to the DAY ONE plaque.

While Pepys slept, neighbors gathered in Pudding Lane to fight the fire that consumed the bakery. According to a local lawyer, Lord Mayor Bloodworth was on hand but refused the locals' pleas to involve the city forces. Pish, he said, a woman could put it out.

"Sounds like the mayor was no help."

"Agreed." Gwen was reading the next column over. "Pepys caught up with Bloodworth later and relayed a royal order to make a firebreak by pulling buildings down. He says the mayor whined 'like a fainting woman' that the fire overtook his men faster than they could work. Then the mayor gave up and returned to his apartments, miles away in Covent Garden."

"Could that be the betrayal Farriner complained about in his confession?"

"Perhaps, but it sounds more like ineptitude." Gwen ran a finger down a note in the margin. "According to this, the Lord Mayor's initial assessment could even be considered reasonable. Fires in London were common, and Bloodworth had demanded bonfires be maintained in the slums the year before—an effort to smoke out the plague. His fires burned day and night in the worst tinderboxes of the city, and there were only a few minor flare-ups."

"Which makes me wonder why this fire, which started in a brick house, was so different." Jack skipped ahead to Pepys's own description of the fire, hours after it began.

So I down to the water-side. and there got a boat. . . . With one's face in the wind, you were almost burned with a shower of firedrops. . . . The churches, houses, and all on fire and flaming at once; and a horrid noise the flames made, and the cracking of houses at their ruins.

A second eyewitness account followed, a diary entry from a friend of Pepys's named John Evelyn, who had watched from the southern bank of the river.

Oh, the miserable and calamitous spectacle . . . The noise and cracking and thunder of the impetuous flames, the shrieking of women and children . . . was like a hideous storm.

Across the cupola Gwen read out loud from the northern balcony's display. "'Day three: The stones of St. Paul's flew like grenades, the melting lead running down the streets in a stream.'" She glanced over her shoulder at Jack. "That's Pepys's friend Evelyn describing the lead roof of the cathedral running down Ludgate Hill like molten lava. Other eyewitness accounts over here report balls of fire flying over the rooftops. They thought the French were attacking."

"Why would they think that?"

"This was Restoration London," said Gwen with a shrug. "As in the *restoration of the monarchy* after Cromwell's failed commonwealth. England had just survived a brutal civil war. The European sharks were circling. Some Londoners even thought the king's brother, the Duke of York, was a French sympathizer—not a bad theory, considering he would later invade England with a French army." She turned back to the etchings. "Witnesses claimed they apprehended French arson suspects and handed them over to the chief magistrate—who happened to be the Duke of York—only to have the suspects mysteriously disappear from the country."

"Fireballs," muttered Jack. "That's what I saw in the glass. But no one was throwing them. They were . . . unnatural."

"Jack, what you saw was—"

He sighed. "Muddled. I get it. But I know what I saw—solid stone exploding, fireballs burning through brick, massive pillars of flame. Nothing about that fire was manmade. Some kind of force was . . . feeding it."

The clerk met his eyes, and he could see that she finally believed him. Both of them said what they were thinking at the same time. "The Ember."

Gwen leaned her forearms against the green copper rail, gazing out at the city. "If the Ember burned down London all those years ago, what do you suppose the Clockmaker plans to do with it now?"

Chapter 28

"**WHAT PEPYS SAW . . .**" Gwen strode to the western balcony and the entries from the fourth day. "Pepys couldn't have seen the Ember start the fire. He wasn't anywhere near the bakery, but he saw *something* that Farriner wanted us to know about. If it wasn't the beginning of the fire—"

"It was the end." Jack joined her at the rail and read the first panel. Pepys described the moment he climbed Barking Tower, the very tower they were standing in.

> *5th (Wednesday) . . . I up to the top of Barking steeple, and there saw the saddest sight of desolation that I ever saw . . . the fire being spread as far as I could see it.*

"This is the last set of panels and the fire *isn't* ending," said

Jack, looking up from the etching. From that balcony, he could see the gold flame at the top of the Monument, half a mile away. "According to Pepys, the flames were as strong as ever, moving east against the wind to engulf the whole city."

"Perhaps." Gwen examined the next column of text. "But listen to what Evelyn had to say a few hours later. 'But it pleased God, contrary to all expectation, that on Wednesday, about four or five of the clock in the afternoon, the wind fell; and, as in an instant, the fire decreased.'"

Jack bent down to read the words for himself. *As in an instant*. And next to the quote from Evelyn, Pepys's own account suddenly reversed from doomsday to hope.

> *Here I met with Mr. Young and Whistler . . . and received good hopes that the fire at our end; is stopped. they and I walked into the town. and find Fanchurch-Streete. Gracious-Streete; and Lombard-Streete all in dust.*

Gwen stepped back from the etchings and scrunched up her brow. "Samuel Pepys climbs this tower on the fourth day and sees the entire city ablaze. The flames are eating up the city, traveling *against* the wind to reach Barking Tower. Then, a few hours later, Evelyn sees the fire suddenly drop. At the same time, we find Pepys wandering around on the ashes of Lombard Street at the heart of the hot zone. How did a two-mile stretch of unnatural, apocalyptic flame, fireballs, and exploding brimstone suddenly drop into nothing?"

"Someone contained it." Jack straightened up from his reading. "Someone got control of the Ember."

"And we know who that someone was, don't we? *The cobbler saved us*. That's what Farriner's confession said. The cobbler has to be the one who reined in the Ember, and Pepys must have seen him do it." She pointed to the floor. "From this very spot." Gwen grabbed the copper rail and hopped over, landing gracefully on the narrow ledge on the other side.

"What are you doing?"

She let go with one hand and reached into her pocket. "You need to spark, Jack."

"Yeah. Well . . . I can do that from this side of the rail."

"I'm not talking about the copper. Metal memory is too short, remember? Weeks at best. And this cupola was a post-war addition, anyway." Her free hand emerged from the pocket holding a substantial screwdriver. "We need to get to the bricks underneath."

Feeling the rush of the breeze a little more than before, Jack stepped over the rail one leg at a time. The ledge could not have been more than two feet wide. Dozens of cars and pedestrians passed by six stories below. If only one of them would look up, see the crazy children, and raise the alarm, Gwen would have no choice but to retreat. But no one looked up. Jack pressed himself back against the copper. "I don't see any screws."

"Me neither." The clerk shoved the flat edge of the screwdriver into a joint between two long copper plates and cranked down, using the screwdriver as a makeshift pry bar. The aged copper let out an angry *squeak*. After a number of excruciating cranks she had it up several inches.

"That's plenty," Jack insisted. "I can fit my hand in. You can stop breaking the church now."

"Oh. Good." The clerk stopped her attack and hopped back over the rail, leaving him alone on the ledge. "Being out there was totally freaking me out."

The edge of the bent plate was so sharp that Jack figured his hand would remain safely up on the tower, even if the rest of him fell off. Still, he could see no other way to get the information they needed. He took a deep breath and slid his palm into the gap.

"Wait!"

Jack yanked his hand back in surprise, wincing as the copper scraped the skin from his knuckles. *"What?"*

174

"I should probably warn you that brick is . . . different. The spark might be a little scary."

"I'm *already* scared, Gwen." Jack rolled his eyes and slid his hand back in. Then he stopped, his palm a millimeter above the brick. "Um . . . just so we're clear. What exactly do you mean by 'scary'?"

Gwen wrinkled her nose. "Brick is weird. It's not like other stones. In fact, it's a conglomerate of stones—a hodgepodge."

Jack didn't like the sound of *hodgepodge*. It bore too much resemblance to *higgledy-piggledy*. "You mean like the glass?"

"No. Not like that. But there are dozens of different minerals in there, and their memories don't always match up. It might seem a little disjointed. Don't freak out, that's all."

Jack glared up at her. He was about to sink his brain into who knows what, while kneeling on a two-foot ledge six stories above a busy street, and he had just learned that sparking on the wrong material could take away his capacity for speech or put him in a coma. *Don't freak out. Sure.* He cringed and let his skin touch the brick.

Shapes shifted and jerked through the street below—the shards of a broken vase, hastily put back together and set into motion. Sounds came to him like a hundred recordings, all played backward. He recognized one of them. The wailing was jagged and inconsistent, but it was the same air raid siren he had heard on Pudding Lane.

A building across the street from the tower exploded in a ragged plume of black and gray, threatening to knock him off his perch. If he fell in his vision, would he fall off the real tower? Or would he simply never wake up again? Spark or not, hanging around in the middle of a bombing raid did not seem like a good plan. Then he remembered his desperate push during the chaos of the glass, the push that had taken him all the way back to the fire.

It was worth a try.

Another explosion. A shape hurtled up from the street below. In the split second that Jack focused on the shadow, it coalesced into a black sedan, flipping right at him. He pushed. Hard.

The falling sensation, combined with being precariously perched on a tower, was almost more than Jack could bear. But he jolted to a stop a heartbeat later, still kneeling on the ledge. He had the feeling of pitching forward from the force of the landing, and yet something held him fast to the tower. The push had worked. If for no other reason, he knew he was deeper in because the brokenness of the vision had increased. And *hodgepodge* didn't come close to describing it.

The brick building that had blown up across the street was gone, replaced with a wall of disjointed black flame, dancing with spasmodic, staccato rhythm. A massive lake of obsidian fire stretched as far as Jack could see. He found it strangely beautiful, and certainly more peaceful than the war zone he had just escaped. There were no screams or cries, no wailing sirens—only the dull, distorted roar of the inferno.

A shape moved toward the fire. Focusing, Jack broke out the image of a man marching resolutely forward, directly into the wall of flame. He held an object out before him, carrying it at arm's length like a holy relic. To Jack's astonishment, the flames parted. The man continued forward into a tunnel of fire, and the curtain of flames closed behind him.

The street fell silent again. Jack waited for something to happen, but there was no change. He wished he had a remote for these things. Why couldn't he rewind or fast-forward? Then it occurred to him that he could.

If pushing pressed Jack deeper into the brick's memory, maybe pulling would do the opposite. He tried pulling his hand away from the brick. Nothing. He could neither move nor affect the spark. Jack wanted to scream in frustration, but he couldn't do that, either. All he could do was let go, relax, and try again. After taking a moment to open his senses the way Gwen had taught him, Jack concentrated on another pull, this time making it more mental than physical.

It worked.

Too well.

Jack's mind rushed upward through the memory of the brick, right back to the bombing—right back to the moment he had left. The flipping car was inches away. "Aaah!"

Daylight. The whistling breeze. A street full of people oblivious to his cry. Jack was hanging out over the edge, his hand already free of the gap Gwen had made. "Help me!"

"What do you think I'm doing?" grunted the clerk, who had him by the collar of his jacket. "You might consider piping down and helping yourself."

Jack scrambled backward into the copper rail and held on tight, staring down at the traffic below. "That was—"

"Cool?"

"No."

"Brilliant?"

"No. It was—"

"Epic?"

"Terrifying." Jack glared at her. "I was going to say terrifying. And you *knew* I was going to lose all sense of reality out there. You should have held on to my collar the whole time."

Gwen gave him a freckle bounce. "I did."

As she spoke, a flash of reddish brown caught Jack's eye from a hilltop plaza across the street. A man in a suede duster raced toward a Tube station at the center of the square. Another man, all in black, was hot on his heels.

Chapter 29

"WE HAVE TO help him!" Jack sprinted across the busy street, dodging traffic, doing his best to block out the angry chorus of honking horns.

Gwen was close at his heels. "Him, who? I didn't see—" A scooter beeped and she stopped short, going up on her toes as it shot between them.

"It was Dad, and the Clockmaker was after him. I swear it," breathed Jack, taking the steps up the hill two at a time. At the top, he tore across the plaza, straight for the Tube entrance. The wall of turnstiles came up fast. As he planted his hands to vault over them, he caught a flicker of black ahead. The Clockmaker—it had to be—disappearing down a tunnel marked DISTRICT LINE. Jack touched down on the other side, adjusting course to follow, and smacked into a heavyset man who had come through the next barrier down. He pinballed off the big pedestrian and tumbled to the floor.

"Watch it, kid!"

Jack picked himself up and sidestepped Mr. Angry-big-and-tall, but he had lost precious ground. When he reached the tunnel, he saw no sign of either his dad or his tormentor among the crowd in the narrow passage. Fortunately, there were no other tunnels leading off to either side—there was nowhere to go but straight ahead.

The sound of Gwen's apologies followed in Jack's wake as he slipped and shouldered his way through the commuters. He saw an escalator up ahead, a bottleneck for the passengers, but the stairs next to it were wide open. Jack launched himself onto the rail, fingers gliding along the steel as he slid down.

The man in reddish brown ran through the passage below, barely a stride ahead of the Clockmaker, along a line of archways that led to the platforms on either side. He glanced back at his enemy, and for the first time since Jack had come to London, he saw his father's face.

"Dad, it's me!"

Neither man looked up at him. They took a right through

the last archway, heading for the east platform. Jack followed less than three seconds later. He stopped at the edge of the tracks, breathing hard, looking frantically up and down the line of waiting passengers. His father and the Clockmaker had disappeared again.

"Jack, you have to stop." Gwen came panting up beside him. "You're acting insane, drawing too much attention."

He didn't answer. What did it matter if he drew the world's attention now that he had found his dad? He jogged along the line of bewildered pedestrians, searching their faces. "Dad! John Buck—"

Jack lost his footing.

Pain shot through Jack's ribs as he slammed down onto a steel rail. He tried to groan, but the impact had knocked the wind from his lungs. The people on the platform shouted for him to get up. A moment later, Gwen was on her knees above him, offering a hand. "Don't touch the center rail! You'll complete the circuit and electrocute yourself."

He nodded, still unable to speak. As Jack carefully pressed himself up, a light appeared in the tunnel, along with the echoing rush of an approaching train. The shouts above him became more insistent.

"Now, Jack! Get out of there!" Gwen dropped to her

stomach to reach for him. But Jack saw something else in the light—a dark figure, much closer than the train. The figure paused for half a second, then melted into the tunnel wall.

Jack got up and raced after him.

The platform wall came and went. The shouting people fell behind. And Jack was in the tunnel, alone with the oncoming train. His bruised ribs screamed in protest, but he kept up his pace. He had no other choice. Either the door was there, or Jack was going to die.

Brilliant white light and earsplitting sound engulfed him. Sparks flew as the driver applied the brakes. Then Jack saw it—a greasy push bar in an otherwise black wall. An instant later, he was through, fighting for his balance at the top of a steep, pitch-black stairwell. He pawed at the wall to keep from falling forward. The train, brakes squealing, flew past, daring him to fall backward and be obliterated. Finally, he steadied himself, let the door close behind him, and stepped down into the dark.

Jack descended three long flights, gaining confidence and speed as he went. Despite the utter darkness, he knew what lay ahead. He could read the translucent blue echoes of his own footsteps bouncing off the walls and the stairs. He saw a door at the bottom, the push bar outlined in rippling blue, and he hit it on his first try, hoping John Buckles was on the other side.

He was. And so was the Clockmaker.

Fire shot from a brass tube protruding from the Frenchman's sleeve, backing Jack's father into a wall of yellow tiles. The chase had led them to an abandoned platform, lit by a few emergency lights over the tracks. Old papers were strewn about the floor; several were burning.

"I don't have it," said Jack's father. As soon as his back hit the wall, he pushed off, trying to jink around the Clockmaker, but another burst of flame forced him back again.

"Stop!" shouted Jack. "Leave him alone!"

The Frenchman didn't turn around, didn't even acknowledge Jack's presence. "What kind of fool do you think I am, Buckles? I have won. You have lost. Accept it. Hand over the Ember, and I will let you live." He took another step forward, leveling the flamethrower. "Refuse, and I will take it from your ashes. Then I will recover the amplifier you stole and the people of London will finally pay for their crimes."

At that moment, Jack saw his father's eyes narrow, his jaw set. He knew that look. It was the same look his dad got when Sadie had him against the ropes in a video game, the same look he got when the light turned yellow at an approaching intersection. John Buckles lowered his shoulders to charge, and immediately vanished behind a veil of flame.

"No!" Jack rushed out into the open, and came jogging to a stop in total confusion. The Clockmaker had faded away, leaving nothing but cold, scorched papers and blackened tiles behind. His father was gone too, vanished without a trace.

Jack dropped to his knees on the empty platform and cried.

Chapter 30

A BEAM OF BLUE-WHITE light washed over Jack. He jumped to his feet and turned, fists up.

"It's Gwen, Jack." The clerk shined the light on her own features as the stairwell door closed behind her. "It's only Gwen. You remember me, don't you?"

Jack lowered his fists, wiping his cheeks with his sleeves. He did not want her to see his tears. "He killed my dad," he said, trying to steady his voice. "The Clockmaker had a flamethrower . . . a flamethrower!"

She approached him slowly, staring into his eyes like he was a puzzle that needed solving, brow scrunched up in confusion.

"What part of that didn't you get, Gwen? My dad was right here. I watched the Clockmaker kill him with a flamethrower and then vanish into thin air." Another tear escaped his eye and he quickly wiped it away. "I lost him all over again."

Gwen coldly stepped around him, shining her light on the scorched wall. "You sparked."

"What?" Jack blinked, trying to determine why she would say such a thing. "No. I saw them. You saw them too. We chased them, Gwen. How could that have been a spark?"

"It was several, actually. Jack, what you saw wasn't real." She knelt to the ground and inspected the charred papers. "Well, it was real, but it didn't happen today." She picked up a paper and gently blew across the burned edge. A few black pieces crumbled away. "See? No glowing red, no lingering heat. This paper has been cold for twenty-four hours or more." She let it fall. "Think, Jack. Where were your hands when you saw your dad from the tower?"

Jack wasn't sure if he wanted to believe her or not. He closed his eyes, remembering the moment he saw his dad sprinting across the square. At the edge of the memory he could see his own hand holding tight to the balcony rail. He winced.

"Yes. Now you've got it. You were touching other metal objects each time you saw them, weren't you?"

He thought back through the chase. There was the

187

aluminum ticket barrier he had vaulted over, and the stair-well rail, and the Tube track. When he had seen the fight, both his hands had been on the push bar. That was why the Clockmaker and his dad had faded as soon as he had run onto the platform. He'd let go of the steel bar, let go of its memory. Jack let out a long breath. "What about the train?"

"That's the tricky part, isn't it? Those trains run every two minutes. You may have seen a train in your spark, but the one you played chicken with was as real as you and me. And that means we have to get out of here." Gwen took him by the elbow and steered him toward a set of brick stairs at the back of the platform. "You can't jump in front of a train and expect the world to be happy about it. The authorities will be down here any second. Come on."

"You know another way back to the surface?"

They topped the stairs and Gwen pulled him left down another tunnel. "We're not going to the surface. We're going to the ministry Archive to get your father's journal. We've been following in his footsteps the whole time, Jack. We'll have to skip ahead a bit if we want to find the Ember before the Clockmaker's deadline."

The Ember. The name alone made Jack want to scream. He quickened his pace and stepped in front of the clerk, stopping her at the intersection with the next passage. "It's over, Gwen. My dad died, just like you said. Forget the Ember. Take me back to my sister."

"No, it isn't over at all." Gwen eyes lit up like Jack hadn't seen all day. "There's more hope now than ever. Don't you see? Your spark proved me wrong. It *proved* your dad didn't die at the Tower of London. If he made it out of there alive, why not here?"

"But the flamethrower . . . No one could have—"

She stomped her foot. "No buts, Jack! You held out hope that your dad was alive against all the evidence, against everything I told you. I'm *not* giving up on that hope now." She brushed past him and continued down the passage. "Are you coming, or what?"

Jack watched her march away, flashlight swinging back and forth, shining its blue-white beam alternately up and down the tunnel. He sighed. She asked him that a lot, but she never really gave him a choice.

By the time Jack caught up, Gwen had stopped at an old ticket booth, struggling to budge the remains of a magazine rack that sat against the wall. "This is Mark Lane Station," she grunted as she pushed. "Closed in '67. But they never sealed the entrance."

"And so you plan to finish the job by blocking it with that magazine rack?"

Gwen kept pushing. "Not . . . the Tube entrance." The rack let out a long *scritch* as it suddenly gave way and shifted to the side, exposing a low, arched portal in the wall. The clerk dusted off her hands and grinned. "*This* entrance. It's an old Ministry Express line."

On the other side, she found a large, two-pronged electric switch and flipped it up into its housing. It sparked, and hummed, and the magazine rack slid back into place, sealing them in.

"Now what?" Jack asked the darkness.

Gwen was not rattled. She elbowed his bruised arm. "Wait for it . . ." As if by her command, green fluorescents flickered on, revealing a station unlike any of the others Jack had yet seen. There were no tracks beyond the old turnstiles, just five rusty cylindrical cars suspended over rectangular pools of black water, each oriented in a different direction.

"Spares for the maglev?"

Gwen laughed. "Hardly." She hopped the turnstiles and began inspecting the pools, moving from one to the next. "Believe it or not, these cars date back to days long before the Ministry of Trackers. The Ministry Express used them well into the 1900s, even though the maglev came on line during Tesla's prime."

Jack hopped over the barriers behind her. "Nikola Tesla worked for the ministries?"

"Not at all." The clerk seemed to find the pool she was looking for. She knocked on the car above it with her flashlight, sending a musical *pong* echoing through the station. "Tesla had nothing to do with the Elder Ministries, but that didn't stop the spooks from stealing his work."

Jack joined her by the pool, giving her a flat frown.

She shrugged. "What? I told you they were cheats." Gwen tugged him to the side and pulled a rusty lever on the car, bringing its door crashing down on the lip of the pool. The impact sent up a cloud of dust, but when it cleared, Jack saw that the hatch doubled as a set of stairs. Gwen gave him a tilt of her head. "Up you go, then."

He took a seat on a bench of stiff leather padding, so ancient it felt like wood.

The clerk handed him a strap with a buckle on the end and nodded to the other half, lying on the seat beside him. "You'll want to put your seat belt on."

Jack did as he was told, though he couldn't see why. The maglev hadn't required seat belts. This car, as old as it was, didn't look much different. He pulled the belt tight and glanced over at Gwen, who was securing her own. "And what are the seat belts for?"

She grabbed a T-handle that hung from the ceiling above them.

"For this."

Gwen gave the handle a good yank and the hatch-stairs closed with a tremendous *bang*, forced up as the car dropped through the platform, plunging into the black water below.

Chapter 31

JACK DUG his fingers into the leather. Water surged around the bubble windows at either end of the cylindrical car. "What did you do?"

"Oh, relax," said Gwen, unperturbed. "This form of transportation is quite reliable."

"Right. And that form is gravity, guaranteed to take us straight to the bottom." Jack glanced around the car. He didn't see any tanks or ventilation. "Don't we need oxygen?"

The clerk shook her head. "We have all we need in the car itself."

A green glow developed at the edges of Jack's vision, illuminating the algae-covered bricks passing by the windows. He unbuckled from his seat and walked unsteadily to the nearest bubble, trying to determine the source.

"Bioluminescent bacteria on the outer hull," said Gwen, shutting off her flashlight and letting the glow envelop them. "Activated by motion through the water." She joined Jack at the window as a perfectly round tunnel rose into view. The car eased forward through the opening, caught by the current, lighting up the bricks as it entered. "See? The steel frames of the bubbles are covered in the stuff, like headlamps. The faster we go, the brighter they get."

The current picked up speed in the tube, and soon they were sailing down the center, their green bacterial lights casting flying rings along the bricks ahead and behind, making for a strange and beautiful ride. Gwen gave Jack a smile and a wink. He nodded and did his best to relax, watching the show. He was almost enjoying himself, until he felt the cold touch of frigid water seeping through his sneakers.

"Gwen! The floor!"

It took only a moment to identify the leak. With their attention focused out the bubble at the front, neither of them had bothered to check the door. A flat stream shot up through the seal at the base of the hatch. And the water was deeper on the bench side of the car. Jack glanced out the forward bubble. The bioluminescent glow reflecting off the bricks was a hair brighter on the lower left, the wall a hair closer. Their ancient aquatic Tube car had abandoned the exact center of the line. "We're listing." Jack took his seat and buckled up. "And we're losing altitude."

Gwen sat down next to him, her calm not so pronounced as before. "It's a short trip. The flow around the cylinder will act as a cushion, keep us off the bottom." She chewed her lower lip, staring down at the leak.

"Sure it will."

Jack and Gwen both tilted their heads as they watched the car list farther off-center. Up ahead, Jack could see a disk of light blue, the end of the tunnel.

"We're almost there," said Gwen, tightening her belt. "These cars use drop weights for surfacing. Once we're through the exit, we'll lose the weights and float right to the surface."

Jack wasn't so sure. "Assuming we're not too heavy, thanks to all this water." He felt the cold of it creeping up his ankles. "We should drop them now."

"No. If we drop them too soon, we'll grind along the top of the passage and get—"

Both children lurched sideways. The aquatic car had hit

bottom. There was a horrendous grind of steel on wet brick as it slowed to a crawl, green lights dimming. The front end passed through the exit and the bottom slammed down on the edge, leaving them less than halfway out into open water. A rivet popped. A new spring bubbled up from the floor. Jack started to unbuckle.

Gwen grabbed his shoulder. "Not yet. Once we're free, the trip to the top might be . . . exhilarating."

Jack glared at her. "You know how I feel about exhilarating!"

"And that's why you should stay strapped in." She pointed at Jack's knees. "The weight release lever is in the bench between your legs. Pull it now."

He crunched forward in his seat and found the T-handle, recessed into the steel face of the bench. He pulled. Nothing happened. The water continued to rise, freezing his calves. If they didn't get out soon, the weight of it was sure to hold them down, drop weights or not.

"Come on, Jack. Pull!"

Jack counted to three in his head, mustered up all his strength, and jerked.

The T-handle broke free.

Two resounding *clanks* echoed through the car as the weights dropped off from either end. The front, free of the tunnel, slowly pitched upward, sending all the water to the back. They inched forward, back end screeching along the bricks, until the roof of the cylinder banged into the upper lip of the tunnel. The car stopped, wedged there.

Chapter 32

"WE HAVE TO make it move." Gwen rocked violently side to side in her seat.

Jack joined in, synchronizing with her movements, but the car remained wedged halfway out of the tunnel, tipped upward and canted several degrees to one side. Through the bubble at the front, he could see the shimmering ripples at the surface, twenty feet above at the most. They might easily swim for it, except the tunnel was still blocking the hatch.

"Wait!" Gwen grabbed Jack's shoulder, stopping his movement. "This is getting us nowhere." She stared down at the water flowing to the back for several seconds, then snapped her fingers. "Right. Got it. To the front, quick as we can." She unbuckled, motioning wildly for Jack to do the same.

At first, Jack didn't get it, but the car tipped forward as soon as he followed the clerk to the front. The floor bounced against the lip of the tunnel and started up again, inching them forward.

"Again!" shouted Gwen, pulling him backward.

They scrambled downhill into the cold water, then up again, and again the car pitched down and bounced. It screeched forward along the bricks and wedged itself at an even higher angle. Water kept flowing in. The rear bubble was entirely full.

"It's not enough!" shouted Jack on their way downhill.

"Yes it is. Once more!"

Down into the frigid water and back up again. This time the screeching continued long after the front end had tipped back up. The car inched forward. Then the screeching stopped and it snapped to vertical. Jack grabbed the top edge of the bench, throwing an arm around Gwen as they shot for the surface. The forward bubble—and most of the car—burst out into soft daylight.

When the car splashed down, it rolled back and forth, water sloshing all around the children as if they were mismatched socks in a giant washing machine. Finally, they settled, bounced off an unseen obstacle, and came to rest against a hard shore. Gwen pulled herself up and yanked down on a release lever, sending the hatch crashing down, and Jack followed her out onto a dock made entirely of red granite. He hunched over, fighting nausea and struggling to find his land legs. When he finally looked up, he almost lost them again.

An old sailing ship towered high above them, dwarfing their cylindrical transport. Two rows of cannon poked out from the sides, and the tallest of the three masts rose more than a hundred feet in the air. For a moment, Jack wondered if he had accidentally sparked again, back to the age of pirates and privateers, until he felt Gwen take his arm and pull him along. "The *Red Dragon*," she whispered. "First flagship of the Honorable East India Company. Don't gawk, Jack. It's so utterly American."

They were not on an outside dock as Jack originally supposed, thanks to the ship and the daylight. Beyond the broad pool where the tall ship rested stretched a massive hall. Statues of all makes and materials lined the walls. Granite columns rose like giant redwoods, branches joining across the ceiling to form a lattice of red stone and frosted white glass.

"A network of shafts bring daylight in through the panes," whispered Gwen, pulling Jack's chin down so he would stop staring upward as they walked. "The array captures light from all angles to give the illusion we're on the surface."

"We're still underground?"

"Sort of. We're above the level of the Thames, but we're inside the northeast face of Ludgate Hill, west of the public Guildhall and underneath the London Stock Exchange. This is the *real* Guildhall, Jack, the headquarters of the Ministry of Guilds."

They passed the edge of the *Red Dragon*'s pool, leaving wet footprints in their wake, and Jack noticed small gatherings of toppers dispersed throughout the hall, turning to look in their direction. The sheen as each man moved in the light showed lines of color in his otherwise black suit. It seemed the toppers flocked according to their colored patterns. "Are they on teams or something?"

Gwen wrinkled her nose at him. "Guilds, Jack. Each colored pattern represents a guild. We also call them liveries. London has loads of them. If you ask the toppers, every skill, every service—everything, actually—has a price. And they're always there beneath the surface to steer the money, making sure that at least some of it gets steered into their own coffers."

Jack nodded sagely, as if he were actually keeping up with her explanation. "Are all of the guilds represented here?"

"Not remotely. The Thieves' Guild is banned from the hall, for obvious reasons. A few of the others, like the Magicians' Guild, are too secretive to come here. The Tinkers' Guild, in particular, wish to be left to their own devices."

Jack gave her a sidelong glance.

Gwen gave him a freckle bounce.

Throughout the hall, the looks from the toppers were turning from curious to hostile. "Um . . . do they know I'm a thirteen? Are trackers even allowed to come here?"

"I told you, they don't care which John Buckles you are. And it's not as if we're staying for tea." Gwen glanced down at her watch. "Though it *is* about that time." She nodded toward the other end of the hall. "The Archive of the Elder Ministries happens to be next door, with a Ministry Express maglev station on the other side. We've taken the back route, that's all. The toppers will tolerate it. They owe us."

Given the evil stares they were getting, Jack wasn't so sure. "Um . . . how, exactly, do they owe us?"

"Well, they owe the trackers, anyway." Gwen inclined her head back toward the *Red Dragon*. "That thing was at the bottom of the ocean for two hundred years. Who do you think found it for them?"

Despite her claim, Gwen kept up a pace that told Jack she wanted out of there quickly. He wished they didn't have to rush. The giant statues were too incredible to pass without a longer look—epic figures in stone or metal, engaged in everything from shipbuilding to basket weaving.

One in particular caught Jack's attention. He felt drawn to it, perhaps because it was the only one with moving parts. A mass of copper gears in the pedestal drove hands around a central dial that rested between the feet of a giant golden statue of Father Time. There was something else drawing him as well. Moving letters appeared in Jack's mind, adding up to a phrase he couldn't quite put together. As they passed the sculpture, he lingered. He grabbed the clerk's scarf, pulling her back like a dog at the end of its chain.

"Hey!" Gwen whipped around and scowled. "Yes, I nearly drowned us, Jack, but that's no reason for a hanging."

He pressed his lips together and made two quick head tilts toward the statue. The turning gears were about to bring a jumble of silver letters into alignment. Gwen turned to look just as they clicked into place. She read the words aloud, her tone shifting from an annoyed whisper to utter disbelief. "The Worshipful Company of the . . . Clockmakers."

Chapter 33

"IT'S A COINCIDENCE. Has to be." Gwen turned to leave. "Our Clockmaker is French."

Jack didn't move. There was more. *Bloodworth*. The name flashed in his mind. It had to be there somewhere. The pedestal was a study in clockwork—moons drifted across the stars, ships bucked on copper waves, a cat chased a mouse down a set of stairs. As the cat reached the bottom, the stairs split and a lens came down between the two halves, magnifying a column of names. Jack recognized not one but two of them. He pulled Gwen back by her scarf again.

Her eyes widened with frustration. "Okay, now you're just being mean."

"What does EIC LC mean?"

She frowned at him, readjusting her scarf, then nodded toward the ship at the other end of the hall. "EIC is the East India Company, the same group that sailed the *Red Dragon*. And LC is the Levant Company. One sent ships to Asia, while the other traded in the Mediterranean, but they shared a list of investors—the same investors that funded a good many of the guilds."

Behind them, Jack sensed a murmur of whisperings. He didn't have to look back to know that the angry toppers were creeping closer. He ignored them, pointing out the column of names to Gwen as the magnifying glass made another pass. "It looks like those investors included our two prime suspects for starting the fire: the Duke of York and Lord Bloodworth."

"Really?" The clerk looked genuinely surprised. She leaned in, reading the heading above the names. "'EIC LC Sponsors of Foreign Masters.'" She gasped, straightening. "Oh, well done, Jack."

He shrugged. "What? What do *those two* have to do with the Clockmaker?"

"Perhaps nothing. Perhaps everything." She chewed her lip for a long second, glancing back at the converging toppers.

Then she pulled him into motion. "Time to go. We've overstayed our welcome."

Gwen rushed Jack to a set of brushed nickel doors, which looked like every set of elevator doors in every office building he had ever seen. She took the platinum card from his pocket and passed it over a disk on the wall before handing it back to him. A red LED bulb lit up above the door.

"What about the names?" whispered Jack. "You figured something out, didn't you?"

"Later." Gwen shot another glance at the toppers, who were neither advancing nor retreating. "Right now you need to know about the Archive. This place we're about to enter is very old, Jack—ancient in the purest sense of the word. The Archive was once a drago stronghold, and they didn't build it so much as carve into it. The rules are different in there."

"Rules? Like the silence-is-golden rule in the Ministry Express?"

She rolled her eyes. "No, not *those* rules."

With a soft *ding*, the LED changed to green and the doors slid open. Still looking at Gwen, Jack stepped forward, only to discover there was no elevator—and no floor, either. He reeled on the brink of a giant well formed entirely of book-shelves, at least fifty feet across.

Gwen yanked him back by the collar before he fell. "Must you *always* do that?"

Before Jack could think of a retort, soft yellow lights descended into view—lanterns hanging from the open gondola of a spherical hot air balloon. Fire flared from a burner to arrest the balloon's descent, and the deck kissed the floor right at Jack's feet. A blond woman in dark glasses, seated at the gondola controls, pushed off with a high-heeled boot, sending her stool gliding around the rail to the children, skirt flowing in her wake.

"Mind the gap, please." The woman opened the gate and withdrew a pair of gold-wrapped bars from her waistcoat, holding them up for Gwen. "Something to eat as we go?"

"Yes, thank you." Gwen took the bars and handed one to Jack as they stepped on board. He tore into it, suddenly realizing how hungry he was. But he was disappointed to find the same choco-nutty-shellfish concoction Gwen had offered him on the Ministry Express.

"To the Tracker Collection? Joining your friend, I presume?" The blond woman pushed off again, gliding back to her original spot, keeping her eyes fixed straight ahead the whole time. A long-haired calico, lounging atop a pile of books, took a lazy swipe at her as she passed.

"Friend?" Gwen gave Jack a questioning look.

He shrugged. He was standing on a hot air balloon in an impossible well of books. How was he supposed to know anything at the moment?

Gwen turned back to the blond woman. "Um . . . no. Not just yet. First, we need the list of master candidates from the Clockmakers' Guild. The 1600s, please."

"Clockmakers' Guild." The woman pulled one of several gold ropes that hung above her head. "Down it is, then."

A jet of gas escaped the side of the balloon, sending them drifting across the well in a slow descent. Try as he might, Jack could not see the bottom. The only light came from the lanterns hanging from the gondola itself, and there were no balconies or walkways—only endless stone bookshelves broken by the occasional door.

"Are you enjoying your first visit to the Archive, John Buckles?"

His eyes whipped up to the blond woman. "How did you—? But you're blind."

Gwen dropped her forehead into her palm. "Oh, Jack."

"Jack, is it?" One eyebrow rose behind the round glasses.

"That's new. Just because one is blind, Jack, does not mean that one cannot see. You of all people should know that."

"Then you're a tracker."

"No. Nor am I a spook, a topper, or a drago. I am the Archivist of the Elder Ministries, so I cannot play loyalties." She smiled. "Although, I sometimes play favorites."

The calico cat let out a discontented *browl* as the gondola bumped against the shelves. The Archivist pulled down a thick volume, feeling the cover with her fingers. *"Worshipful Company of the Clockmakers, 1601 to 1700."* She hefted the book in her hand before passing it to Gwen. "Busy century."

Jack hardly heard her. He had left his seat to examine the strange stone of the well, his nose inches from a decorative half column carved between the shelves. He thought he could see depth behind the polished surface, chasms of dark gray and midnight blue. Deep within, rivers of opalescent red flashed back at him, changing course as he shifted his head from side to side.

"Go ahead," said Gwen, opening the book across her lap. "You can try. We call it dragonite. No tracker has ever managed the tiniest spark from that stuff."

Whether Gwen had given him permission or not, Jack

would have touched the stone. He *had* to. He laid a hand on a half column that divided the shelves, closing his eyes and willing the dragonite to tell him its secrets. He tried pushing, pulling, everything he had learned so far, but he could not spark. All he got was an odd warming sensation passing up his arm. When he let go, he caught the Archivist looking at him, dark glasses turned in his direction for the first time. "That *is* new," she said, turning her sightless gaze forward again.

The Archivist gave her pedal a quick punch and the balloon ascended a few feet, where she pulled another volume from the shelves. "Jack's father requested the same Clockmakers' Guild records four days ago." She handed the second book to Jack. "He also requested this."

"Shipping Manifests of the Honorable Levant Company: 1661 to 1670." Jack looked up at the Archivist. "What did Dad want with shipping manifests?"

"He didn't say. Your father and Percy kept a tight lip about this case."

"Oh." Jack stayed there, looking at her. He wanted to ask her something else, but he wasn't sure if he should. Finally, he lowered his eyes. "Did . . . did he say anything about me?"

"No, Jack. I'm sorry." The Archivist pulled one of her gold

ropes, simultaneously flaring the burner, and the balloon began a slow climb through the well, inching toward the opposite side. "I'm afraid your father was tight-lipped about you, as well. Always was."

An awkward silence followed, and Jack knew his question was responsible. He searched for a way to change the subject, eyes settling on the calico. "Um . . . I like your cat."

"That is *not* my cat." The Archivist's somber expression shifted to one of mild annoyance. "He came with the Archive."

The cat raised its head, swishing its tail with mutual disdain.

Jack wasn't sure whether he'd made the mood on the gondola better or worse. "Oh. Well, he's pretty." He set the manifests down atop the pile of books and scratched the calico's ears.

Gwen glanced up from her reading. "I wouldn't do that. He's a bit temperamental, that one."

The cat purred contentedly, rolling its head against Jack's hand.

The clerk frowned. "Well, he is when *I* try to pet him, anyway."

"What do you call him?"

The Archivist snorted. "Monster, mangy creature, nuisance—I try not to call him at all."

"I've found it!" Gwen raised a finger, then rested it on a page full of flowing calligraphy. "Robert Hubert. *He* is the connection between the Great Fire and the Clockmakers' Guild."

The cat dropped to the floor to take a stroll around the gondola, leaving dozens of fine hairs clinging to Jack's fingers. He wiped them on his jacket. "Hubert. That sounds familiar."

"Because I've mentioned him before. He was the Frenchman who confessed to the burning of London." Gwen propped the book up in her lap so Jack could see. "It seems the merchant investors sometimes recruited foreigners for the guilds—new blood and all that. They offered passage on merchant ships, sending their candidates out to seek exotic materials and the like before bringing a masterpiece to London. If the guild accepted the masterpiece, the candidate would become a master, and the investor would get a share in his future profits."

"So . . . Hubert was a French clockmaker applying to the guild?"

"A *pendulier*, Jack, just like that nutter who has your father." She tapped an entry near the center of the page. "Look, it's right here: Robert Hubert received sponsored passage on the *Marigold*, sailing from Istanbul with a proposed masterpiece entitled *Aeterna Flamma*."

The Archivist let out a little chuckle.

"What?" asked both children at once.

"I believe the title is a play on words—if you're a clock-maker obsessed with time, that is." She pressed her pedal, sending up a burst of blue fire from the balloon's central burner. "*Aeterna Flamma* is Latin for 'Eternal Flame.'"

Chapter 34

THE CIRCLE OF LIGHT from the gondola lamps rose through the well of books, passing the sliding nickel doors to the topper headquarters. There was a matching set across the well that led to the Ministry Express. Leaning out from the rail, Jack could see another door in the darkness far above, flush with the books. He could not see much detail, only a thin crack of yellow light at the threshold.

The calico reclaimed his lazy perch on the stack of books, laying his paws across the shipping manifests. Jack gave its ears a little rub and returned to his seat. "The clock was called Eternal Flame," he mused, wiping the new crop of cat hair on his jeans. "What if the Ember was part of the masterpiece? Maybe it powered the clock."

Gwen laid her hands on the open book. "That would mean Hubert knew how to control it."

"Maybe, but not very well. We know he confessed to burning the city. Maybe he unleashed the Ember by accident. Either way, I think *our* Clockmaker is an admirer, trying to finish the job."

"I'll grant you the Clockmaker." Gwen leaned back against the gondola rail. "But not Hubert. You've forgotten the most famous mystery surrounding his confession."

Jack hated how she always knew more than he did, and lorded it over him. "Famous in *your* country, maybe." He folded his arms. "Okay. Out with it."

Gwen gave him her know-it-all grin. "Hubert was exonerated. *Everyone* knows *that*. A few days after he was hung"—she grimaced—"*and* torn limb from limb, the captain of the ship that brought him to London came forward with the proof. He was a bit late, to be sure, but his evidence was rock solid." She pointed to the date the *Marigold* arrived in London. "Hubert's ship arrived on September fourth, 1666. Two days *after* the fire began."

"If Hubert arrived in London after the fire started, how could he have caused it?"

"Exactly." Gwen slapped the book closed, startling the

calico. It sat up and glared at her, swishing its tail. "*That's why your father needed the shipping manifests.*" She stood, reaching out for the book at the top of the calico's pile. The cat hissed and swatted her hand away.

Jack was sure Gwen had skipped over something. "Wait. I'm not sure I'm following you."

"Do try to keep up, Jack." The clerk kept her eyes on the cat, staring it down. "The Levant Company had regular trade with Istanbul—several ships. What if Hubert had *already* sent his masterpiece to his investor? What if the clock containing the Ember arrived *before* the Frenchman?"

"Of course. That would explain why he felt responsible for a fire he couldn't have started. So, if we want to track the Ember, we need to know who the investor was." He pursed his lips, finally getting it. "And the manifest of the *Marigold* should tell us."

"Precisely." Gwen gave him a nod, reaching for the manifests again. The cat flattened its ears and batted her hand. She stopped, took a breath, and forced a smile. "Niiiccce kitty."

The calico glowered at her, putting one paw against the binding of the text. The moment the clerk's fingers moved again, it pushed the book to the edge of the pile, inches from the open space between the rail supports. A low moan rumbled from deep in its furry chest.

"You wouldn't."

The cat raised its head and perked up its ears, removing the offending paw from the book.

"Of *course* you wouldn't. Goooood kitty. You were just playing." Gwen straightened up, pretending to lose interest. "Me too." She turned partially away, then made a quick grab for the manifests. It was a big mistake.

The calico shot out its paw, smacking the book over the edge long before Gwen's fingers reached it. The book bounced off the deck and dropped through the rail, vanishing into the infinite darkness below. Jack never heard it hit the bottom.

"Bad kitty!" Gwen stomped her foot, shooing the cat off the remainder of the stack. It hissed, retreating between Jack's legs.

The Archivist sighed. "Do you see what I have to deal with? That's the second one this week." She pulled one of her ropes, arresting the balloon's ascent. "Dropped books, hairballs on the seats—three days ago he used a fifteenth-century manuscript by Edward of Norwich as a scratching post."

"Hairballs?" asked Gwen, glancing back at the bench where she had been sitting.

The gondola bumped against the dragonite, its deck touching the threshold of the door Jack had seen from below. An engraving above read MINISTRY OF TRACKERS PRIVATE COLLECTION. Gwen opened the gondola gate for Jack, and he pushed the door inward.

A huge form stepped into the frame.

"Well, look 'oo it is. Mrs. 'udson sent me 'ere to find out wot that drone pinched from the Chamber. Guess I've done 'er one beh'er, now, 'aven't I? I found me the kid wot 'ijacked the drone in the first place."

Chapter 35

THE SIGHT of the oversize sixteen-year-old from the Chamber gave Jack a knee-jerk desire to run. Then something clicked. Over the course of the day he had faced gas explosions, fireballs, and specters of the dead. He had survived a game of chicken with a subway train. Shaw no longer measured up. Jack scowled. "Where's my sister?"

"Where's my artifact?"

"He didn't take it." Gwen passed Jack and bulled right through the warden, heading for a big walnut desk at the center of the room. "He's helping me track down the man who did, some nutter calling himself the Clockmaker."

Shaw followed her into the collection. "But I thought 'e was—"

"You thought wrong."

Suddenly finding himself alone with the Archivist, Jack mumbled an embarrassed "Thank you" and rushed after the others, entering a small, three-story library. Spiral staircases at the four corners wound up to railed walkways that wrapped around the room, allowing access to the volumes on the upper levels. "Sadie," he insisted, catching up to Shaw. "Where is she?"

The big warden reversed course, forcing Jack to pull up short. "Your li'l sister's still at the Chamber, going on an' on 'bout 'ow 'er big brother is finding 'er daddy. She 'as a captive audience, as it were. All the doors and 'lectronics are still locked out, thanks to you."

"If the Chamber is still in lockdown, then what are *you* doing here?"

Shaw's scowl sagged a bit. "Since the computers was fried, Mrs. 'udson wanted a warden to go out through an air shaft and get to the paper ledger, 'ere in the Archive, to find out wot the drone took." He heaved out a sigh. "I was the only one small enough to fit."

"Small enough?" Jack leaned sideways to catch Gwen's eye.

The clerk was busy pouring herself some tea, reading a wide ledger that lay open next to the silver tea service. She looked up and nodded, returning the kettle to the platter.

"Okay . . ." Jack returned his attention to Shaw. "So, what was stolen?"

"Nero's Globe." Gwen answered for the warden. "According to the entry, it was a sphere of dimpled glass, infused with a blue-green metal."

"Blue-green," muttered Jack, "like the beetles."

Shaw's thick eyebrows knitted together. "Like the one you brought to the Chamber, eh?"

"I told you, it wasn't mine." Jack pointed at the book. "Who wrote that entry?"

"Your dear departed dad, as it were," replied the warden with a grin.

The flippant reference to his dad felt like a smack in the face. Jack bit off an angry reply and stepped around the warden, heading for the desk.

Gwen took a sip of tea and continued reading. "John Buckles Twelve signed the globe into storage more than two weeks ago. According to this, he and Uncle Percy liberated the artifact from a private residence in Calais."

"Um . . . liberated?" Jack stood across from her, placing his hands on the desk.

"Stole, Jack. Did you really think the ministry finds the

world's most dangerous artifacts lying around in caves?" Gwen lowered her cup. "Most often they've already been discovered, changed hands a number of times. If an artifact can't be purchased, the rules permit more *covert* methods of acquisition." She pushed the ledger aside and slid a second book in front of her.

"Oi! Leave that alone." Shaw lumbered around the desk, towering over the clerk with his gargoyle scowl. "That's *my* research. Took me forever to find it 'mungst all this lit'rature."

"*Your* research?" Gwen's freckles flattened into an ironic frown. "If you could even spell research—or spell *lit-er-a-ture* for that matter—I might take you seriously." She planted five fingertips on his chest and pushed him back to the end of the desk. "The professionals are here now. Keep out of the way and let us work."

"Professionals," mumbled Shaw. "Not likely." But he remained where she had put him.

A soft padding brushed the edge of Jack's hearing and he glanced up to see the calico settling on the second-story walkway, bushy tail slipping down through the iron balusters. "The Archivist left the cat," he said absently.

"More likely, the cat left *her*." Gwen carefully lifted a yellowed page, checked the other side, and laid it down again.

"This text says the globe was a weapon of Ancient Rome. The statue called *The Colossus of Nero* depicted the emperor holding it in his left hand, sculpted to look as if stars"—her eyes shifted up to Jack—"or *embers*, were shooting out from all sides."

Jack didn't buy it. He may not have known British history, but every American kid had to study Rome. "*The Colossus of Nero* disappeared a thousand years ago. Nobody knows what it looked like, so how could the ministry possibly know what was in his left hand?"

Both Shaw and Gwen stared at him with flat expressions.

"Unless, of course, a tracker found it."

Gwen gave him a freckle bounce. "Your grandfather, actually. He found it inside one of the Seven Hills of Rome." She returned her eyes to the text, muting her voice with her teacup. "Lying in a cave, it seems." After turning the page and reading for a bit, she cleared her throat. "The mad emperor Nero used the globe to destroy Rome. Three hundred forty years later, a similar device appeared in Constantinople, right before that city burned to the ground as well."

"Constantinople," Jack said slowly. "Isn't that—?"

"Istanbul. Spot-on. The same city where Robert Hubert created his Eternal Flame clock."

"But the globe can't be the Ember. The Clockmaker already has it."

"No. It can't." Gwen sidestepped along the desk, returning to the ledger. "In his entry, your father postulated that Nero's Globe required a power source. He suggested an expedition to find it." She set her cup down on the platter. "That power source *must* be the Ember. I'm betting Robert Hubert separated it from Nero's Globe and used it to power his clock."

"Which he sent to London," added Jack. "Where either Lord Bloodworth or the Duke of York lost control of it—or used it on purpose—burning five-sixths of the city. But . . . if the Ember burned the city on its own . . . why does the Clockmaker need the globe?" Jack's brain stalled. His thoughts kept winding back to the confrontation between his dad and the Clockmaker. He closed his eyes, trying to see the vision again.

I will recover the amplifier you stole and the people of London will finally pay for their crimes.

"The amplifier." Jack repeated the phrase out loud, stopping the vision before it reached its horrible conclusion. "The Clockmaker accused my dad of stealing an 'amplifier.' I think he meant Nero's Globe. Maybe it magnifies the Ember's effects."

"Exponentially, it would seem." Gwen patted the book.

"This text tells us that Nero used the globe to burn Ancient Rome, a city with more than a million people, spread over an area seven times the size of Old London. A fire that size could burn all the inner boroughs of London, from Kensington to Canary Wharf, with Buckingham at the epicenter."

"Burn Buckingham?" Shaw's ruddy features had turned ashen, as if he had finally grasped the severity of the situation. He sank into a leather chair beside the desk. "A million in Rome. An' 'ow many people live in the inner boroughs, then?"

Gwen closed the text and clasped her hands together, resting them on the cover. "Three and a half million."

Chapter 36

"WE CAN'T LET the Clockmaker have the Ember."
Jack stared across the desk at Gwen. "So how are we going
to get my—?"

The clerk cut him off with a glare, eyes subtly shifting to
Shaw and back again. Jack took the hint. The warden did not
need to know they planned to trade the globe's power source
for Jack's dad, especially now that Shaw understood what the
Ember could do.

Gwen left the desk, motioning for Jack to follow. "We'll
figure it out. But first we need to find the blasted thing. For
that, we need your father's journal." She led him to a tall
cabinet at the rear of the library, unremarkable except for a
bronze sphere mounted on the top.

When she opened the doors, Jack expected to see shelves of journals. Instead he saw what looked like an antique typewriter, with odds and ends crowded into the spaces around it—a large crank wheel attached to a glass sphere, a brass box with jars of yellow liquid, and tons of copper tubes and wires.

"I don't actually know where the journals are kept. I'm only an apprentice clerk, after all." Gwen pulled a telescoping stool out from beneath the contraption and nodded for Jack to sit down. "But this will locate them for us. We call it the *Findomatic*, invented in 1749 by William Watson, the first scientist to send data via electricity. It would have replaced card catalogs two hundred years before computers if not for a small incident in the Royal Society library."

"Incident?" Jack eyed the typewriter, then gently lifted the black paper spilling out from the spool to read the latest entries—phrases like *Cloud-Busting Umbrella* and *Black Prince's Ruby*, typed in silver ink. Three of the four most recent lines were failed attempts to type *Nero's Globe*, with only the fourth spelled correctly. "This your work?" he asked, glancing back at Shaw.

The big warden glared at him from his chair. "Shut it, you."

Gwen cranked the wheel several times, spinning the glass sphere against a fur cloth. After a few turns, the yellow liquid in the jars began to bubble. Jack felt his hair stand on end. "Type in 'John Buckles,'" said Gwen, releasing the wheel and stepping back. "Better make it 'John Buckles the Twelfth,' actually. Otherwise we might get quite a few results."

Jack did as he was told, carefully pressing the round, ivory keys. Each one sent a hammer up to smack the paper with a sharp report, leaving a silver letter behind. When he finished, he slid his pinkie to the return key, but Gwen blocked him. "One moment, please." Then she turned and shouted, "Clear!"

Shaw groaned. "We're the only ones 'ere, Gwen." As he said it, though, the calico dropped from its perch, landing on the carpet with a heavy *thump*.

"And that's why we have rules." Gwen ducked down behind Jack. "All right. Go ahead."

Wondering why he suddenly felt like a human shield, Jack pressed the return key. The carriage slid to the beginning of the line and the paper rolled up one notch, aligning the new entry with a pair of small copper spheres on either side of the page. Nothing happened. The bubbling yellow liquid settled to silence. Gwen squeezed Jack's arm. "Wait for it . . ."

Jack jumped in his seat as a spark danced across the paper, tracing the letters. Four thick lightning bolts launched out from the sphere above the cabinet, connecting with smaller spheres sticking out from the shelves. The cat raised its head and perked up its ears, following the streaks of electricity as they worked their way through the books. Finally, a glass-windowed cabinet flew open and a small book popped out, seated on its own brass tray.

Gwen hurried over to the journal, and Jack could tell she was dying to look inside. But she let him be the one to remove it from the tray. The first thing he noted as he thumbed through the pages was the detail of the drawings. Jack had never known his father to be an artist, yet he saw swords and cathedrals, gargoyles and angels, maps of mountain passes, castles, and canyons, each with an X marking some mysterious spot.

Sensing Gwen's patience fading, he flipped to the last few entries. A triangle diagram covered two pages, three lines connecting three drawings. On the left was an old mantel clock that looked as if flames were climbing up its sides, and on the right, a dimpled sphere that could only be Nero's Globe. At the top of the triangle, drawn over the binding, was something that looked like a sun. It originally had a label that read *The Heart*, but Jack's dad had crossed it out. A newer label read *The Ember*.

"He was close, wasn't he?" asked Gwen, reading over Jack's shoulder.

He nodded. "I never saw the clock in any of my sparks. Maybe Dad found it."

Gwen drew in an involuntary breath and slapped Jack's bruised arm.

"You wot?" Shaw swiveled around, eyes locking on Gwen. "Wot did you tell him?"

"Nothing . . . really." She glanced at Jack, giving him a what-were-you-thinking look. "He fell down and it sort of happened."

"Not just a thirteen," Shaw muttered to himself, "a thirteen that can already spark." He thrust his broad chin at Jack. "The ministry'll be very int'rested in that li'l tidbit, won't they?"

Gwen punched Jack's bruised arm again as the two returned to the desk with the journal. Apparently he had given up damaging information, but he couldn't ask what the big deal was with the warden still listening in. He let it go and laid the journal down on the desk between them. On the next page, there were more written notes, but the opposite page was blank. He thumbed through the remainder. The rest of the journal was empty. "This is the last entry."

"'Great Fire Suspects,'" said Gwen, reading the top line.

Chapter 37

JOHN BUCKLES had named three suspects in the final entry of his journal: Thomas Farriner, the baker; James, Duke of York, the king's brother; and Thomas Bloodworth, the Lord Mayor. He had already scribbled over the baker's name, writing *too obvious* in the margin.

In the notes beneath the duke's name, Jack's dad quoted historians that called him a tyrant, and cited evidence that he had invested in several French candidates for the guilds—though none of them was Hubert. The notes also referenced the same allegations Jack and Gwen had found at the top of Barking Tower—witness statements claiming several French arsonists had been handed over to the duke, then promptly disappeared.

"This looks bad for the duke," said Jack, frowning at the page. "But read what Dad wrote in the margin."

Gwen scrunched up her nose. "'Inconclusive.'"

Jack rested his chin in his hands and sighed. "We're getting more questions than answers." He shifted his eyes down to the single note under Bloodworth's name, and found it even less helpful. Instead of something useful like *Bloodworth did it, the Ember is in his basement*, his dad had written nothing but a long string of numbers. "And what is that supposed to mean?" he asked, tapping the entry.

Gwen flipped to the inside cover, showing Jack a label with its own set of digits. "I thought it might be a reference number like this one, a location to help us find a book in the collection, but the string is too long."

They both stared at the number for several seconds. Then Gwen suddenly straightened. "Unless . . ." She ran to the Findomatic and cranked the wheel. "Clear!"

There was another *thump* as the calico dropped off its perch, giving Gwen a look of pure exasperation. The clerk was too focused to notice. She typed in an entry and pressed RETURN.

Jack ducked as white bolts shot across the library, lighting up the shelves with streams of electricity. A thick volume popped out on the third level.

"It isn't *just* a reference number," exclaimed Gwen, setting the journal back on the desk as she rushed by on her way to the nearest spiral stair. "It's a reference number *and* a page."

Jack hesitated, processing what she meant. Then he jinked around Shaw's chair and ran for a different stair, closer to the book. He, Gwen, and the calico all reached it at the same time. The title on the binder read AN ACCOUNT OF CURIOS-ITIES OF THE LORD MAYORS OF LONDON BY JOSEPH FOWLER VI 1845.

Gwen showed none of her previous patience. She pulled the book from its brass tray and started paging through. "Two twenty-four. Two twenty-four," she repeated as she flipped through the text. "Those were the last three digits in your father's number." When she finally got there, it was clear someone else had already dog-eared the page. Page 224 was the start of a new chapter, with the heading THOMAS BLOODWORTH 1665–1666. Above the heading was a black-and-white portrait of a portly man wearing a stern expression and a long curly wig.

The clerk paced down the narrow walkway as she read, stepping over the cat, which had stretched itself out across her path. "Several passages are underlined"—she reversed course at the stairwell, giving Jack a sour look—"in *pen*. Do you know how old this book is?"

"Gwen, what does it say?"

"Oh. Right." She strode toward him, nose down in the book again. "Lord Bloodworth made some quirky moves in his time. In 1665 he had a glass booth installed in his London offices. He feared the commoners all carried the plague, so he would sit inside the box whenever one came to see him."

"A glass box." Jack flattened his expression. "Dad was really grasping there."

"He was building a profile." The clerk came to a stop in front of Jack, feet together. "Which is simply good detective work." She made an about-face and continued pacing. "Bloodworth also used press-gangs to roust the poor out of the city, and he set those bonfires we read about on Barking Tower, attempting to smoke the plague out of the slums. Another of his brilliant ideas was to order the slaughter of eighty thousand cats."

"Cats?"

The calico lowered its ears and moaned.

"I *know*," said Gwen, acknowledging the animal as she passed on her circuit. "*That* blunder allowed the rats to flourish, probably making the plague exponentially worse."

Jack was growing impatient. Glass boxes and dead cats were great, but he had hoped for a smoking gun. "Is there anything about the artifact or Robert Hubert?"

"Not exactly. But the writer does say that Bloodworth sponsored foreign candidates for the guild. He favored basket weavers, gun makers, and—"

"Clockmakers."

"Who else? And then there's this." Gwen turned the book around so Jack could see, indicating the last sentence in the chapter. His dad had circled it twice.

```
Lord Bloodworth despised the poor, often
commenting that they had brought the
plague to his city, robbing him of the
dignity of his office.
```

"So Bloodworth hated the commoners." Jack dismissed the text with a shrug. "Circumstantial."

"Hearsay, actually." Gwen closed the book with a definitive *whump*. "But Farriner said, 'The mayor betrayed us.' That's *got* to mean Bloodworth's our man."

"Unless the baker only wrote that because he blamed the mayor for refusing to help him fight the fire." Jack sighed and checked his watch. The afternoon was passing too quickly. "We have to make a decision. We don't have time to look into both Bloodworth *and* the Duke of York."

"Personally, I favor the Duke of York," Shaw piped in from below, thumbing through the journal. "Wot, with 'im sympathizin' wi' the French? An' all those arsonists vanishin' into thin air? Now, that's a dodgy bloke if ever I saw one."

The other two, along with the calico, turned from their conversation to stare down at the warden in shock.

"Di'n't think I was payin' attention, did ya?" Shaw let out a swinish snort, leaning back in the leather chair and placing his hands behind his head, stretching the limits of his tweed jacket. "Anyways, I don't favor the mayor for it, turnin' up at the bak'ry so quick like that. That'd be returnin' to the scene of the crime, now, wouldn't it?"

A piece of the puzzle floating through Jack's mind suddenly snapped into place. "The scene of the crime," he said quietly. He turned to Gwen. "I need a map of London—one that shows us what it looked like the day before the fire."

Chapter 38

"WAIT." The Archivist held up a warning hand, keeping Shaw from stepping out onto her gondola. She motioned for Gwen and Jack to board first, and the cat reclaimed its position atop the books. When the Archivist finally did allow the warden to step on, the balloon dropped of its own accord, without any venting of air.

"Jack needs to see the Map," said Gwen, settling down onto the gondola bench.

The Archivist nodded as if she knew exactly *which* map, but Jack couldn't see how. Gwen had offered no other explanation. "One from the 1660s," he added, just to be sure.

"Relax, Jack." Gwen's freckles rose into a grin. "She knows the Map you need."

The elevator-style doors to the Ministry Express and the Guildhall rose through the light of the lanterns, passing above them, as did the empty spaces where the old book from the Clockmakers' Guild and the shipping manifests had rested on the shelf. And still they descended.

Gwen lowered her voice. "We're entering the section dedicated to the Ministry of Secrets. Below these shelves are the oldest records of the Archive, those belonging to the Ministry of Dragons."

If they were nearing the Ministry of Dragons section, they were nearing the bottom. Yet, looking over the side, Jack still could not see the floor. He was dying to know what was down there. "If we're close," he offered, "why not go all the way down and recover the manifests?" He did not bother to whisper, and earned a harsh look from Gwen for the offense.

"That would *not* be a good idea," said the Archivist. "Not all mysteries are meant to be solved, Jack." Even she kept her voice low, which Jack found particularly unsettling. As if to punctuate her warning, a grating rumble rose from the black. Jack pulled back from the rail and looked wide-eyed at Gwen, but the clerk was studying her hands, chewing her bottom lip.

Before Jack could ask any more questions, the Archivist punched her pedal and the gondola bumped to a stop against the wall. Where Jack expected to see a door, he saw a flat slab of dragonite instead. "Um . . . ," he whispered, not wishing to be rude to the blind woman but not knowing how else to phrase his concern. "I think you missed."

The Archivist gracefully kicked her stool around and laid a hand on the stone. To Jack's astonishment, the dragonite dematerialized, exposing a door behind, made entirely of midnight-blue marble. "Magic," he breathed, before his brain could catch up to his mouth.

The Archivist sniffed. "Don't be absurd." She stood back, pulling open the gate. "Mind the gap, please."

Jack was first through the door, into a small chamber. The walls were made of the same dark blue marble, with shelves carved into them, as empty as the niches in the baker's tomb. A simple iron chandelier hung low over the center, gas flames quietly hissing, casting a pool of yellow light over what Jack assumed must be *the Map*.

It seemed more like a big copper box than a map table, with sheer sides instead of legs, each a patchwork of plates joined by little hinges. Copper plates also made up every detail of the model of London on top, right down to the river winding its way through the center.

"I think you're going to like this." Gwen strode past on her way to the map table, then Shaw and the Archivist, leaving her balloon hovering outside. The calico came last, skirting around the Map. It disappeared down a passageway in the shadows beyond.

"Where—?"

"I believe he keeps his litter box back there," answered the Archivist before Jack could finish the question.

"The cat keeps his litter box in the Ministry of Secrets section?"

"Where else would he keep it?"

Gwen guided Jack around to the other side of the table, where four crank wheels of steadily diminishing size were attached. On the table's edge, engraved between a pair of rearing dragons, were the words LONDON, 1066 TO THE PRESENT, and a rolling date counter set to 7 p.m., 20 March 1413.

"'To the present.'" Jack read the words aloud as if that would help him make sense of them. "How can a map cover an indefinite period?"

"September second, 1666. At midnight, please." Gwen tugged Jack out of the way as the Archivist cranked the largest of the wheels, rolling the years forward. Hundreds, maybe thousands, of gears ground within the box. The city sped forward through time.

Plates rapidly clicked, folding upon themselves and unfolding again in new shapes. Lines of houses collapsed while others rose up from empty fields. The copper Thames roiled. Then, as the Archivist moved to each successive wheel, the rate of change slowed. The counter rolled to 12 a.m., 2 September 1666 with a slow and final *click*.

Jack walked around the table. "This is London right before the fire?"

Gwen nodded.

The streets were so cluttered with ramshackle tenements as to be useless. The houses had grown together, the upper floors reaching across the streets so that the roofs nearly joined, making caves of the lanes below. Shacks and hovels clung to the buildings like fungus, blocking off whole roads. Just west of Pudding Lane, where the greatest clutter had grown, a single narrow gate led to a slum that covered dozens of acres, with a labyrinth of interior alleys and court-yards. How could anyone have escaped such a place once the flames hit?

Gwen hovered at Jack's shoulder. "They called that

Little Tyburn, named for the gallows outside the city walls. Laws did not apply in there. The wooden walls kept the authorities out, and tens of thousands of the city's poorest tenants in."

"And where is Covent Garden? The neighborhood where Bloodworth lived."

"Why?"

Jack almost smiled. Gwen hadn't figured it out yet. "Just show me."

The clerk moved down the map, a good distance from Little Tyburn, until she came to the spot where the Thames took a hefty turn to the south. She pointed to a well-organized collection of streets, lined with tall row houses. "Here."

Jack let his eyes drift between the two neighborhoods, taking in the distance and the growing jumble of shacks that clogged the streets the closer he got to the baker's house. "How could Bloodworth have made it to the fire so quickly?" he asked, walking slowly along the Map. "It would have taken a messenger an hour to get through all this mess, and at least another hour to drag our drunken mayor back to Pudding Lane."

Realization washed over Gwen's face. "But Bloodworth was there well before the fire spread to the nearby houses.

He had to have been there within the first few minutes. And that's not possible, unless . . ."

Jack came to a stop next to Shaw. "The Lord Mayor didn't return to the scene of the crime at all," he said, slapping the warden on the back as hard as he dared. "He never left."

Chapter 39

GWEN STARED at Jack across the table, looking crestfallen. His hands fell to his sides. "Wait. What's wrong? I figured it out. I thought you'd be impressed."

Her freckles bounced, but not quite high enough to form a smile, even a fleeting one. "I am . . . sort of. It's just that . . . you know . . . you're the tracker. You make the observations. I'm the one who makes the deductions, at least the big ones. That's our thing, isn't it?"

He frowned. "We've known each other like six hours. We don't have a thing."

"And if *you* start making the big deductions, where does that leave me?"

Shaw's big head turned from one to the other, his mouth

slightly open. "'Ave you two gone bonkers? Three and a 'alf million lives're on the line, remember?"

"Right. Of course." Gwen held a hand out over Covent Garden. "So Bloodworth sponsors a French clockmaker applying to the London guild, hoping to share in his profits. But when the masterpiece arrives, powered by this incredible source of heat, he's inspired." She moved to Little Tyburn. "He sees a way to end the plague that's ruining his career—a better way than killing cats or ordering bonfires in hopes that one would get out of control."

"It's midnight. No one's around." Jack jumped in to continue her stream of thought. "Bloodworth seizes the moment and tosses his prize through the window by the ovens, releasing the Ember from whatever casing Hubert built to control it."

The clerk shot him a glare. Apparently Jack was still in trouble for beating her to the big deduction. "*But*," she said, continuing on her own, "the Ember is more powerful than Bloodworth expects. The fire burns through the slums and keeps on going, burning five-sixths of the city." Gwen nodded slowly. "So that's how the Ember got to the bakery." Then she furrowed her brow, looking down at the Map again. "But where did it go from there?"

"The cobbler!" exclaimed Jack. "*The cobbler saved us*. We

know Farriner was right about the mayor. Maybe he was right about the cobbler, too. If the mayor started the fire by releasing the Ember, then the cobbler put the fire out by regaining control of it." He spread his hands. "We have to find the cobbler. We find him, we find the Ember."

Gwen's jaw dropped. "You did it again. *Stop that*." She frowned at him for a long time, then turned to the Archivist. "Roll the hours forward through the fire, please."

The Archivist nodded, taking the hour reel and slowly cranking forward. At first, the only movement was the copper plates of the Thames, gently rolling with the current. Then the bakery collapsed, from the center of the roof outward, then the buildings around it and the buildings around those, and so on. The fire spread like the plague Bloodworth had wanted to stop.

Jack bent closer to Little Tyburn as the clicking epidemic spread. The walls of the slum went first, as if the fire wanted to encircle its victims. As Jack watched, the flash of the copper became the flicker flames. He could see shadows running back and forth, fire hemming them in on every side, ripping through the tumbledown labyrinth.

"Jack?"

He blinked, jerking upright. The flames were gone,

replaced with bright, oiled copper. The model city had become a wasteland. He glanced around at the stares of the others, then recovered his composure and fixed his eyes on Gwen. "What did you say the death toll was for the fire?"

"Jack, I don't know how that's going to help—"

"Just tell me."

"Six," interrupted Shaw. "Ever'one knows that. Less than wot fell to their deaths from top o' the Monument itself." He gave Jack his gargoyle grin. "Ironic. That's wot that is."

Gwen shook her head. "The official death toll and the census taken a few years later don't agree. The census was a hearth tax, meaning they counted apartments and houses rather than individuals, but somewhere between seventy and a hundred thousand unnamed poor had gone missing. It's the biggest mystery of the Great Fire."

"Or the biggest secret," Jack said quietly.

A hint of a smile formed at the edge of the Archivist's lips. "There's only a tiny difference between the two, isn't there, Jack?"

Gwen cleared her throat. "Let's get back to the Ember, shall we? Let's assume our cobbler really did stop the fire. To contain the Ember, he would first need to acquire from Bloodworth the piece of Hubert's clock that kept it under control, wouldn't he?"

Jack could see she already knew the answer to that question. "That sounds right."

"Of course it does. Bloodworth and the cobbler *had* to have crossed paths *after* the fire started and *before* it ended."

Jack scanned the copper wasteland. "So where could the two of them have met while London burned? Where would a snobbish aristocrat have gone to seek shelter from the fire?"

"Oh!" Gwen took a step back as if the copper table had given her an electric shock. "I've got it! *The ravens keep their secret*. Why didn't I see it before?" She looked from Jack to Shaw to the Archivist and back to Jack again. "'The *ravens* keep their secret.' The famous denizens of the infamous castle where snobbish aristocrats and commoners alike could tread." She punched Jack's sore arm. "Who's making the big deductions, now, hmm?"

Jack pressed his lips together, rubbing the bruise. He didn't get it. And judging from the look on the warden's face, Shaw was equally in the dark. "What denizens, Gwen? What castle?"

Gwen's face was almost giddy. "The *ravens*, Jack, at the only castle in the city."

Chapter 40

JACK PREFERRED to part ways with Shaw, but Gwen seemed to think keeping him close was a better idea. Despite Jack's obvious nonverbal cues, she invited the warden to join them, convincing him that Mrs. Hudson would want him to go after Nero's Globe and the Ember rather than reporting back to the Lost Property Office.

The three of them took the Ministry Express from the Archive to the black granite hub near Pudding Lane, and on to a small station Jack had not yet seen. There, they crammed themselves into a circular lift, with Jack squished against Shaw. The tweed vest was musty, and a little moist. "You couldn't have taken the next one?" Jack asked, tilting his head awkwardly sideways to look up at the journeyman warden.

"Shut it, you. This is a ministry lift. A thirteen shouldn't even be here."

Jack sighed. "Yeah. I've heard."

Moments later, they tumbled out of a round brick structure onto a stone plaza. The walls of a fortress rose before them, right in the middle of the city. Jack pulled his hat on to shield his ears from the cold wind. "The Tower of London. This is the castle with the ravens?"

"Ever since the reign of King Charles the Second." Gwen gave him a triumphant freckle bounce. "The same king who reigned during the Great Fire."

The clerk led them to a long square that ran between the fortress and the Thames, its wrought-iron rails all decorated with lighted garlands and bows. With darkness falling, only a few people still braved the wind and the cold, too huddled up to pay any attention to the children. Gwen steered the boys toward a vendor with a steaming cart, parked in the shadow of a tree that overhung the Tower moat—the only tree without a string of lights.

"Candied peanuts, love?"

Gwen snapped her fingers twice at Jack, which he understood as a request for his platinum card. The vendor examined it, raised an eyebrow at Jack, then shrugged and pulled the cart back, revealing a hidden stairway.

"And some nuts as well," said Gwen, handing him a folded bill.

The vendor touched a finger to his wool cap. "Much obliged, love." He handed them each a paper cup of warm candied peanuts as they passed. The scents of caramel and cinnamon floated across Jack's brain in ribbons of deep red, flecked with gold.

The stairs took them down to a short wall between the dry, grassy moat and a channel of water flowing under the square. The water continued into the Tower through an archway blocked by a portcullis, where a small sign read TRAITORS' GATE. "Why is it the 'Traitors' Gate'?" whispered Jack as Gwen waved them through a black door on the other side.

"Because this is where the condemned entered the Tower." She pulled the door closed behind, shutting out the light from the square. "You know, prisoners about to get the ax."

Jack pulled his hands away from the stone walls. "Great."

Moving in and out of the light, Gwen led them up stairwells, through creaking doorways, and down cobblestone lanes until they finally emerged on a grand inner courtyard. Timber and plaster houses lined the defensive walls, interspersed between stone towers, making Jack feel as if he'd stepped into a village from another century. It *was* a village, it seemed, with real residents. He noticed lights in several of the windows.

"Keep your voices down and stick to the shadows." Gwen sank her chin down into the coils of her scarf as she led them along the edge of a green yard. "The yeoman warders live here full-time. They won't be too keen on three children running amok in the courtyard."

In the quiet that followed, Shaw's tweed jacket buzzed. Jack half expected him to pull out some anachronistic bronze contraption, with vacuum tubes and copper coils, but the warden produced a very ordinary-looking smartphone. He held it up, showing them Mrs. Hudson's stern face, looking as if she disapproved of the camera. The label above the picture read LOST PROPERTY. "Chamber must be out o' lockdown," mumbled the warden, raising a heavy thumb to answer the call.

"Don't!" Gwen tried to take the phone, but Shaw pulled it back, letting it buzz.

"And why not? We're well in front o' tha' Clockmaker fellow, ain't we? Time to call in the pr'fessionals." His glare shifted to Jack. "Besides, I think it's time Number Thirteen 'ere should face the music, don't you?"

"The music?" Jack didn't like the sound of that. Gwen had said the ministry would hold him, but what else would they do? The British wrote the book on *civilized*, didn't they? Then the reason for Gwen slapping his arm in the Archive came to him. Jack had revealed to Shaw that he could spark well before his time. The ministry would want to know why. How would they find out? Torture? Experiments? "What music?"

Shaw curled his thick lips into a sneer. "Just you wait." He touched the screen to answer Mrs. Hudson's call, but the phone had stopped buzzing. It went to voice mail. "Not a problem. I'll just ring 'er back, then, shall I?"

"Please, Shaw. This isn't *only* about Jack. We need the Ember to save his father."

"You wot?"

Gwen's lips were pressed together, trying to hold the explanation in. But the pressure burst and it all came flooding out—Jack's father, the Clockmaker, the exchange at midnight.

"You'd be a hero," she said, finally taking a breath. "Think of it: saving a tracker's life, bringing in a pair of *seriously* dangerous artifacts—the ministry might even promote you to full warden. But you can't call them about Jack, not yet."

Shaw slowly pocketed the phone, turning his glare on Jack. "Millions o' lives, Mr. Thirteen. Buckingham. Those're the stakes. I s'pose you 'ave a plan, then?"

"I . . . uh—" Jack shot a glance at Gwen. She nodded vigorously and then pretended she was stretching her neck when the warden's eyes drifted her way. Jack cleared his throat. "Of course I do. I'm a tracker, right?"

Shaw glared at him a few moments longer, then emptied the cup of candied nuts into his mouth and crunched down. "Aw'right, *tracker*. I'm in. Where do we go next?"

"We . . . um . . ." Jack caught Gwen making subtle flapping movements with her hands. "We follow the ravens, of course." He scanned the courtyard. There was a lot of ground to cover, nooks and crannies everywhere. "But where are they?"

"Usually right here." Gwen nodded toward a wooden perch in the grass, on the other side of a memorial with a glass pillow at the center. "This is the lawn where the condemned used to get their heads chopped off. The ravens favor it."

Shaw snorted. "And the ghosts."

"Don't be ridiculous. There are no ghosts in the Tower."

A fleeting shadow caught Jack's eye, a shift in the light beneath a barren tree at the corner of the grass. "I wouldn't be so sure."

Chapter 41

JACK RACED AHEAD of the others, tossing his paper cup into a bin as he passed, frowning at his own foolishness. Specters had followed him since Pudding Lane. They had popped up at the Monument, at Barking Tower, and in the Archive. Now, finally given the chance to turn and run from a ghost, he was chasing it down.

Gwen caught up at the tree. "What did you see?"

"Just give me a sec." The cold made it harder for Jack to think, to see. A white cloud shrouded everything. He let out a long breath, waiting until pieces of data rose from the mist.

A dead leaf scratching across the cobblestones: not the movement he'd seen.

Initials carved into the tree: puppy love immortalized in thoughtless graffiti.

A shadow in a doorway to his right: insubstantial. Human. *Release us.*

Jack's eyes snapped to the doorway, but the shadow was gone. The wooden door, banded with iron, stood cracked slightly open. He hurried across the narrow lane.

"I don't think the ravens go inside the towers," protested Gwen as Jack eased the creaking door inward.

He knelt down in the darkness and picked up a black feather, holding it up for the others to see. "Really?"

"You saw that in the dark, did you?" asked Shaw, squinting at the token.

Jack pushed the door all the way open, turning away to enter the tower. "Not exactly."

An empty, vaulted chamber opened before them, lit by city lights seeping in through arrowslits. Before Jack could wonder what to do next, he heard a flapping of wings reverberating from a spiral stair to his left. He rushed up the steps to follow.

After a full turn of climbing, Jack saw a strip of light projected on the steps above him, presumably from an arrowslit around the next bend. He stopped and caught his breath, holding out an arm to keep Gwen from passing. A shadow grew within the light, tall and sharp, with the distinct form of a head and shoulders.

"Tell me you see that," whispered Jack, touching Gwen's sleeve.

She nodded in silence.

They crept upward, keeping tight to the inside wall, and both let out a relieved breath at the same time. Their ghost was a raven. The black bird stood in an arrowslit, casting its ghostly shadow on the stairs. It regarded them with shining black eyes, and cocked its head as if trying to understand a question the children had yet to ask.

"You found one!" panted Shaw, coming up behind them, out of breath from the climb. The bird flapped out the window.

"Oh, well done," huffed Gwen, slapping his arm.

"That ain't right." The warden stared after the bird. "Ever'one knows the ravens of the Tower don't fly. The ravenmaster clips their wings to keep 'em from flappin' off."

"They *can* fly," argued Gwen, "but only short distances." She turned to head back down the stairs. "We can follow him if we hurry."

More light spilled down the stairs from above, and Jack

caught a hint of movement, like the shifting light beneath the tree outside.

"Up," he said, catching Gwen's sleeve. "We need to go up."

A pointed archway at the top let them out into another chamber, big and empty. There were alcoves that might once have held furniture, and a tall, yawning fireplace. Jack shivered, suddenly feeling as if his jacket no longer kept the frigid air at bay.

"I thought we was chasin' the bird," said Shaw. "Wot're we doin' up 'ere?"

Jack walked the perimeter of the room, running a hand along the stones. Several were carved with etchings that looked more like classical art than graffiti. "Who made these?"

"Young Lady Jane Gray, for one," said Gwen, eyeing one of the simpler carvings, "not long before the headsman took her life in the yard below. A good number of lords and ladies waited for their deaths here, kept in style until their executions."

Shaw folded his arms. "An' *that's* why this place 'as so many ghosts."

"Lords and ladies," muttered Jack. "Wrong ghosts." A whisper drew his attention to the fireplace, and the shadow beneath the mantel coalesced into a silhouette. It beckoned to him. *It is time. Release us.* Then it twisted into a wisp of smoke, disappearing up the chimney.

Jack didn't have to ask if Gwen had seen the specter. She had been looking right at the hearth and hadn't reacted at all. He ran to the spot where the ghost had vanished. What did it want him to see?

Soot: left by the fires of a half-dozen centuries.

A handprint in the black: ancient, hardly there.

A breath of air: an airy whistle, a string of light gray blowing across his mind, definitely not coming down the chimney.

Jack passed a hand along the wall, an inch from the stone, until he found the air stream. "Help me," he said, leaning a shoulder against the bricks.

Gwen didn't question him. She stepped right into the hearth to help, but it wasn't until Shaw lazily pressed a hand against the bricks that a section of the wall gave way. The hidden door shifted outward, grating against the stones below, and Jack squeezed out into the wind.

Chapter 42

THE DOOR in the fireplace opened onto a hidden section of the ramparts—a wedge-shaped space of ancient walkway, trapped between the tower they had just climbed and a timber building that had been built right on top of the fortress's original defensive wall.

"We're behind the Queen's House," said Gwen, touching a wooden beam. The timber structure pressed right up against the crenellated battlements that had once served as cover for archers standing on the wall. She glanced back at the open fireplace. "That passage has to have been there since the days before the Queen's House was built. Do you think any of the royal prisoners knew about it?"

Shaw stood next to her, peering over the battlements at

the long drop to the cobblestone lane that ran between the inner and outer walls of the Tower of London. "Wouldn't 'ave done 'em any good. Even if they 'ad a rope to climb down, they'd still 'ave to get over the second wall. More likely it was for the comings an' goings of the torture master—to keep 'is work on the lords an' ladies out o' sight."

"Quiet." Jack shushed him, holding a finger to his lips.

"You wot?"

"Be *quiet*, Shaw." He heard a scratching sound, faint but definite. Jack ignored the angry look from the warden and leaned out to look along the back of the long timber house. A black vapor swirled above the battlements, untouched by the wind. It moved a little farther away and hovered there. He climbed up onto the stone parapet to follow.

Gwen grabbed the leg of his jeans. "What are you doing?"

"It wants me to follow. You don't have to come."

"Who wants you to follow?" She leaned out to look around him. "Oh! You found the raven!"

"It's not a raven. It's something else." Jack pushed her hand away and sidestepped across the first gap in the battlements, pressing his face against the back of the Queen's House. The cold wind beat against him, trying to tear him off the wall, and the vapor swirled just out of reach. It drifted farther away each time he inched closer. "Where are you taking me?"

"It's not taking you anywhere, Jack. It's only a bird. We should go back, look for the rest."

Jack couldn't turn his head to look back, but he knew from the proximity of Gwen's voice that she had followed him out onto the ledge. "I told you, it's not a raven," he called into the wind. "It needs me to follow."

Her hand touched his. "Then I'm coming with you."

"I'll just stay 'ere, then, shall I?" Shaw called from the walkway. "Keep watch, an' all that? Per'aps I'll call the 'earse for you once you fall to your deaths."

Jack was so focused on following the black vapor that he didn't notice a chimney until he was almost upon it, built into a gap in the battlements so that its bricks jutted out past the stones. The black vapor hovered at its edge.

"Don't," breathed Jack. "Please don't."

The vapor swirled around to the other side and disappeared.

"Of course you did."

"What?" Gwen called out behind him.

It dawned on Jack that she couldn't see around him. She hadn't seen the chimney blocking their path. "Nothing! It's just . . . going to get a little hairy ahead. That's all."

"As if this isn't hairy enough!"

Jack reached the end of his foothold and leaned his head back far enough to see around the bricks. The chimney was barely more than three feet wide. He could make it. Maybe.

Getting a hand and a subsequent foot to the other side was easier than he imagined—too easy. Once Jack got himself into that spread-eagle position, hanging on to the chimney for dear life, he was stuck. He glanced down at the cobblestones below and the world spun. He laid his head against the cold bricks, closing his eyes.

"Jack, I'm not sure about this," said Gwen, reaching the end of the ledge behind him.

"Neither am I." He went for it, praying for some sort of handhold in the wall on the other side. There was no wall. Jack's reaching hand touched nothing but air. He fell.

"Jack!"

"I'm okay." On the other side of the chimney was a sort of alcove, an indention for one of the windows of the Queen's House. Jack had tumbled into it. As he stood, dusting himself off, he saw that the window hung partially open. The black vapor disappeared through the gap.

Jack poked his head out from behind the bricks. "Come on, Gwen. I've got you." He pulled her across the chimney and she dropped off the battlements, right into his arms.

"Oh!" Gwen looked up into his eyes as he set her down. "Um . . ."

Jack quickly turned away and crawled through the window, hoping the shadows were enough to hide the red in his cheeks. "In here. Come on."

"Right." Gwen's hands dropped to her sides. "We'll just carry on, then, shall we?"

Jack stepped down into an attic with sloped timber beams and a wood floor running the length of the Queen's House to form a long hall, broken by narrow patches of light shining in through the windows. He heard a light tapping in the darkness. "Hello?"

Release us.

Odds and ends were scattered about the space—tall paintings, old toys, ancient furniture covered in white sheets. Jack took a step toward the tapping sound and bumped into a rocking horse. It creaked as it rocked back and forth.

"Do try not to break anything, will you?" whispered Gwen, appearing beside him. "There are five centuries of royal history up here." She took his hand as they crept through the room. "What is that sound?"

"A ghost."

"There are no such things as ghosts, Jack."

He stopped, gripping her hand a little harder. "Really? Then what's that?" Ahead, in a wide shadow between the pale patches of light from the windows, stood the black figure. *Now, Jack. Release us.* It sank into the floor.

Gwen pulled her hand away. "It's only a raven, silly."

Jack squinted at the spot where the specter had disappeared. She was right. He saw the same large raven they had seen in the tower. How had he not seen it before? The bird pecked at the wood plank beneath its feet, making the tapping sound they heard from the window. As Jack approached, it backed away, head cocking this way and that. Five others fluttered down from the shadows to join it, forming a semi-circle around the plank, watching with focused intensity.

The floor seemed to rise in Jack's vision, the pattern of the planks becoming more apparent. The central plank, the one the raven had pecked, was different. The gaps around it were wider than the gaps between the others, and the nails holding it down had square heads. All the other nails in the attic were round. Without turning to look at her, Jack held out a hand to Gwen and snapped his fingers. "Give me your screwdriver."

"What? Why?"

"Gwen, please."

She complied, and Jack shoved the screwdriver into the

floor to pry up the plank. It came up an inch with a terrible *squeak*. Gwen gasped. He looked back and frowned. "Tell me how this is different from what you did at the top of Barking Tower."

Her mouth snapped closed again.

After two more cranks, the plank came free and Jack carefully set it aside. The hole beneath was deeper than he expected. He couldn't see what was down there. He winced as he put a hand down into the hole, praying that he would not touch the cold, white silk of bone, or the grit of human ashes. He found neither. Jack's hand closed around a thick cloth bundle instead.

Six ravens hopped attentively in Jack's wake as he carried the bundle to the light. Black vapors hovered around a thick roll of red cloth. *Release us.*

He glanced at Gwen. She couldn't see the vapors. She hadn't heard the whisper. But her expression told him she recognized the worry on his face. "No ghosts, Jack," she whispered, nodding at the cloth bundle. "Only answers."

The two sat down on the wooden floor, and Jack unfurled the wrappings. One of the items inside clunked to the floor, a large medallion on a gold chain. A sapphire the size of a walnut was set in the center.

"I told you there were no ghosts." Gwen picked up the necklace, letting the jeweled medallion twirl back and forth, sparkling in the light.

"And you were wrong." Jack held up a second item from the bundle for her to see, a thick sheaf of papers, bound in soft leather. He read the title burned into the cover. *"Great Fire of 1666. The Rolls of the Silent Dead."*

Chapter 43

CAREFULLY, Jack leafed through the yellowed pages. "Names. They're all names." He stopped at the center, examining the first few entries on the page.

Fryght, Anne
Fuller, Geoffrey
Matilda (Wife)
Unknown Daughter (Infant)
Fynch, Henry
William (Son)
Unknown Son

On it went, column after column, family after family. Some were listed merely as numbers in a tenement, with only a profession listed—*mason, smith, fuller,* and the like.

"There are hundreds of pages," whispered Gwen, clicking on her flashlight, "each with five columns. There must be tens of thousands. The official death count really was an error."

"Or a lie." Jack kept turning the pages. "Why weren't the bodies ever found?"

"Cremated. Burned to ash along with everything else. The bigger question is, who collected all these names?" Gwen nodded down at the book. "Check the last page. A seventeenth-century author would have signed at the end of the record, not at the beginning."

Jack turned the book over and opened the back cover. Beneath the names on the last page, he found a final, cryptic inscription.

Compiled by a nameless cobbler and a humble baker. Recorded that the dead might someday be remembered. Kept secret at the behest of our king. May God have mercy on us all.

He shook his head. "Nameless. Great. Now how are we going to find the cobbler?"

"And what does this medallion have to do with the list?"

Gwen held the jeweled disk in her open palm, letting its gold chain dangle through her fingers. "It can't be the Ember."

"Or can it? Is it hot or anything?" Jack stretched out a hand to feel the sapphire. The moment his fingertips touched the cool, hard stone, his body dropped through the floor.

Jack had learned enough to know a spark when he felt one. He landed on his feet, standing at the open window of the attic, looking out at a wall of flame engulfing the city. The charred, black scent of burning debris filled his nostrils. He could see every detail, the grit of battlement stones before him, the grain of the smoke rising in the distance. Like the cobblestones on Pudding Lane, the sapphire had taken him deep into the past. But these were no shadows. Jack could see everything as clear and sharp as if he were really there.

Without any thought or desire to do so, he turned from the window. He was a captive of the sapphire, and it seemed the jewel was hanging around someone's neck. Two guards in red-and-blue regalia approached, dragging a man between them. They tossed him down onto the wood planks and he scrambled to his knees, adjusting a wig of sooty curls as he looked up. Jack recognized his face from the book in the Tracker Collection. He would have breathed out the name in disgust if he could speak. *Bloodworth*.

"It was him, sire." A second man took a knee beside the mayor. Jack knew him instantly. The black grime in the lines of Thomas Farriner's face made him look unnervingly like the effigy covering his tomb. "My maid witnessed him throwing the cursed thing through my window. She would not leave the house for fear of the malice in his eyes, and she perished because of it. So have many, thanks to this devil's sorcery."

Bloodworth glowered at the baker and opened his mouth to reply, but he was interrupted by a calm, commanding voice, one that seemed to come from Jack himself. "What precisely have you done to us, my Lord Mayor? And how do you propose to stop it?"

The anger fell from Bloodworth's face, replaced with sniveling fear. "I ended the plague, Your Majesty. I rid my city of its vermin. But now I cannot stop the flames. I know not how. The jewel from the clock controls them. They are not natural."

The mayor reached into his cloak, causing the guards to take a step closer, but what he withdrew was no weapon. He held out a blue-green box with a broad window of glass in the lid. "This was the heart of the clock, Your Majesty. It held the infernal jewel, the . . . ember . . . that made the fire. The box itself has some power to push back the flames. I tried to go back for it, but the heat"—his eyes fell to the floor—"and the churning storm of smoke and sparks. It is worse than any tempest you can imagine. No man can find his way through the conflagration."

Farriner suddenly stood, eyes widening. "I know one who can! He is well known in Little Tyburn, Your Majesty, for tracking lost items, even children, with uncanny skill. Give him the Lord Mayor's box and he can track this Ember through the flames."

Both men fell silent for several seconds. Then the commanding voice returned—the voice Jack knew belonged to the king. "Tell me this hunter's name, Master Farriner, that I may send men to the shelters at Moorfields to find him."

"He has no given name, sire. And he is no hunter. He was an orphan who took trade as a cobbler. He used to say that the brass bindings on a good pair of boots were the only thing that shined in Little Tyburn." The baker shrugged. "Most people call him Johnny Buckles."

Chapter 44

JOHNNY BUCKLES.

Jack reeled at the sound of his ancestor's name. The cobbler he had been looking for all day was the first of the Buckles line. The baker, Thomas Farriner, and Jack's own family were tied together in history. The realization threatened to sever his connection with the sapphire. White light flashed, obscuring the spark. He felt a familiar rising sensation, pulling him out of the past. He wasn't ready. Not yet.

Jack pushed, straining his synapses, trying to stay in the seventeenth century. He needed to see more. He wanted to see the cobbler's face. His head screamed. The light became a sheet of solid white, blocking everything. He was losing.

The effort to hang on tensed every muscle of the body

Jack had left behind. A cry startled him, distant—not his own voice but familiar. He couldn't focus on it. He had to keep fighting. Then, suddenly the bright light was gone, and so were the mayor and the baker.

Jack was back in the attic room, but he was still standing. The scent of smoke still hung heavy in the air. A man in a long leather coat, blackened with soot, knelt before him. Strings of grimy brown hair hung down, hiding his downcast face.

"Well," said the commanding voice of King Charles, "the fire has fallen. You must have found what I sent you for."

The young man's face lifted, and Jack would have shouted if he could. The cobbler was a younger version of his dad, or maybe an older version of himself. Without a word, Johnny Buckles pulled the Lord Mayor's blue-green box from his coat and held it up before the king. "Do not open the box, Your Majesty. The jewel feeds on the air and comes alive with fire. It is nigh impossible to reclaim once unleashed."

Jack noticed his ancestor's hands were bandaged. The cuffs of his coat were not merely blackened—they were charred. Retrieving the Ember had come at some cost. A hand beset with rings appeared from the periphery of Jack's vision, pressing the box away. "Open it? I will not even hold it. This Ember is too dangerous a thing for ambitious hands to carry.

I charge you, cobbler, with its safekeeping. Hide the jewel where even you would trouble to find it."

The cobbler bowed and turned to go, but the king commanded him to stay.

"Wait. Service such as yours demands reward."

The vision jerked and shook. Jack thought he was loosing his hold again, but he quickly realized the sapphire was on the move. Soon the medallion hung from the cobbler's neck. Jack looked up at a man he could easily have mistaken for Captain Hook, if he did not already know better, down to the coiled black wig and the curled mustache. Yet the gold trim of the king's coat was singed, his elbows blackened. Even he had been out among the flames.

The king nodded to someone out of Jack's view, a guard perhaps. The interview was drawing to a close. "We will call upon you soon, young . . . Buckles. The Crown has need of a skilled tracker. In the meantime, you will not speak of this Ember, or the Lord Mayor's part in the fire. With the late civil war and the treasure lost in this calamity, we are greatly weakened. Rumors of a dangerous weapon in our hands and whisperings of a terrible atrocity committed by a knighted lord would embolden enemies both without and within. England would not survive."

The cry Jack had heard before encroached on his vision. He lost his hold on the spark, accelerating upward until he reached lightning speed, with the noise growing louder the whole time. Then he was back, sitting in the dark with Gwen, his hand clasped over hers, her lips parted in the midst of a yelp. "Ow! Not so hard. That thing is sharp!"

Jack felt the pain as well and quickly released her.

"You're a tracker," said Gwen, massaging her hand. "I know you don't have to squeeze so hard to tell if something's hot."

Jack stared down at the impression the medallion had left on his hand. "I saw it. I saw the real Ember. It was right there, inches away from me."

"You sparked." Gwen nodded. "That explains the grip. But I'm still mad . . . sort of. What did you see?"

Jack placed the rolls of the dead back on the red cloth and wrapped them up again. "I know why these names were kept secret so long."

"To cover up the scandal of mass murder by a landed lord, of course. I put that much together on my own." Gwen got to her feet and offered him a hand. Then she pulled it back. "Easy does it this time, okay?"

"I'm not going to spark off your fingers, Gwen."

"Right. Okay." She extended the hand again. "What about

279

the cobbler? Did the spark show you where he took the Ember?"

"Not exactly, but I saw and heard enough." Jack let her help him to his feet. Then he took the medallion by its chain and carefully added it to the cloth bundle.

"Well?" Gwen was still waiting for him to elaborate.

He walked over to the window, gazing out at the lights of modern London. "The Ember is hidden in the one place I absolutely cannot go."

Chapter 45

"**JOHNNY BUCKLES** could have buried the Ember in the woods south of the Thames," argued Gwen, folding her legs up onto the seat of the Tube car they were riding in. "Or perhaps a cave in the Scottish Highlands. For all we know, he took it out of the country."

"He didn't. He would have kept it close." Jack stared at their reflections in the bowed window. It worked like a funhouse mirror, giving them each two heads, one above the other, like the king and queen in a weird deck of cards. "King Charles charged him with keeping the Ember safe. He would have hid it someplace where he could keep an eye on it."

The car was empty except for the three children, slowly making its way westward stop by agonizing stop. The

Ministry Express would have been faster, but Gwen had insisted it would be too risky. Using Elder Ministry resources had been fine while the Chamber was in lockdown. The other ministries didn't know one tracker from another. But now that the lockdown was over, the Chamber would be watching the maglev. The last thing the children needed was to let the wardens know they were headed straight for the Ministry of Trackers—that the Section Thirteen was about to sneak into the Keep itself.

The train slowed and the revolving-door-Tube voice spoke in her obnoxiously calm tone. "This is . . . Great Portland Street. Change here for connections to the . . . Metropolitan . . . and . . . Hammersmith lines. Mind the gap, please." The doors opened. Jack looked to Gwen to see if they were getting off. She still hadn't told him exactly *where* the Keep was.

The clerk shook her head, letting the doors close. "What do you plan to do about the book of names?" she asked, rocking sideways as the car lurched into motion again.

"I'm not sure." Jack had set the book and the medallion back in the hiding place beneath the floorboard, while the ravens looked on with what he felt were disapproving glares.

Even if he wanted to release the names, no one would take the word of an American kid. The best he could do to satisfy the specters would be to call the right archeologist with an anonymous tip. "Who am I to let such a big secret out? On the other hand, those ghosts *really* want their names released."

"You didn't see any ghosts, Jack."

"Per'aps 'e did," interrupted Shaw, whose oversize frame was taking up most of the bench catty-corner to the others. "I'm bettin' a thirteen 'tracts all sorts of undesirables."

Gwen gave the warden a withering scowl. "He saw a *raven*, Shaw. I saw it too."

Jack frowned. "I'm not talking about the Tower. I mean, I am, but . . ." He cast a glance at Shaw. He didn't want to discuss the rest in front of the warden. Of course, Shaw already knew he could see fields of data and spark before his time. Why not add communing with the dead to his list of Section Thirteen offenses? He sighed. "The ghost in the Tower wasn't the first one I saw today."

While the warden listened with poorly feigned disinterest, Jack told Gwen about the wraiths in the cobblestones and the skeletons in the Monument, about the man he saw in the stained glass window and the people he saw in the Map.

"I've been seeing ghosts all day. They all wanted me to find that book."

The clerk remained unconvinced. "In all the literature I've read about trackers, I've never seen any evidence that they can see or hear ghosts."

"But *I* saw—"

"Visions, Jack. That's all. Images in your head." She glanced up at the map of Tube stations above the windows, eyes shifting from one location to the next. "On Pudding Lane, you touched the ashes from the Great Fire. At the Monument, you picked out bones in the sculpture that time had washed away. At the Tower, you saw a raven and heard the wind whistling through the joints of the secret door." She dropped her eyes to his. "The ghosts were manifestations of your subconscious, Jack. All of them. Your subconscious recognized the clues and put them together into visions to help the rest of your brain catch up."

Jack turned back to his strange, two-headed reflection, trying to decide which would be worse: having the curse of seeing the dead or the curse of a subconscious with a mind of its own. "If none of it was real . . . then how do I know what to do with the names?"

"But you already do, don't you?" Gwen placed a hand on

his knee. "If your own subconscious gave you the visions, then you've already decided. You simply haven't accepted it yet."

"Is this ghost of yours the one tellin' you we'll find the Ember in the Keep?" asked Shaw, folding his arms and crumpling up his tweed. "Not that I'm complainin'. The Keep is where you belong"—he leaned forward, bushy eyebrows pushing together—"permanently."

"No. That part I figured out on my own." Jack turned to Gwen and frowned. "But I still don't know where the Keep *is*."

Gwen chewed her lip, glancing at the doors as the car began to slow. "It's not too late to turn around, Jack. Shaw is right. If we go in there, you may never come out again. And that won't do your father any good, will it? How can you be so sure the first John Buckles hid the Ember at ministry headquarters, anyway?"

"Because that's what I would have done."

The clerk nodded. "Then I guess we're here."

Out the window, Jack saw a familiar mural as the train coasted into a station—a wolfish dog pouncing on a terrified man, while two other men raced to help, one wearing a bowler hat. The revolving-door-Tube voice made her serene announcement. "This is . . . Baker Street."

Chapter 46

"THE KEEP is underneath the Lost Property Office?" Jack tried to contain his anger as he followed Gwen up the stairwell leading out of the station. "Why didn't you tell me?"

"I *did* tell you, Jack. I told you the Lost Property Office was the tip of the Ministry of Trackers iceberg. Remember? It's not *my* fault you didn't take it literally."

Jack couldn't believe she was trying to turn this back on him. "You *knew* the ministry would hold me prisoner if I learned about my family. You told me I couldn't go to the Keep. But I had already been inside, hadn't I—inside the Chamber? And *you're* the one who pushed me through the door. What was your plan, Gwen, take me prisoner and get some sort of reward?"

"Not likely." Shaw let out one of his swinish snorts, tromping up the steps behind Jack as if to make sure he didn't turn and run.

Gwen topped the stairs and headed for the turnstiles. "Mrs. Hudson would have found out you were a thirteen as soon as you filed that paperwork. She would have shut you out, Jack, turned you away without explaining anything." She paused at the barrier. "You were so close to the truth, but you were minutes from walking out the door without ever learning who you really were."

"The truth?" Jack's voice echoed in the station. "Which truth? That my life would be over as soon as I stepped through the big metal door? Or the truth that you wanted a captive playmate so you could pretend to be a quartermaster?"

A Tube cop seated on a stool in the corner looked up from his newspaper with concern. Jack lowered his voice to a growl. "What did you think would happen, Gwen? Did you think we'd be some kind of twisted team? That you'd bring mysteries down to whatever dungeon they buried me in and we'd solve them together? How fun for you."

The Tube cop went back to his reading. With nothing but the *Times* between him and the guard, Jack hopped the turnstile and stormed out onto Baker Street.

Jack marched up the sidewalk toward the Lost Property Office. He didn't have much of a plan. His DNA would open the door to the Chamber, which he now knew was the first level of the Keep, but an army of Shaws was waiting for him on the other side. Maybe he could get past them. Maybe not. At least Sadie would be there.

"Wait!"

Gwen chased after him. Jack could see her without looking back, by the echo of every footfall, by the snap of her scarf—a shadow approaching through the white haze of the cold. She had awakened parts of his senses he could not turn off, and Jack wasn't sure if he was better or worse off because of it. He knew Gwen had kept things from him throughout the day, but he had never thought she meant to betray him right from the start.

"Jack, *stop*." Gwen came up beside him, breathing heavy. "You can't go in that way. You won't get two feet past the door and you know it."

He kept going, refusing to look at her, two storefronts from the Lost Property Office.

"I'm sorry. All right? Is that what you want to hear? I used you, Jack, and I'm *sorry*. I always wanted to be something more, *do* something more than file paperwork. And then you walked in, all tracker-ish and totally impossible and . . . and . . ."

"And what?" He stopped, inches short of the windows of the Lost Property Office.

Gwen shrugged, looking down at the pavement. "Well, it was a lot for a girl to handle, that's all." She let out a long breath. "I thought your DNA could get me into the upper-level computers, get me answers about my uncle. And I ignored the consequences for you and your sister." The clerk fell silent for several heartbeats. When she finally looked up again, her eyes were wet but determined. "Don't go through that door, Jack. Not if you're doing it to punish me. I won't let you give up the chance to save your father."

"What am I supposed to do? The Ember is in there. I have to get in somehow."

She sniffed, wiping away a tear with her scarf. "How about trying the back door?"

Minutes later, all three stood on the stoop of an ordinary London row house, half a block up Baker Street from the Lost Property Office. The address read 221B. Jack turned to

Gwen with a flat expression. "You do realize your back door is a front door, don't you?"

"I've 'eard of 221B," muttered Shaw, taking hold of the knob at its center. "It's a utility access." He pushed, grunting with the effort, but the door didn't budge. "It's locked."

Gwen pulled the warden back by his tweed jacket. "Of course it is. And 221B wasn't *always* a utility access. For more than two hundred years this was the main entrance to the Ministry of Trackers—secret, until it wasn't. Once word leaked out, Londoners came calling day and night, with everything from missing persons cases to owner-less hats. Dr. Doyle was the Minister of Trackers then. That's when he came up with the idea of the Lost Property Office."

"If it's locked," asked Jack, "how are we supposed to get inside?"

"Don't know."

He looked down at Gwen in surprise.

"I said there was a back door. I didn't say I knew how to get through it."

Jack frowned, considering the door. If it was a utility access, maybe someone had used it recently enough that he could spark on the knob. Maybe he would see evidence of a hidden key or a secret combination. He stretched out a hand, but the door swung inward on its own before his fingers reached the knob. A lantern appeared, then a face next to it, small and innocent. Jack couldn't believe his eyes. "Sadie!"

Chapter 47

"**WHAT ARE YOU** doing here?" asked Jack, pulling his sister into a hug. "Where is Mrs. Hudson?"

Sadie hugged her brother back for a long time before pushing away and answering. "Mrs. Hudson got really busy once all the computers were fixed. She sat me down and told me to stay put. But I got this feeling you were on your way."

"A feeling?"

His sister nodded, placing a small hand over his heart. "I could feel your heart. Just like I can feel Daddy's. So I came looking for you."

"You mean you wandered off." Jack was not sure whether to laugh or cry. He shot a glance down Baker Street. "Come on. We need to get off the street."

Inside 221B they found an ordinary English flat, all wainscoting and wood trim, complete with photos hanging on the walls. The four children huddled around Sadie's lantern at the base of a set of red-carpeted stairs. Jack took his sister's hand and squeezed it in both of his. "Can you lead us back the way you came?"

"She doesn't have to." Gwen studied the pictures. "I know the way from here."

Shaw let out another snort. "Not likely. You've never been 'ere before and you know it."

"You're right, of course." Gwen came to a photo of a man playing the violin, hanging slightly off-kilter. She straightened it, causing a pronounced *click*, and the floor began to descend beneath their feet. "But I *have* read all the schematics." She winked at Jack. They had been standing on a hidden elevator the whole time.

They descended a good long while through wood, brick, and stone before the elevator finally jolted to a stop within a cage of iron-grate panels. The overlapping grates to the left slid apart, and their little company filed out into a tunnel hewn from black rock. The rush and pound of falling water echoed down the passage. Beneath the natural sounds, Jack sensed something manmade as well—a constant, pulsating drone. He could feel the hairs on the back of his neck standing on end. "Gwen? What is this place?"

Before the clerk could answer, Sadie hurried ahead, turning a corner and vanishing from sight, leaving them all in darkness.

"Not this again," moaned Jack, and ran after her. He turned the corner and skidded to a stop at the edge of an iron bridge that stretched across an underground river.

Sadie had stopped at the center. She held her lantern out over the rail. "Look, Jack! Isn't it amazing?"

He stepped out into the mist rising over the bridge. A torrent of water poured down from above, turning three massive, gleaming wheels through great half circles of copper. Gwen came up behind him, resting her forearms on the rail. "This is the River Tyburn, a tributary to the Thames that runs beneath Baker Street. Your ancestor chose this place for the Keep because the river would provide a concealed source of power and transportation."

An aquatic carriage, like the one that had nearly drowned Jack and Gwen, was suspended on a chain between the bridge and the falls. It had rusted in place halfway across the river, on its way to what Jack assumed must be the departure side of an old Ministry Express station. "Transportation?" he asked, eyeing the steel carriage. "You mean the leaky-tubes-of-death?"

The conversation was interrupted by a loud *creak* as Shaw opened an iron box at the near end of the bridge, exposing a pronged switch. "Cool. I'll wager the power is still connected."

Jack walked back along the bridge, shaking his head. "Don't touch that, Shaw."

"I don't take orders from thirteens, now, do I?" growled the warden, and shoved the switch up into its housing. Creaks and groans echoed from beyond the rock walls. The carriage jerked into motion. Then it stopped again, amid a hideous, ringing grind.

Sadie covered her ears.

"Shut it down!" shouted Gwen.

Shaw hastily reversed the switch and the noises stopped—all but the low, rhythmic groan as the carriage bounced slowly up and down on its chain.

They all stood and stared. Jack saw particles of red dust lazily rising with the mist. Hairline fractures stood out in his mind, so that he wasn't sure whether he saw them or could simply hear the cracking as they spread through the chain links. Either way, he knew what was about to happen.

Jack was already moving when the first link failed. The

horizontal car dropped to vertical, swinging on the chain and slamming into the chasm wall. The impact broke the other connection and it plunged into the river. The carriage bobbed, carried by the current, then toppled straight toward the control panel where Shaw was standing.

"Look out!" Jack pushed Shaw back into the stairwell passage as Gwen yanked him the other way by his collar. The big steel tube smashed through the rail between the two boys, sending up sparks on either side, knocking them down onto their seats.

Everyone froze.

With a long, terrible groan, the iron bridge began to fail.

Chapter 48

JACK SPRANG UP, following Gwen in the race to the other side, pulling Sadie with him. The failing bridge carried them sideways, bending into the river's flow, and the iron plates at the end began to tear away from the stone. "Jump!" shouted Jack. All three made a final, desperate leap for the passage, and tumbled into a heap on the stone floor.

"How cool was that?" Sadie sat atop her brother, holding her lantern high.

Jack set his sister aside and got up in time to see the remains of the bridge sink beneath the water. The carriage floated off into the darkness with Shaw staring blankly after it, stranded on the other side.

"Oh, well done," shouted Gwen. "What do you think will happen when it hits the sewer lines, hmm?"

"The ministry shouldn't 'ave left it 'angin' there, should they?" Shaw gave her a shrug. "Bound to go sometime. Miracle no one was 'urt."

Jack screwed up his face. "Right. A miracle. You're welcome." He gestured at the remains of the bridge. "You've cut off our escape, genius."

But Gwen leaned close to his ear. "Don't worry. There are other ways out of the Keep. Locked doors are easier to manage from the inside. That's what Uncle Percy always says." She turned back to Shaw, raising her voice over the pound of the waterfall. "We'll have to carry on without you. We'll find the Ember and then meet you at Baker Street Station, quick as we can."

"Quick as you can." Shaw nodded his agreement, but his words sounded more like a warning. He backed away into the darkness.

Jack stared after him for a few seconds, then turned from the river and followed Gwen and Sadie into the new passage. "How do we know Shaw isn't running back to Mrs. Hudson right now to sell us out?"

"We don't." Gwen shrugged, looking over her shoulder.

"But he's been dying to bring you in ever since the Clock-maker's beetle interrupted him this morning. I think he'll wait a little longer so he can finish the job in person, and perhaps nab the Ember in the process."

A dozen reflections of orange flame flickered on the wet floor at the far end of the tunnel, where soft light poured in from an open chamber. "Maybe he won't get the chance," said Jack, slowing his pace. "It looks like someone left the lights on for us."

Gwen pushed ahead. "Gas lamps. Always burning. No need to worry. Not yet, anyway."

If the original entrance to the Ministry of Trackers had been designed to intimidate and impress, the builders had succeeded. A broad path stretched from the mouth of the passage across a monstrous cavern of green pools and dripping stalactites. On the far side, a five-story wall of black granite blocks stood exposed, curving away at the edges, as if a Gothic tower had crashed into the earth, drilling down through the middle of the cavern. Jack read the Latin phrase engraved above the huge double doors. *"Populus, Thesaurum, Refero."*

"People, treasure, answers." Gwen proudly translated the motto. "We find them."

Jack raised an eyebrow. "Treasure?"

"Not all treasure is gold and silver, Jack. I should think you had learned that by now."

One of the two doors was bronze, and stood partially open. The other was cut from a giant slab of opalescent quartz, polished to a glassy shine. Jack didn't have to ask the reason for the two materials. One door could tell a tracker exactly who had passed through it in the last few days—maybe weeks if he was skilled. The other, he assumed, had a deeper memory. "Is there someplace where the Buckles family kept their stuff?" he asked, ushering Sadie through the doors. "A storage room, or a locker, or something?"

"A locker?" Gwen snorted, following Sadie inside. "Right. Something like that."

The grand hallway beyond the entry had the feel of abandonment—once a broad thoroughfare for important Londoners in need of the ministry's services, now a forgotten back alley of the Keep. "Everything's wood," breathed Jack, running a hand along the carved molding.

"That's for—"

"The trackers. I get it. The Chamber was the same, and the Tracker Collection. You can't have your primary employees confusing visions with reality every time they lean against a wall."

"Precisely. They might do something crazy, like play chicken with a train."

Jack ignored the jibe. His attention was fixed on the dusty odds and ends cluttering the shelves built into the walls—framed medals, swords and spyglasses on brass stands, *and old photographs*. His brain registered a face he recognized. Jack saw his mother.

He stepped closer, zeroing in on the picture. Mary Buckles was barely out of her teens, seated in the front row of a small group. "Gwen, who are all these people with my mom?"

"Your *mum?*" For all her knowledge about Jack and the ministry, Gwen seemed genuinely surprised. She rushed to his side. "That can't be right. Where?"

"Front row. Third from the left. That's definitely Mom."

"I've seen this picture before." Gwen pulled the photo from the shelf, pointing to a man with sandy hair and freckles like hers. "That's Uncle Percy. And the rest are quartermasters—class of 2000." She slowly lowered the picture. "And, Jack, the woman seated third from the left is *Mary Fowler*. She was your father's first quartermaster."

He pursed his lips. "No. That's Mom. And her maiden name is Smith—Mary *Smith*. She didn't meet Dad until he immigrated to New York fifteen years ago."

"Right." Gwen gave him an ironic chuckle. "And I'm sure that's what the ministry believed as well. But I'm betting that story is a lie."

"You're telling me Mom was part of the ministry too?"

Gwen placed the photo back on the shelf, angling it just so. "Not just part of the ministry, Jack, the daughter of another tracker family—ministry royalty, if you will."

Jack paced back toward Sadie, who was too busy examining the knickknacks to follow the conversation. "If Mom knew about the ministry, why didn't she go to the Lost Property Office the moment we arrived in London?" Even as he uttered the question, Jack realized his mom *had* known. Of course she lied about where she had gone. She had been lying to him his whole life. His eyes narrowed. "Gwen, did you see my mom yesterday?"

"No one has seen Mary Fowler for fifteen years. She quit. Disappeared. And now we know why. There are rules about this sort of thing."

Jack didn't like the tone in her voice. "*What* sort of thing?"

"Marriage, Jack—within the tracker ranks. Section eight, rule six: 'The tracker bloodlines shall never be joined under any circumstances.' *Never*, Jack." Gwen joined him in the circle of light from Sadie's lantern. "The ministry fathers understood the potential of tracker abilities, and they were deathly afraid of what the union of two tracker lines might produce."

"*Produce.*" Jack repeated the word. "Wait. You're talking about me. *I'm* the genetic freak they feared." He drew in a breath. "Is that why I can see ghosts?"

"You can see ghosts?" exclaimed Sadie, so loud that her voice echoed down the hall.

The other two turned to shush her.

"Yes," said Jack.

"No," said Gwen at the same time. They frowned at each other.

Sadie held the lantern up to her brother's face. "Cool."

Jack pushed the light down again. "Mom and Dad broke the rules. That's why she disappeared and changed her name—so she could marry him in secret. Why would she do that, knowing what it might do to her children?"

Sadie smiled up at him. "Why don't you ask her?"

"Mom's not here, Sadie." Jack was sure he had experienced this conversation before.

His sister gave him the same incredulous look she'd given that morning in the café. "Of course she is. She's right here, in this building."

Chapter 49

FOOTSTEPS interrupted Jack's train of thought—heavy footsteps that reverberated in his head like bowling balls thrown into a pond. "Someone's coming." Down the hall, at the intersection of another corridor, a long shadow fell across the wood floor. "Someone big."

The clerk pushed open a panel between the shelves. "Through here. Quickly."

As Jack backed toward her, a huge man came into view, dressed all in tweed, lowering a head the size of a basketball as he passed beneath an archway to enter the grand hall. He turned in Jack's direction just as Gwen yanked him sideways through the wall. She shut the panel and covered Sadie's lantern with her scarf. "Are you *trying* to get us caught?"

Footsteps thumped their way, coming to a stop outside their panel. All three held their breath. Then the footsteps thumped on and the great bronze door groaned. Giant-tweed man had gone out into the cavern. Jack let out his breath. "The ministry knows we're here. They're looking for us."

"No. They're looking for Sadie." Gwen uncovered the lantern, illuminating the landing of a stairwell. A wooden stairway curved slowly out of sight above and below. "She wandered off when Mrs. Hudson turned her back. Remember? But that warden *will* come back. Thanks to Shaw's handiwork at the bridge, he has nowhere else to go." She handed the lantern back to Sadie and took her hand, starting down the steps. "This is the Great Stair. It winds around the perimeter of the Keep, all the way to the bottom level. Which is where I think we'll find that locker you're looking for."

A good many steps below, they came to a landing. It led inward for several yards before the stairs resumed, next to a door labeled SUBLEVEL 6. Gwen explained that the Keep narrowed every few levels, like an inverted wedding cake.

"And how many levels are there?" asked Sadie.

"Twenty-six in all, varying in size. One of them is more than ten stories tall."

Jack considered the long stretch of steps below, slowly winding around the giant underground tower. "Isn't there an elevator or something?"

"Lift, Jack. You do have *some* British blood, don't you? And they all have cameras. We wouldn't descend a single level before the Chamber froze the lift and sent in the wardens."

"What about an inner stairwell? Anything would be faster than this."

Gwen paused, turning to look up at him from the step below. "Jack, this is a three-hundred-year-old structure, designed and built to house history's most dangerous artifacts and train its best detectives. The inner workings are a veritable labyrinth, and sneaking through the storage levels would be nothing short of suicide." She and Sadie started down the steps again. "No sticky wickets, Jack. We use the Great Stair. Down to the bottom and back up again. Easy peasy."

She was not kidding about the size of the levels. Sublevel Ten, in particular, seemed never-ending. They passed door after door, descending through the alphabet—10A, 10B, 10C, and so on. Not far below 10G, Jack noticed the lantern light had become a cottony yellow sphere around them. The air thickened with a growing fog. At 10K, he saw the source.

Heavy mist poured through the crack at the threshold, billowing down the stairs. "Gwen?"

"Sublevel Ten is the arena," said the clerk, without so much as a pause as she stepped down into the flowing mist. "A little larger than a first-class cricket ground. The ministry uses it for various forms of training—and, of course, the annual Tracker Games."

"Games?" asked Sadie.

Gwen glanced down at her with an officious smile. "Ministry regulations, volume one, section six, rule nineteen: 'Competition breeds excellence.' Our arena is so large that it even has its own weather system—gets a little foggy on cold nights, drizzles in springtime, that sort of thing."

The clerk seemed to be joking about the rain, but Jack wasn't laughing. The mist filling the stairwell beneath him had started to glow. A low, harmonic hum drifted across his mind in spiraling ribbons of blue and white. He recognized the sound from his time in the Chamber. "Gwen, look."

The clerk backed up a step. "I see it."

Jack shot a glance back at the door where the mist was

pouring through. They had descended too far to get back up there in time. "Your scarf. Hurry!"

"I can't, Jack." Gwen shook her head, keeping her eyes on the approaching glow. "Those things are too quick."

"Maybe you can't. But I can." He snapped his fingers, opening his palm, and Gwen placed a loop of the scarf into it just as the bronze mini-drone rose out of the fog, blue light shining within its four circular engine housings. The drone paused when it saw them, hovering a few feet away, level with Jack's eyes. It shifted back and forth with jerky movements, sizing him up.

Jack stared the thing down, widening his senses and trying to pick out its tells. With each movement he caught minute fluctuations in engine glow and tiny shifts in the angling of the circles. He could do this.

Gwen was still backing away, pulling Sadie with her. "Now, Jack. Before it reports us."

Both Jack and the drone moved at the same time. He missed the main body, but the end of the scarf shot through one of the circles as the drone passed over his head. He grabbed the other end and held on, trying to pull the thing down. The drone pulled him up instead.

"Gwen?" Jack shouted, twisting in the mist as it carried him up the stairs.

"I've got you!" The clerk jumped up, grabbing his legs. And still the drone climbed.

Gwen's added weight gave Jack some leverage. He yanked down with all his might, tilting the engine housing and sending the drone careening to the side. It smacked into the wall and dropped several feet, blue lights dimming. Jack and Gwen crashed down on the stairs. Ignoring the pain in his back, Jack gave the scarf another hard pull and steered the drone into the other wall. Broken pieces clattered to the steps.

Gwen was ready when it fell. She lifted a foot high and stomped with a satisfying *crunch*, scowling down at the machine. "I suppose that's coming out of my pay, isn't it?"

Jack rubbed his aching back. "That thing was strong."

"Quantum Electrodynamic Drones," said Gwen, twirling her scarf about her shoulders again. "QEDs, we call them. Borrowed the technology from your American Jet Propulsion Laboratory. They've always been overpowered. I once saw a QED lift a life-size statue of Queen Victoria"—she puffed out her cheeks—"the later years."

Jack laughed, instinctively looking toward the lantern light to see if Sadie got the joke. But Sadie was not with the lantern. She had left it sitting in the mist at the next landing down—one of those that turned inward as the Keep narrowed. From the shadows around the corner, Jack heard a door click closed.

Chapter 50

"YOUR SISTER does this a lot," panted Gwen as she and Jack raced down the stairs.

"You have no idea."

Jack cracked open the door marked SUBLEVEL 11 and peered through. Sadie was twenty feet away, walking down the center of an endless hall of paintings. Many of the figures in the artwork resembled his dad; some, his mother. All of them appeared to be wounded, with an arm in a sling or leaning on a cane. "Sadie!" he called in a harsh whisper.

If Sadie heard him, she didn't show it. She was looking slowly left and right at the doors between the paintings, finger resting on her chin, as if searching for the right room.

Jack ran out into the open, with Gwen right on his heels. "Sadie!" he hissed again.

"Get back here!" added Gwen.

They were too late.

A shadow fell across the crack of light beneath the door to Sadie's left. The lever turned. It opened. Then it paused. "Get some rest," said an aged voice from the other side. "I'll check in on you tomorrow."

Jack and Gwen pulled Sadie into the room across the hall, one door opening as the other closed. Through the gap, Jack caught a glimpse of the person entering the hall. He wore a mirror strapped to his head and a stethoscope around his neck. "Was that a doctor?" he asked, turning to Gwen as the footfalls receded.

Gwen didn't answer. Her eyes were fixed on the room behind them. They were not alone.

They had chosen to hide in a bedroom from a bygone era, moderately furnished with a high-backed chair that faced a small bed and dresser. A man was propped up against the pillows, sandy hair poking out from the bandages that covered half his face.

"Uncle Percy!" exclaimed Gwen, racing to the bedside. "You're awake!"

313

Percy reached for her with a hand laden with IV tubes. "Gwen," he said in a weak, raspy voice. "And you brought your new friends, I see." With the phrase *your new friends*, his one visible eye shifted to the high-backed chair, and Jack realized someone was seated there.

A woman's hand appeared on the arm, clutching a pair of red leather gloves. She rose and turned, still wearing the blue peacoat she had worn when Jack had last seen her. At the sight of her two children, her legs gave out and she dropped to her knees.

Jack forgot about the Ember. He forgot about the Ministry of Trackers. He forgot his anger over years and years of secrets and lies. Nothing remained but the rush for his mother's arms. "I'm sorry," he said, squeezing her tight. "I'm so sorry we left the hotel."

Sadie reached her mother a split second after Jack, hitting them so hard she nearly toppled them both over. "It was my fault. I thought I saw Daddy."

Mary Buckles held her children for a long time before finally standing up to look at them. "It's all right. I know all about it." She dabbed her tears away with her gloves. "At least, I know some of it. Percy has been filling me in." She sniffed, showing Jack that sad smile he had told himself he never wanted to see again. "But I suppose you have a lot of questions for me."

Jack checked his watch. It was past ten o'clock. "My questions will have to wait. We have less than two hours to rescue Dad."

"Rescue your dad?" Percy winced, trying to sit up. "But John is—"

"Alive." Gwen finished the statement for him. She steadied her uncle, leaning him back against the pillows again. "John Buckles Twelve is still alive."

"I can feel him," added Sadie, looking up at her mother. "I can feel his heart."

Jack squeezed his sister's shoulder. "And I believe her. But we think Dad is hurt pretty bad. The Clockmaker has him, and he'll give him back in exchange for the Ember."

"Which means we're on the clock." Gwen rolled her eyes at her own words. "No pun intended. Long story short, Jack thinks the first Buckles hid the Ember in the Keep. And I'll bet you can guess where I was taking him to look for it."

"You were headed downstairs."

The clerk nodded.

Mary Buckles set her features and took her daughter's hand. "Then I'm coming with you." She turned to Percy and tried to speak, but he raised a bandaged hand.

"Ol' Percy'll be fine, Mary. Won't go anywhere without you. I promise."

Fifteen sublevels separated the hospital floor from the basement, where Gwen hoped to find the Ember. During the descent, Jack told his mom the full story, and his mom told him hers. She had been trying to make contact with Percy in secret ever since she had arrived in London, but to no avail, since he was unconscious. Then she had returned to the hotel and found both her children missing. She had searched everywhere, from Edgware Road to Piccadilly, and had been about to turn herself in to Mrs. Hudson and beg for the ministry's help when Percy finally called. He had told her that Sadie was safe and Jack was with Gwen, at large in London and last seen exiting the Ministry Express station at the Tower.

She finished as the four of them reached the bottom of the Great Stair, and Jack let out a long breath, knowing the worry he had caused her. "I'm sorry, Mom. I—"

"No. *I* did this," Gwen interrupted, lowering her head. "If I hadn't interfered, Jack and Sadie would have gone back to the hotel. They would have been waiting for you when you returned."

Jack's mother turned to the clerk with a soft smile. "The *Clockmaker* set all of this in motion, Gwen, not you. He was the one who lured Jack and Sadie away from the hotel and steered them to the Lost Property Office. And if you hadn't *interfered*, the Clockmaker would still have found a way to separate Jack from Sadie and use him to find the Ember." She placed a finger under Gwen's chin and gently lifted. "Don't you see? If not for you, Jack would have had to face all of this alone."

She gave the clerk a little hug and pulled an old brass key from the pocket of her peacoat. Its ornate head formed into the letters J and B. She winked at the clerk. "I'm not sure how you expected to get through without this." Then she slid it into the lock.

The door opened into a great domed cavern, one Jack realized was not actually part of the main structure of the Keep. Far above, in the dim light, he could see the bottom— or perhaps the top—of the great underground tower, jutting down through the ceiling. Its crown of stone battlements pointed down into the cavern, and its eight gargoyles were inverted, looking up at the dome, as if the entire tower truly *had* been shoved into the earth upside down.

Beneath this strange sky rested a tiny neighborhood right

out of the seventeenth century. At the end of a cobblestone lane that led from the stairwell, four timber and plaster houses stood in a semicircle around a small plaza lit by gas lamps, with a bubbling stone fountain at the center. Three were dark, but a warm light glowed from the upper room of the first house on the right.

"Welcome to Tracker Lane, Jack," said his mother. "Welcome home."

Chapter 51

JACK WALKED slowly to the edge of the cul-de-sac. "The trackers live here?"

"Usually . . . so I'm told." Gwen walked beside him, looking as awed by the old houses as he was. "But, as I said before, the ministry is in a sort of minimum-manning phase, treading water until the fourteenth generation. The twelves are dispersed—in Australia, Hong Kong, Switzerland—caring for the thirteens. They only come in for special assignments."

"That's why Dad was always traveling." Jack turned to his mom, a flicker of hope in his eyes. "What about the elevens? Some of them must still be around."

She shook her head. "I'm sorry, Jack. That part of what your father and I told you was true. Both of your grandfathers are gone. It was a terrible year. Three elevens died, not long after the twelves took over, in a series of unfortunate accidents. The fourth, Edward Tanner, is bound to a wheelchair, teaching medieval history at Cambridge."

Jack glanced up at the light in the window. "If everyone is gone, then who's up there?"

The door to House Buckles—that's what Gwen called the house with the light on—opened to the brass key. Jack could practically see the clerk's freckles shining as she crossed the threshold. His mom hung her coat inside the door, lifting a long brass tool from the hook beside it and lighting the gas chandelier in the hall—as naturally as if she were just coming home from a very long trip. She nodded at the stairs. "You and Gwen go on up. Sadie and I will stay down here and see what we can find in the kitchen."

Jack led Gwen up four flights of stairs, trailing his fingers along a banister alive with stalking animals—falcons, panthers, and wolves. The wood-panel walls were hung with eleven paintings of men with eleven variations of Jack's face, dressed in clothes from eleven eras. At the top, he stepped out into a well-lit study that took up the whole of the upper floor, filled with tall bookcases and plush furniture. Jack felt a tinge of disappointment. No one was there. A tiny part of him had held out hope that his father would be waiting for him. Finding his dad in this cozy study, ready to regale his wife and children with a grand story of escape, might have spared Jack the ordeal that lay ahead.

Gwen spread her arms wide as she reached the top of the stairs behind him. "You wanted your family's locker."

He nodded, turning in a slow circle. He couldn't see any containers or hiding places, no chests or cabinets. Even the small writing desk beneath the window had no drawers. "But where would Johnny Buckles have hidden the Ember?"

"How should I know? I've never been here before. To be quite honest, I'm absolutely stunned we made it this far."

There had to be a hidden nook or chamber, a door that Jack wasn't seeing. He walked to the center of the study and took in the room.

Desk: empty except for a writing pad and a painted wooden globe, floating in midair above its base—cool, but not what he was looking for.

Window above the desk: gold stained glass depicting a falcon in flight—ancient and streaked with minerals, like the stained glass at Barking Tower.

A glow: a purple light coming from underneath the book-cases that covered one wall—so dim as to be almost invisible.

Jack approached the shelves and scanned the books, settling his gaze on a large black volume near the joining of the two center cases: *The Polymerase Chain Reaction and Other Great Tales*. Beneath the title was a big silver thumbprint. Jack raised his hand, hesitated because he felt foolish doing it, then pressed his thumb into the binding.

"Welcome, John Buckles." The revolving-door-Tube voice spoke from behind the bookcases. Jack heard a hum very much like the maglev, and the cases before him parted, forcing him to back up. The two great halves of the wall of bookcases swung out, folding at the breaks to form a partial room. White lights flickered on. Long pieces of the floor rose up and tilted out into rows of canted tables, covered in green velvet and packed with shining gear.

"Now, *this* is a locker," breathed Jack, stepping inside.

Racks of vintage clothing filled the left side of the secret room. Jack ran his hand down the sleeve of a red suede duster, his dad's favorite. He'd never realized there was more than one. Next to the duster hung a leather jacket that looked his size. Without really thinking, he slipped off the used coat Gwen had given him and tried it on. The fit of the silk liner felt perfect, tailored just for him. He pulled a bowler hat down from the shelf above.

"Ahem."

Jack turned, bowler touching his hair.

Gwen was shaking her head. "There are very few men in the world who can pull off a bowler hat, Jack Buckles. And there are precisely zero teenage boys who can."

"Right. Sure." He felt his cheeks redden as he set the bowler back on the shelf. "Maybe just the jacket."

The vintage clothes were the least of the secret closet's treasures. Swords and matching daggers hung on the back wall, alongside pneumatic dart guns and ornate canes with glowing chambers in the shafts. All sorts of gear were pressed into the velvet of the tables. There were magnifying glasses with carbon-fiber handles, brass spyglasses and compasses, and several disks and spherical devices that Jack did not recognize. In the middle of the central table was a small sphere of translucent red stone, inlaid with gold lattice. Jack lifted it from its form-fitted impression, holding it up for Gwen to see. "What do you suppose this is?"

"I'm not sure. It may be a scout. They come in a variety of configurations. Scouts are tracker recording devices, from a time before there were apps for that sort of thing." As Jack lowered the sphere, she gazed around the room. "I thought I knew all there was to know about the tracker houses, but this . . . this is amazing."

"And yet there's still no sign of the Ember. Maybe I was wrong."

"Jack. Look at that." Gwen's roving gaze had fixed on the right end of the room, where a large mirror hung on what had previously been the back panel of a bookcase. The sculpted gold frame twisted out into curved handles on either side. At the center of each was a vertical eye, set with a pale green gem as large as the sapphire in the king's medallion.

They exchanged a glance.

Gwen gave him a little shrug. "Why not?"

Jack took hold of both handles, palms pressed into the green gems, and felt himself yanked straight into the bookcase.

Chapter 52

JACK JERKED TO a stop in total darkness, suspended in black space with nothing but the mirror before him. His own reflection had fled the glass, leaving behind an aged man with long gray hair. Jack knew him from his vision at the tower. Johnny Buckles. The tracker's eyes flashed with a hint of recognition. "My son—"

Even as the elder Buckles spoke, Jack shot backward through the dark. The face in the mirror changed as he flew, rapidly shifting through a dozen versions of John Buckles. Some wore a thin smile, some looked grave, but every one of them began a solemn statement with *My son, John,* or—

"Jack."

He stopped again, suspended in the void, staring at the image of his father.

"If you're seeing this, it means I never came home from that trip to London—the one I took when you were thirteen. And it means you're in the Keep, so I guess you know the big family secret everyone has worked so hard to keep from you. What you may not know is that every John Buckles leaves one of these messages for his son." John Buckles Twelve let out a rueful chuckle. "Although, I never expected to leave mine so soon. There's so much I want to tell you, but I'm out of time. I can't let the man who's after me figure out that I've come here.

"You see, Jack, I opened Pandora's box. And now I have to deal with the consequences. It seems the first John Buckles understood that powerful men would always want more power. He knew they would always covet what was inside Pandora's box, wherever they came across it, so he hid this particular version, taking the secret of its existence to his grave. And now, through ignorance and carelessness, I've exposed that secret." He paused to scratch his head, tilting the bowler with his knuckles the way he used to tilt it when Sadie asked him a tough question. "Someone is coming for the box, Jack, and if I don't lead him away, millions will pay the price."

Jack couldn't bear being so close to his dad—so close to the moment when everything changed—and not being able to stop him. *Where is it?* his thoughts screamed. *Just tell me where the Ember is and I'll come get you!*

It was almost as if his dad had heard him. "The ministry will be looking for the Ember after I'm gone. Maybe that's why you've come to the Keep. Maybe they brought you in to help. But I can't tell you where it is, son. I won't. You have to leave it be. You have to let me go." He glanced down, as if checking his watch. "Tell your mom and your sister I love them. I love you, too, Jack. I'll always love you, no matter where I am." He smiled that same sad smile that belonged to Jack's mom. Then he kissed his fingers and pressed them to the mirror.

Don't go, Dad! Please, don't go! Jack tried to press his hand against his father's, releasing his grip on one of the handles. Instantly he was yanked back through the void, right out of the bookcase. His dad was gone, replaced by the reflection of his own tear-streaked face.

Gwen was in the mirror as well, at his shoulder, deep concern in her eyes. "Jack, I—"

He turned away, holding up a hand to stop her as he passed and wiping his eyes with the other sleeve. "My father left a message in the mirror—a good-bye. He found the

327

Ember. But he wouldn't tell me where it was." Jack sniffed and dropped his hands. "Why wouldn't he tell me?"

"I think you know the answer. Your dad didn't want to put you in danger, Jack. Or any civilians. He was ready to make a final stand."

A final stand. Jack turned, slowly shaking his head. "No. He wasn't. Not entirely."

"You just told me he said—"

"This isn't about what my dad *said*, Gwen. It's about what he *did*. Dad took precautions. He planned to survive the Clockmaker's flamethrower. He got help. I know he did."

"*How* do you know? Did he say that in his message?"

"No. But he was wearing a red scarf."

Jack left her standing in the equipment room and walked out into the study. "The Ember *has* to be here somewhere. All I have to do is spark. I can watch Dad's movements from a few days ago. Let him lead me to it whether he wanted to or not." He searched the room for metal objects.

Globe: wood.

Desk: wood.

Swords: hidden behind the bookcases, which were all made of wood.

Everything in the room was covered in wood, cloth, or paper.

Jack let out a frustrated growl.

"Your dad didn't *want* you to find the Ember," said Gwen, more forcefully than before. "He didn't want you coming after him. Jack, this was *his* choice."

Jack's gaze settled on the falcon in the stained glass window, and a solution hit him. It had worked before. He glanced back at the clerk. "Yeah, well, this is *my* choice." Before she could react, he rushed forward and pressed his palm against the glass.

Chapter 53

CHAOS. Total bedlam, like before in Barking Tower.

Jack's head screamed. A roar of multicolored sound attacked his mind. Intense light smashed against his vision. He had no eyelids to shut it out. Everything was squeezed into a two-dimensional plane. And Jack's consciousness was squeezed in with it.

This time, however, he understood what he was facing.

Gwen was wrong. Glass, stained glass at least, reflected, amplified, and confused, but it could record as well, like the sapphire in the Tower and the green gems on the mirror. Three hundred years of sight and sound were recorded in the silicate— all melted and jumbled together, but they *were* there. All Jack had to do was unscramble them. He had done it before.

Maybe he had done it. Or maybe Gwen was right. Maybe what he saw was an illusion. Maybe he had succumbed to the chaos, and the fire and the wraith he saw in the Great Fire glass were nothing more than the creations of his own subconscious.

Jack pushed, the way he had pushed before, and the chaos pushed back. The light brightened to pure white. He felt like his skin was stretched against his skull, so taut that his cheeks might split open. Then a string of lilting blue appeared, quickly contorted into a shriek by the glass. Gwen was shouting at him, adding to the chaos, trying to pull him out of the spark.

He fought against her. *His choice.* That's what he had told her. Suddenly Jack found his own voice and screamed. The bedlam shattered.

The barrier in the Great Fire glass at Barking Tower had dropped away in a hundred shards. This one exploded into a million—a sparkling glass mist. When it finally settled, all that lay beyond was darkness. For a moment, Jack wondered if he had really won, or if the glass had killed him.

As the pain receded, though, detail appeared in the dark. Jack was looking up at the domed rock ceiling above Tracker Lane, except the gargoyled crown of the Keep that should have jutted down through the center was missing. In its place was a vertical cavern, rising up beyond the limits of vision.

Jack's perspective began to shift, lifting and turning, floating through the cave. He saw workers, and a crane of wood and iron. They were lifting the window into place, and him with it. He had gone too far back—way too far. He had wanted to watch his dad's last moments in the Keep. Instead he had sparked back to the day House Buckles was built. Jack had overshot his goal by more than three hundred years. He tried pulling with his mind, trying to rise up through the centuries, but to no avail. After everything he'd been through, he still couldn't control his sparks. Jack was stuck.

The men worked by lantern light. The gas lamps had not yet been installed, nor had the other houses been built. But the fountain was still there, at the center of the cave, and Johnny Buckles paced around it. He was not much older than he had been when the king entrusted him with the Ember. He directed the work on the house, motioning to the crane operator until Jack's window was in place, giving Jack a useless view out over the cul-de-sac instead of into the study. Not only had he overshot his time period, but now he was facing the wrong way.

Jack pushed and pulled, and pushed again, and he suddenly shifted, a sideways rush of black rock and orange lantern light.

When he settled, the workers were still there, building a second tracker house. He heard the sounds of construction above him as well. The Keep was under construction within the vertical fissure. His efforts had worked, sort of.

Jack pushed and pulled again, and again he shifted a little ways through time, to another stage of construction. He repeated the process over and over until the gas lamps burned and the glossy gargoyles snarled down from their inverted perches beneath the finished Keep. All the while, Johnny Buckles aged, his hair growing white. But he never stopped pacing around the cul-de-sac, one eye on the construction and the other—

The gold sheen of the stained glass falcon filled Jack's vision, flying away from him. Then he realized that *he* was the one flying. Jack flew backward, the angry scream still pouring from his lungs, until he hit the wood floor with an abrupt "Oomph!"

Gwen hit the floor with him, arms wrapped around him in a bear hug. She rose up on an elbow and punched him in his bruised arm. "What were you thinking? You could have put yourself into a coma!"

"What's going on?" Both children turned as Mary Buckles crested the stairs. "I heard shouting."

Gwen quickly sat up, backing away from Jack. "Mrs. B. I—"

"We're fine," said Jack, pushing himself to a sitting position. "I fell, that's all. I'm okay."

His mom clearly did not agree. Her face went white as a sheet. Gwen turned back to see what was the matter and drew in a short breath, biting her lip. She reached into her pocket and produced a pale purple handkerchief. "Here, use this."

"For what?"

She put the kerchief in his palm, then gently pressed both his hand and the kerchief up under his nose. When she released him, Jack pulled the kerchief away and saw that it was filled with blood.

His mom rushed over and helped him to his feet, taking over the job of cleaning up his face in a way that he found incredibly embarrassing. "What did you do?" she asked, still dabbing at his nose, though the flow of blood had stopped.

"I took a risk, Mom—like Dad would have done." Jack pushed her hands down. "And it paid off."

Jack hurried out into the courtyard, carrying a bronze falcon-head cane in one hand and a sword as tall as he was in the other. He wasn't sure which one would do the job.

"What did you see?" asked Gwen, jogging next to him, with Sadie and Jack's mother following right behind. The clerk had asked the same question in the study and on the stairs, but Jack was in too much of a rush to answer.

He stopped at the fountain, a simple urn with water bubbling out from a quarter-size hole, spilling over into the small pool at its base. Jack handed the cane to his mother and held his fingers under the water. He smiled at Gwen. "Feel it. The water's warm."

"Of course it's warm. That's a geothermal spring, Jack. Are you certain you're all right?"

He raised his eyebrows, leaning on the sword. "How do you know it's geothermal? This isn't exactly Yellowstone. I'd bet it's a groundwater spring, powered by gravity."

Gwen's eyes shifted to the urn. "And you think the Ember is inside, heating it up."

"In the spark from the stained glass, I saw Johnny Buckles overseeing the construction of this place. The workers didn't dig a hole for the Keep beneath Baker Street. The cavern was already here. My ancestor hid the Ember in the deepest, darkest place he could find. But what if once King Charles commissioned the Ministry of Trackers, Johnny Buckles realized that same deep, dark place could serve as the perfect headquarters?" Jack inclined his head toward the fountain. "Gwen, this fountain was already here, before construction on the houses or the Keep began."

The clerk slowly nodded. "So the Ember *is* in there." Then the pace of her speech began to quicken. "The mechanism for getting it out must be *particularly* cunning. Johnny Buckles would have made it nigh impossible to open the urn. Perhaps it's hydraulic. *Yes.* We stop up the flow and the pressure will open the hatch. *No.* Too easy. Come on, Kincaid. Anyone could have thought of that one." Her eyes widened. "Oh! What about static electricity? I think I saw a pair of electrospheres in your dad's armory. We could—"

As Gwen chattered, Jack gently guided her to the edge of the cul-de-sac, entrusting her to his mom, who gave him a knowing nod. With the other three safely out of the way, Jack returned to the fountain and raised the massive sword, hauling it back as far as he dared.

"What are you doing?" shrieked Gwen, just as the blade made contact.

The urn shattered in an explosion of water and wet stone, sending fragments out into the cul-de-sac. A blue-green box sat within the broken bowl that remained, water bubbling up all around it. Jack dropped the sword and gently lifted the box from the debris. It was warm, almost hot to the touch. He paused only a moment, then unhooked the catch. He had to. He needed to make sure the jewel inside really was the Ember. At least, that's what he told himself.

As Jack drifted back toward the others, he raised the lid. A faceted black gem, a little smaller than his fist, shined back at him from a tight housing of the same blue-green metal. The jewel had the look of obsidian, until glowing veins of orange appeared beneath its surface—growing and connecting, pulsating like the coals of a dying fire fanned by a nighttime breeze. In less than a second, the whole Ember gleamed yellow. Jack could feel the heat of it on his face. He snapped the lid closed and looked up, only to find his path blocked by a wall of tweed.

"Oi. Thirteen. I think you'd better 'and that over, don't you?"

Chapter 54

"SHAW." Jack wished he had not dropped his sword by the fountain. He would never have stabbed the warden, but he would have felt like more of a match for the brute with a weapon in his hand. "How did you get down here?"

"Easy 'nuff without you two slowin' me down. *I'm* not wanted 'round 'ere."

"You got that right." Gwen stood at Jack's shoulder, and his mom and Sadie stepped up on his other side.

Jack frowned. "So you gave us up to Mrs. Hudson."

"Not yet. Not when I can bring in a thirteen an' a dangerous artifact all by my lonesome. An' look"—Shaw's thick lips spread into a grin—"'ere's a thirteen, right 'ere. Wot's 'e got in 'is 'and but a *seriously* dangerous artifact. Guess my job is done, eh?"

"What about my dad? You were going to help us rescue him."

"Your dear ol' dad is *dead*. Time you faced that. Besides, two out of three ain't bad." Shaw cast an ominous smirk at Jack's mom. "An' now I've caught the infamous Mary Fowler as a bonus." He took a step forward, reaching for the Ember. "Awright. Time for—"

"You know what?" Mary Buckles stepped between the warden and her son, stopping the big teen cold despite his advantage in size. She pressed the head of the cane into his chest. "You may be abnormally large for your age, but you're not in charge here. I am."

The warden grabbed her arm and shook it. "An' why should you be in charge, eh?"

In a sudden flash of bronze falcon and blue peacoat, Jack's mom spun out of Shaw's grasp, twirling the cane above her. She brought it down right behind his knees. As the warden's legs buckled, she reversed her spin and the falcon head came around again, swatting him across the chest. Shaw went down hard. She stood above him, holding the cane at his chin. "Why? Because I'm a grown-up. And these are *my* kids."

The episode had rendered both Jack and Sadie speechless, but not Gwen. "*Mary Fowler*," she said, breathing out the name. She elbowed Jack in his bruised arm. "Told you your mum was a quartermaster."

Shaw wasn't finished. As Mary turned to her son, the warden let out an angry growl, pushing himself up. "Now you've done it."

Jack snatched the cane from his mother's hand, spinning it point down and shoving it into Shaw's chest. At the moment of impact, he pressed a brass button beneath the glowing chamber on the shaft. Electricity snapped from the end. Shaw convulsed. The air filled with the acrid scent of burning tweed, and the warden fell back onto the stone, unconscious.

"Thank you." Jack's mom let out a shaky breath. "But how did you know about the stun gun?"

Jack offered the cane back to her. "I didn't. It just seemed right."

"Hang on to it." She pressed the cane back into his hand. "A tracker's cane contains a number of surprises. I think you'll find it comes in handy in a pinch."

As Jack tucked the cane into his belt, he heard a familiar crackling noise coming from Shaw. "Bugs!" he shouted, pulling Gwen to the warden's side. "Help me lift him!"

The two rolled Shaw over, revealing two of the Clock-maker's beetles underneath, already nearing the end of the usual self-destruct ritual. The children each kicked one of the bugs, sending them flying into the wreckage of the fountain, where they burst into flame.

"I never heard them crawling on him. The tweed must have muffled the sound." Jack glanced down at the warden. "Do you think he was . . . ?" He couldn't finish the question.

"No." Gwen shook her head, giving the unconscious Shaw a little punch with her toe. "He's a conniving brute, but he's *our* conniving brute. The beetles must have attached themselves without his notice. They could have been on him since the Archive. We have to assume the Clockmaker knows everything."

"Then we'd better get going."

"Jack," his mom interjected, "let me go instead." She gestured at the wisps of smoke drifting up from the remains of the bugs. "Look what you're up against. This man is a killer."

"No, Mom." Jack handed the Ember to Gwen and took his mother's hands. "You need to stay with Sadie. I've come this far. I can finish this."

"But you're—"

"Not a little boy anymore." Jack set his jaw, the way his dad had set his jaw when he faced the Clockmaker. "I'm a tracker now."

His mom nodded, without arguing any further, and Jack checked his watch. The digital display read 11:15 P.M. He had to get the Ember to Big Ben by midnight, and climbing the Great Stair might take more than an hour. He turned to Gwen. "We need a lift."

"I told you. The lifts have cameras, and most of them only go up or down a few floors. There's an express lift one level up, but that's a secure storage level. The Chamber will see us. As soon as we go for it, the wardens and QEDs will converge."

"Um . . . which will arrive first?" An idea—another option—had materialized in Jack's mind.

"The QEDs, of course." Gwen wrinkled her nose. "What difference does it make?"

Jack almost smiled at the insanity of his plan. "It makes all the difference in the world."

Chapter 55

JACK AND GWEN climbed the Great Stair to the next level up, the lowest sublevel of the Keep proper. Before leaving Tracker Lane, they had returned to his dad's armory for a few extra supplies and a satchel for the Ember. Then they had said good-bye to Jack's mom and Sadie, who planned to seek out Mrs. Hudson as soon as he and Gwen were clear.

Their climb brought them to a small landing, and a vault door not unlike the door to the Chamber. "This is the Keep's high-security storage sublevel," said Gwen, "where we keep our most dangerous artifacts—things like the Ember. Are you sure you want to go in there?"

"How many sublevels before we reach another one with access to the express lift?"

"Five."

"Then I don't see another way."

Gwen nodded, biting her lip. "All right, then, listen up. This sublevel is circular, like all the rest besides the Chamber. Halfway 'round the perimeter hall, we'll find another hall that branches off, leading straight to the express lift. The straight hall is quite long, because the lift comes down from the upper floors, which are much wider than this one. We'll have to keep up a good pace once we go for it. Your DNA will open the door, but I doubt it will deactivate the security drone on the other side."

"That's what I'm counting on." Jack reached for the thumb pad.

"Wait!" Gwen grabbed his wrist. "I wasn't finished. The storage aisles that make up most of this sublevel are arranged like tumblers on a lock, or one of those garden mazes. Whatever happens, stick to the perimeter. Do *not* try to cut through. You'll never come out the other side."

"Because I'll get lost?"

She let go of him, taking a deep breath as he pressed his thumb down onto the pad. "No. Because you'll be killed . . . *or worse*."

The door popped open and the two wasted no time getting

inside, skidding to a stop in the dim, wood-panel hall of the perimeter. "Your secure storage facility is wood too?"

"Ironwood," Gwen answered with a shrug. "As fireproof as concrete, without the risk of sparking."

Jack looked left and right, up and down the long curving hall. "Which way?"

"It's a circle. Pick one."

He took off at a run. Before Gwen could follow, a QED shot out from the maze and hovered between them.

"Go!" shouted Jack, pointing the other way. "I'll keep it busy."

She did, and the drone took off to follow.

"Hey! Don't you recognize me?" Jack yelled after it.

The QED coasted to a hover thirty feet away, slowly reversing course.

Jack backed away, nodding. "That's right. John Buckles Thirteen. You can't have me running loose in the Keep, can you? Go ahead. Call the wardens. Tell 'em all about it. As long as you stick with me and leave her alone."

The drone inched toward him, spreading its cargo pincers, which couldn't have been wider than two of Jack's fingers.

He laughed. "Really? What's your plan—grab me by the jacket and carry me upstairs? I'm not sure those'll do the job."

A panel opened on the underside of the QED, and two more sets of pincers emerged. They opened and closed in rapid sequence, like legs on an angry dragonfly.

"Whoa." Jack's eyes widened. "That *is* your plan." He turned and ran.

Images of varied artifacts flashed in Jack's head as he passed the aisles leading into the maze. The hodgepodge of items differed little from what he had seen in the Lost Property Office display—a table lamp and a top hat, one of those flat robotic vacuums. He half expected to see the creepy clown dummy from the Graveyard. Instead, he saw a bronzed apple with two bites taken out of it and a giant clock with its hands chained in place, a few minutes from midnight. He was almost to the lift hallway when a second QED appeared to block his path. Had it come from the maze or the hall?

"Gwen!"

She was too far away to hear, or too busy to answer, and Jack was trapped, with only one route open to him. Despite the clerk's former warning, he turned at the next corridor, straight into the maze.

As he rounded the corner, Jack was surprised to see light

ahead. Maybe thirteen was lucky after all. It looked like the aisle he had chosen went straight through. On the shelves flying by, he saw a set of rusty shackles, a bronze ax with a white tag that read SARGON II, and a jar full of sickly grapes preserved in brine. None of it looked particularly menacing until Jack passed the grapes. Then *all* of it seemed menacing. He had the overwhelming feeling that he wouldn't make it out of that aisle alive—a feeling that got a lot stronger when he noticed another boy running right at him, wearing the same leather jacket. Jack wasn't running toward an open hall. He was running toward a huge mirror.

He pulled up short before a gilded frame. Sculpted lettering across the base read ERWIN SCHRÖDINGER. "Schrödinger, Sargon, and sour grapes," he muttered. "I must be in the *S* aisle. How organized." Jack turned, hoping to retreat to a cross aisle he had passed before the drones hemmed him in, but his elbow swung over a shelf as he turned, bumping the cobra-shaped head of a long black staff. It clattered to the floor, and transformed into a living snake.

Jack drew his cane and swung it back and forth like a club. "Get back!" The cobra coiled and struck, and Jack connected, smacking the snake under its broad hood with the bronze falcon head, knocking it back against the shelves. The jar of sour grapes tipped and tottered, slowly rotating toward the edge.

The snake hissed and coiled for another attack.

The jar fell.

Two drones sailed down the aisle.

Jack swung again as the cobra made its second strike, and heard a satisfying *crack* when its fangs snapped on the bronze. Instantly, the snake reverted to a rigid staff. A QED snagged it in midair, setting it gently back on the shelf while the other drone caught the falling grapes an inch above the floor. The second QED returned the jar to its place, and both advanced toward Jack, opening their pincers wide.

He backed away, expecting to bump into the mirror. Instead, he tripped over the lower lip of the frame, and fell right through the glass.

"What on—" Jack finished with an *"Oof!"* as his seat hit the floor. He was sitting in front of the same mirror, in a completely different aisle, with no snake staff and no drones. Except the mirror before him wasn't the same. The gold lettering across the bottom read MR. PICKLES. In the reflection, Jack saw a lighted hall, marked with a brass plate with the letters TFIL. It took a moment for his mind to catch up. Then he jumped to his feet, shouting, "Lift!"

The QEDs approached from the side as Jack raced across the perimeter hall, heading into the long passage. Up ahead, the doors of the express lift were open wide, but there was no sign of Gwen.

Chapter 56

JACK SLAMMED into the back of the lift and whipped around to see the two drones speeding down the hall. He poked the close button repeatedly with the end of his cane. "Come on. Come on."

The doors finally activated, closing at an excruciating rate. Above him, the camera hung by a wire, its mounting broken. He recognized the work of Gwen's scarf.

With the doors only inches apart, the lead QED turned on edge, pulling up its pincers and zipping through. Jack cringed as the other one crashed into the barrier behind it. The drone that made it jerked back and forth above him, exploring the four corners of the car before finally settling at the center and lowering its pincers. It started a slow descent, coming down to claim its quarry. Jack tucked his cane into his belt and backed into the corner. There was nowhere to go, but running had never been his plan in the first place.

"Gotcha!" he cried, jumping up and grabbing the two forward pincers. The QED rose up in confusion, lifting him from the floor, and Jack kicked the lift's emergency stop button as he passed. "Now, Gwen!"

A panel in the ceiling slid back. Gwen peered down. "You called?" With nowhere else to go, the QED rose through the gap, and she caught hold of the rear pincers, letting it lift her off the roof in its climb. Together they rose up through the shaft.

"It worked!" Jack looked up at the glowing circles of the engines carrying them up toward the surface. "I can't believe it really wor—" He stopped short when he lowered his gaze and his eyes met Gwen's, mere inches away. She did not look happy. "What?" he asked. "What'd I do?"

"All that equipment in your father's armory and you couldn't find a single breath mint?"

Jack gave her a flat frown. "You're one to complain. I'm not the only one with choco-nutty-shellfish breath around here."

She giggled, but the breath jokes only covered the first two levels of the long climb. After that, things settled into uncomfortable silence, the two of them facing each other, their noses nearly touching.

"Ahem." Gwen cleared her throat, looking off to the side. "Took you long enough. I suppose you simply *had* to cut through the aisles, if only because I told you not to."

"How do you know I cut through?"

"It's written all over your face."

Gwen brought her eyes forward again, and Jack felt the need to look up, feigning interest in the shaft above. "I fell through a mirror."

"Really, which one?"

"Does it matter?"

"Absolutely. Seven people have fallen through Mr. Pickles's mirror, and we have no idea where they went—whether they're alive or dead."

He thought she might be joking, but she looked perfectly serious. "I fell through the other one."

"Right. Of course."

"Um . . . Gwen?" He was looking up again, and this time his interest was real. As they had talked, the drone had been accelerating, and now the blue glow of the engines illuminated the ceiling of the shaft, racing down to meet them at breakneck speed.

Gwen looked up to follow his gaze, and both children screamed. "Aaaaah!"

There was a resounding *clang*, but without the expected pain of a crash or the gut-wrenching plummet back down to their deaths. Jack felt the white rush of cold wind on his cheeks. He opened his eyes, one at a time, and saw a grate lying open below them.

"Are we dead?" Gwen's voice was muffled, her head still tucked into her arm.

"No!" Jack shouted over the gale that was already carrying them east of Baker Street. "But we have a new problem. Don't look down!"

She did, and yelped, wrapping her legs around him. The motion caused the drone to bobble. It struggled to correct itself, lurching south before settling in its eastward drift again.

"Now what do we do?"

Jack's attention was on the drone and its movements. "I need you to turn around."

"Seriously?" Gwen shouted back. "You're making breath jokes now?"

"Just turn around, will you?"

Using Jack for support, Gwen managed to turn, hand by

hand, and face away from him. The drone lurched with every shift of her weight, sliding left and right before recovering control.

"Now lean left!" shouted Jack, and they pulled on the left-hand pincers together. The QED moved left under their command. "Right!" Again, the drone responded. Jack smiled despite the cold and the ache in his arms. "We can steer this thing!"

It took a great deal of trial and error to find their rhythm, but soon Jack and Gwen were flying over the lights of London, dodging steeples and high-rises, toes dipping into the tops of the trees in the parks, though they did that on purpose only once. Gwen gave the directions, sighting land-mark after landmark on the way southeast to Big Ben.

"The Clockmaker might be expecting us!" Jack shouted over wind rushing past their ears. "But he won't be expecting this!"

Chapter 57

JACK AND GWEN flew right across the top of West-minster Abbey, pulling up their feet to keep from kicking its spires. Up ahead, the Great Clock Tower rose above the Thames, glowing gold in the lights shining up from below. Beyond the river, Jack could see the blue ring of the Millennium Wheel, and beyond that, a quarter moon hanging over the eastern horizon.

Gwen gave an exaggerated nod toward the tower. "We can land on the balcony above the clockface! The one Parliament lit up with those gaudy green spotlights!"

But the green balcony was drifting to their right.

Jack suddenly understood the full difficulty presented by the wind. Sure, the gale had made the flight cold and loud, but now it had become a control problem as well, driving them off course. Steering the QED toward the tower felt like steering a canoe toward a dock on a rushing river.

Gwen had seen it too. "We're not lined up! We're going to overshoot!"

The eastbound gale was too strong, and the balcony coming too fast. Before they could work any farther south, they were passing the northwest corner. In desperation, Jack let go of a pincer and grabbed for the rail. He missed. His fingers hooked the nose of a dragon gargoyle instead, the northwestern extent of the structure. The QED jerked to a halt with a disturbing *crick* from Jack's spine, swinging Gwen closer to the rail.

The clerk pulled herself onto the dragon's back. She knelt between its wings, hooking an arm around the stone baluster beneath the rail and reaching for Jack. "Take my hand!"

As if he had other options. She hardly got out the words before his grip on the pincer failed. His arm dropped. Gwen caught his hand. Inch by inch, Jack scrambled up onto the dragon's back, and the two climbed over the rail together, into the glaring green of the balcony spotlights. As soon as Jack had let go, the QED had shot away with the wind, fighting its way north in a futile attempt to return to the Keep.

Apparently it wanted nothing else to do with a thirteen.

There was a great ratcheting *click* from the clockface below, and Jack peered over the edge. 11:47. If they failed to hand over the Ember within the next thirteen minutes, the Clockmaker would kill his father. Jack hurried to the nearest of the tall, arched windows surrounding the belfry and peered in.

The balcony spotlights shone through the windows, casting eerie green light into the square brick chamber, pitting shadow against shadow on the floor. The belfry was empty except for its five iron bell platforms, bolted to the floor beneath the five bronze bells. Jack saw no evidence of the Clockmaker or his dad. "It's clear," he whispered, cracking open the window and motioning for Gwen to follow him through. Inside, he blew into his hands and rubbed them together, grateful to be out of the wind. "Okay. We're here. Where is this guy?"

Gwen gestured at the floor. "Where else? He told us to meet him at the Great Clock." She pointed to the central bell, the largest of the five by far. "*That's* Big Ben. The Great Clock Tower is what we're standing in, and the *real* Great Clock is a big jumble of gears in the chamber beneath our feet."

On the next level down, they found a narrow walkway

that led between the four faces of the clock and the four big walls of lightbulbs that stood behind them. The Great Clock itself, Gwen explained in a whisper, was in an inner chamber behind the walls of lights, and the only entrance they could find was a small wooden door on the eastern side.

Gwen pulled Jack away from the door, whispering in his ear. "How are we supposed to sneak up on the Clockmaker if there's only one way in? He hasn't left us any options."

Jack squinted up at the wall of lights above. At the very center, a heavy gear shaft projected out from a large hole, to power the hands in the clockface. The other three sides would be exactly the same. He backed away from Gwen and looked her over from head to toe, evaluating her size. "Or maybe he has."

Seconds later, Jack threw open the chamber door.

"Ah, Lucky Jack. Right on time." The Clockmaker leaned against the rail of a pen filled with slowly turning gears, grinning at his own pun. His hand rested on a wheelchair, where John Buckles the Twelfth sat with his blackened suede duster folded neatly in his lap and his head slumped to his chest. There were blistered burns on his cheeks.

Jack took a hasty step into the chamber.

"Stop! Not another step." The flared brass barrel of the

flamethrower emerged from the Clockmaker's sleeve, an inch from his captive's head. His grin became a snarl. "I hope for your father's sake that you have brought my prize, *mon ami*. Otherwise, this meeting will be short and tragic. Most tragic, indeed."

It was all a ploy, and Jack knew it. The implication, however veiled in threats, that either Jack or his dad had any chance of getting out of there alive was an obvious lie. As soon as Jack produced the Ember, the Clockmaker would fry him with the flamethrower, or release his clockwork beetles, or hit him with something equally deadly that Jack had not yet seen.

But Jack had thought of all that.

His gaze shifted to the structure above the Clockmaker's head—a set of crossed I-beams running from wall to wall, supporting the shafts that powered the hands outside. An echoing *click* filled the brick chamber and the shafts rotated, turning the hands of all four clockfaces at once.

"That is another minute passed," said the Clockmaker, holding out a gloved palm. "I told you before. I am on a schedule. Where is the Ember?"

"Take it easy." Jack bent sideways to reach into his satchel with both hands. "I have what you asked for." He fumbled in the bag, stalling for as long as he dared, then whipped both hands out at once. In one hand he held the box containing the Ember; in the other, a four-barrel dart gun with the wicked, serrated tips of its bolts protruding from the barrels. He leveled the brass weapon at the Frenchman. "But you won't get it until my dad is safe. Now step away from the chair."

The Clockmaker laughed long and hard, making Jack regret his effort to take command. He turned the flame-thrower in Jack's direction. "Do you really think your little darts will make it through the flames? Oh, Lucky Jack. You are not *that* lucky."

Jack swallowed his fear and frustration and took another step toward his dad, keeping his weapon up. "Maybe you're right. Maybe you can stop my darts." He thrust his chin at the wall above and behind the Frenchman. "But there's no way you can stop hers at the same time."

Gwen had made it through. She was perched on the I-beam next to the hole where the shaft went through the wall. As the Clockmaker turned to look, Gwen raised her own four-barrel weapon and aimed it at his head. "I believe *Lucky Jack* told you to step away, chum."

"Shoot me," growled the Frenchman, returning the barrel

to his prisoner's forehead. "Go ahead and try. Your father will be dead before your missiles find their marks."

Jack had anticipated such a threat. "But they *will* find their marks, so you'll be dead too." He held up the Ember. "My dad was ready to die over this thing, Mr. Clockmaker. Are you?"

The gears ratcheted through another minute, filling the room with another echoing *click*.

Chapter 58

"**FINE,**" snarled the Clockmaker. "I will play your game."
He moved away from the chair as Jack came forward. Each
faced the other as they passed. Jack shot a glance at the overcoat folded in his dad's lap and saw a flash of shimmering red
from the lining. Unconsciously he bit his lip, daring to hope.
"Dad! Can you hear me?"

John Buckles made no reply. He didn't move at all.

"All right, Lucky Jack." The Frenchman had reached the
doorway. "You have your father. Now give me the Ember."

Jack could hear Gwen drop to the floor behind him and
creep to one side, changing her angle, using the pen full of
gears as a partial shield. Even so, the Clockmaker still had his
flamethrower. Oiled gears would not be much of a defense.

If it came to shooting, Jack was certain at least one of them would get fried. He could only see one way out of the standoff. "Fine. You want it?" He eased open the catch on the Ember's box. "Then take it!"

Jack thrust out the box, causing the lid to flap open and sending the Ember sailing toward the Frenchman. The jewel instantly brightened, igniting the air, an arch of flame trailing behind it.

The Clockmaker didn't even flinch. He reached up and caught his blazing prize, and his glove and coat instantly caught fire. Soon he was howling with pain, utterly engulfed in flames.

Wasting no time, Jack snatched up his dad's duster and held it up as a shield. The shimmering red liner matched those he had seen in the dragos' coats at the Ministry Express station. The liners were made of dragon scales—they had to be. That was how his dad had survived the flamethrower.

Jack advanced, praying he could contain the Ember before it burned down the whole tower. But he only made it a few steps before stopping in stunned confusion. The Clockmaker's terrible howl had become a cackling laugh. He lowered his makeshift shield and saw the flames receding. Mystified, he retreated to his dad's side. "It's not working, Gwen! Shoot him!"

Both shot dart after dart into the fire, but they couldn't see their target, and the laughing continued. Finally, the smoke and flames dispersed, leaving behind the blackened ruin that the fire had made of the walls and floor around the doorway. And the Clockmaker stood at the center of it all, transformed.

The black gloves and coat were gone, along with the wide-brimmed hat. His clothing had burned away, exposing a suit of plaited blue-green armor, complete with a mask. At his feet lay the discarded remains of the flamethrower and its miniature tanks. He held the Ember enclosed in a metallic fist. With his other hand, he held Nero's Globe on high. "Did you think I was not prepared for the Ember's power, Lucky Jack? Hadn't you guessed? It was *my* ancestor, Robert Hubert, who discovered its secrets. It was *he* who unearthed the globe and learned how the alloy within its glass controls the jewel. Did you think I would not have continued his work?"

Click. The Great Clock advanced another minute.

"Midnight approaches, and justice must be dealt on a schedule—that is the British way, is it not? At the stroke of midnight, London will learn the true meaning of justice." The Frenchman lifted his mask with a knuckle, revealing a twisted grin. "Good-bye, Lucky Jack. I am afraid your time has run out."

With that, he opened his fist, exposing the Ember. Rivers

of fire gathered inside the jewel, as if drawing heat from the air itself. Then flames shot out across the room.

"Get down!" Jack raised the overcoat to shield himself and his father. He felt the heat against his arm—intense heat, as much as he could bear—but the flames did not break through. When he lowered the smoking duster, the floor before him was blackened. The oiled gears behind him flickered with blue flame. And the Clockmaker had vanished, leaving a swarm of clockwork beetles in his place. Jack fired the last of his darts, dropping one of the bugs, but that did nothing to deter the rest. The swarm advanced into the room.

"Jack . . ." Gwen stood up behind the flaming gears.

"I see them." He threw the dart gun aside and reached into his satchel. His hand wrapped around a copper ball—something like a yo-yo—and he let his finger slip through the ring on its chain.

The clerk drew a similar ball from the pocket of her coat. "Wait until they're close."

The beetles spread their formation, crackling with anticipation. Jack's eyes widened. "I think they're close enough, don't you?"

"Now!" shouted Gwen, and both tossed their spheres at the same time.

The spheres snapped from the ends of the chains, spinning the magnets inside as they sailed into the swarm. The clockwork bugs attacked them with relish, sending out purple bolts of electricity. To their surprise, the copper targets fired back. Spidery patterns of lightning struck out from each ball. More than a dozen beetles dropped to the floor and exploded. The rest fell back, retreating through the door.

Gwen punched the air. "Well done! I knew the electrospheres would come in handy."

Jack wasn't ready to celebrate small victories. He turned and knelt before the wheelchair, gently taking his father's hand. "Dad, can you hear me?"

"Jack, there's no time for that." Gwen rushed around the gear pen and checked his father's pulse and breathing, nodding at her findings. "He's all right for now, but you heard the Clockmaker. He's going to combine the Ember with Nero's Globe at midnight. He's going to burn London. None of us will be all right for long if we don't stop him."

Jack didn't answer. "Please, Dad. I can't do this without you." He reached into his satchel and withdrew the red-and-gold sphere he had found in the armory—the one that had been at the center of all the gear. "Look. I brought this with me. It's so beautiful. It *has* to be important, right? We can use it to stop the

Clockmaker. All you have to do is wake up and show me how."

Click.

Gwen took a step toward the door. "It's 11:53. Seven minutes. We have to go."

"Please, Dad. I need you." Jack opened his father's palm and pressed the sphere into it, lowering his forehead to their joined hands.

"Jack?" The voice was not Gwen's.

Jack looked up and saw his father gazing down at him with tired eyes. "Dad!"

"Son, the Clockmaker, he—"

"He's gone. He took off with the Ember. But we can get it back . . . you and me, together."

"Jack, I can't . . ." His father let out a labored breath. "I know you wanted to save me, son, but millions of lives hang in the balance now. This is so much bigger than you and me, and it's up to you to see it through."

"Jack, what are you doing?" asked Gwen. "We're running out of time."

"Just give me a second!" He glared over his shoulder.

Click.

"Go, son," he heard his father say. "You're a tracker now. You can do this."

By the time Jack turned back, his dad's eyes were closed again. Behind him, Gwen had reached the exit. "*Now*, Jack!"

He picked up the duster and ran after her, stopping her at the door. "Fine, I'll go, but I need you to stay with my dad."

"What? Don't be absurd."

"He's hurt, Gwen. He needs looking after."

She didn't argue. She didn't say anything, even though her lips had parted.

Jack saw the shift in the clerk's expression at the same time he felt the blood slipping from his nose for the second time that night. He pulled a cloth from his satchel and wiped it away. "It's nothing. Stay here. I'm going after him."

"No way. You're hurt. You can't possibly—"

He didn't wait for her to finish. Jack backed into the hall and slammed the blackened door between them.

Chapter 59

JACK CROUCHED BESIDE the stairwell door, the green light of the belfry spilling over the threshold. The bleeding had stopped, for the moment. He tucked the cloth away and pulled the last of his little tricks from the satchel, a brushed nickel sphere that Gwen had told him was most definitely a scout.

He twisted the two hemispheres of the ball, winding it up, then tossed it through the door. The upper hemisphere snapped open into a set of propellers, spinning to keep it in the air. After a count of five, Jack held up a second sphere, a powerful magnet, and the scout zipped back into the stairwell. He snatched it from the air with his other hand, and instantly sparked.

The Clockmaker had opened the floor-to-ceiling windows on the eastern side of the belfry, exposing the one balcony that was sheltered from the wind. He had set up a bronze pedestal at its center, and was about to set Nero's Globe in the bowl at the top.

The spark ended with another ratcheting *click* from the present. 11:55. In five minutes, the Frenchman would place the Ember into the globe and unleash its amplified power on London. With the gale outside, the flames would be unstoppable. But what could Jack do?

He did the only thing he could think of.

"Hey, Zippo!" Jack raced out into the belfry, diving for the platform beneath the nearest chime. A line of flame shot out from the Clockmaker's palm, roaring around the plate iron structure. Only his father's coat kept Jack from being singed. He poked his head up when the fire receded. "What is your problem?"

The Clockmaker finished placing the globe and laughed. "Lucky Jack, are you still here?" He opened his hand, sending another blast of fire at the stand. Smoky haze drifted through the air, colored green by the spotlights.

"You got past my little friends," said the Frenchman, closing the Ember in his fist again. "Applause for you, *mon ami*. But it matters not. In a few minutes the small bells will chime and then the great bell will ring. And, on the stroke of twelve, the amplifier will release a thousand of the Ember's children to the wind. There is nowhere for you to run. All of London will burn. Even the mighty Thames will boil."

Jack made a dash for the large, central bell platform, dropping into a roll as fire shot over him. He made it to the shelter of the larger stand and threw his back against the iron plate. "Good!" he shouted, breathing hard. "Then we may as well chat while we wait for your apocalypse. We have nothing better to do." The stand was halfway between the stairwell and the Clockmaker. If Jack could make it to the balcony, get past the fire and the beetles, maybe he could knock the globe over the rail, take away at least some of the Clockmaker's power. He coughed in the thickening smoke. "So . . . tell me . . . *why* is it so important that London burns?"

Click. The hands in the four faces advanced another minute.

"Why? How can you ask why, Lucky Jack, when it was you who found the names of the dead? Or would you prefer to cover up the truth, like the first of your cursed line?"

"Johnny Buckles didn't want to cover up those deaths." Jack cautiously peered around the stand, gauging the Clockmaker's position. "But the scandal of Bloodworth's treachery would have broken England. He did what he had to do for his country. He was a patriot."

"Wrong!" The Clockmaker paced in front of his pedestal, fists clenched in rage. "He was a traitor to his kind. Hubert was the true patriot. He sacrificed himself out of sorrow for the slaughter of his fellow commoners."

A bolt of electricity snapped above Jack's head. He swung out with his cane, smacking the beetle across the belfry. The Clockmaker was distracting him, keeping him from developing a plan. But why hadn't he sent the whole swarm?

Click. Three minutes to go. Jack leaned out to take a peek.

The Frenchman stopped his pacing directly between Jack and the pedestal. His remaining beetles hovered at his shoulders. "The new London rose from the ashes of nameless thousands. Legions of this city's poorest citizens became the very mortar of its buildings, and for three hundred fifty years, the millions that followed them have pretended the slaughter never happened—just like your ancestor." His fist began to open, revealing the fire pulsing within. "A Hubert took the punishment in 1666. And so a Hubert will deal out the punishment now!"

The Clockmaker sprayed the belfry with flame, moving

his arm in an arc. Jack thought the move was a purposeless gesture of anger until Gwen tumbled to the floor beside him, her wool coat on fire. He pulled it from her shoulders and tossed it out into the belfry, attracting a second line of fire that burned it to cinders in seconds.

Jack pressed the clerk back against the stand. "What are you doing here?"

"What am I doing here?" Gwen coughed, waving her hand in a futile attempt to get the smoke away from her face. "How about, 'Are you okay?' Isn't that the usual opener after one's friend is nearly barbecued while coming to one's aid?"

"Welcome, *ma chère*," said the Clockmaker as another blast of flame hit the stand.

"See? Even the villain knows how to deliver a proper greeting."

"Gwen, what about my dad?"

"Your mother's with him."

"My *mother*?"

Gwen ducked as more flames lit the belfry around them. "She came ahead of the rest. Mrs. Hudson was rallying the wardens when she left, but, Jack—"

"I know. They won't get here in time." He sighed and

peeked over the stand, quickly dropping again to avoid the incoming fire. "I can't get to him. He sees every move I make."

Click.

"Two minutes until the bells, *mes amis*. And then you will see justice served. That is, if you live that long!"

A long blast of fire licked the platform, bending around the iron stand and forcing Jack and Gwen to squeeze together. As soon as the flames subsided, two more beetles buzzed into view, flanking them from either side, and Jack was too busy shielding Gwen with his father's coat to knock them away. They lashed out with electric bolts.

To Jack's surprise, both bugs missed wide. Way wide. Gwen knocked one away with a snap of her scarf. The other dove at Jack, but he hardly had to dodge at all. He shifted his head to the side and the bug smacked into the iron plate, dropping to the floor and flopping about. Jack ground it into the stone with his cane and kicked it away before it exploded.

Jack and Gwen stared at each other for half a heartbeat, trying to process what had happened. Then light dawned on Gwen's face. "The smoke . . . confused their cameras," she said, coughing into her arm.

She was right. The smoke in the belfry had grown as thick as it had been in the burning flat. If not for the green light cutting through the haze, Jack would not be able to see the clerk at all—not with his eyes, anyway. He lowered his voice. "I have a plan. If we can lose these lights, both the bugs and their master will be totally blind."

Gwen tied the scarf behind her head, covering her mouth and nose. "Yes, but so will we."

"You will. *I* won't." Jack scooted to the corner of the platform and risked another peek, encouraged by the fact that the Clockmaker did not seem to see him. He scanned the green haze, trying to settle his senses despite the choking smoke.

Ropes: one of them burning.

Bell hammers: ready to strike the apocalyptic hour.

Conduit: running along the ceiling above the northern windows.

Yes.

Jack traced the copper line to a pillar, where it descended into a common electrical box. "I see the breakers," he whispered, retreating from the edge, "in the northeast corner of the belfry. But the Clockmaker is standing by Nero's Globe on the eastern balcony, not twenty feet away. I'll have to run right through the line of fire to get to the box."

Click. One minute to go.

"Wait." Gwen suddenly shifted to the other side of him, inches from exposing herself to the Frenchman's fire. "Let me go. If I distract him, running for the box, perhaps you can hit him from the other side."

"You don't have to do that, Gwen. You've already done enough."

"Actually, I do." The clerk raised her eyebrows. "Joint regulations, volume one, section one, rule one: 'Defend the Realm against all enemies, even at the risk of life and limb.'"

Jack chuckled, which mostly came out as a cough. "You're always quoting the rules, Gwen, but you never follow them. Why start now?"

"I beg your pardon." The clerk looked taken aback. "I follow *all* the rules, all except one."

The chimes in the four corners began to play, counting out the last twenty-five seconds before the stroke of midnight. Thick bronze ripples filled Jack's vision. "Oh, really?" he shouted over the clanging bells. "And which one is that?"

"Haven't you been paying attention?" Gwen shouted back. She leaned in and kissed him on the cheek, snatching up the cane and his father's coat. Then she gave him the brightest freckle bounce he had seen all day. "It's you, Jack Buckles. You're my broken rule."

Before Jack could say another word, Gwen raced into the open. The Clockmaker raised the Ember, directing it her way.

"No!" Jack grabbed the iron platform and pulled himself up, scrambling into a run toward the opposite corner.

The Clockmaker looked from one to the other, confused by the split attack. He let out a maniacal cry and swung his arm toward Jack as he opened his fist. Fire sprayed across the belfry. But the flames missed both targets. Gwen reached the box a millisecond later and jabbed the cane straight through the lid, activating the stun gun. Sparks flew in all directions. The green lights went out with a *bang*, and the bells disappeared in the darkened haze.

"What are you doing?" shouted the Clockmaker. "Darkness will not stop me!" He coughed in the smoke as he stumbled toward the moonlit balcony, heading for the globe.

Jack closed his eyes. He no longer needed them. The ripples from the chimes reflected off the stands and the bell hammers. They reflected off the windows and pillars. And they reflected off the Clockmaker and his beetles, too. Jack saw every bug as he raced to intercept the Frenchman—scarab-shaped silhouettes formed of glowing bronze. Lightning struck out from every one of them, but the bolts were easy to dodge.

The Frenchman reached the pedestal and shoved his hand into the globe, opening his fist. The Ember glowed a vibrant yellow. Dozens of smaller versions appeared on the faceted glass.

"Gwen!"

The clerk, glimmering in Jack's vision like a golden angel, turned his way and hurled the cane in a blind toss, end over end.

The Clockmaker heard the shout as well. He yanked his hand from the sphere and turned toward the sound, dousing the miniature embers. "You are finished, tracker!"

But Jack was already past him. He jumped, using the brick frame of the arched window to launch himself up and catch the cane, reversing direction in midair. As he came down, he pulled the shaft from the falcon head, unsheathing the sword inside. He brought the blade down on the wrist joint of the Clockmaker's armor, putting all the force of muscle and gravity into the swing.

The Frenchman screamed in pain, a real scream this time.

He stumbled backward onto the balcony and knocked over the pedestal as he passed.

The globe fell to the stone and shattered.

The severed fist, enclosing the Ember in an iron grip, dropped at Jack's feet.

The Clockmaker toppled backward over the rail.

Chapter 60

"I CAN'T *believe* the wardens never found him." Gwen plopped down in a high-backed chair, not unlike the chair from the room where she and Jack had found her uncle. "Not to mention Scotland Yard. Do you think perhaps he survived?"

Jack only shrugged, slipping his hand into his father's, careful to avoid the mass of tubes descending from the rack next to the bed. "They never found the clockwork beetles, either."

A troop of the largest men Jack had ever seen had stormed the belfry not long after the Clockmaker went over the rail—every one of them dressed in tweed, and not a few wearing bowlers. They had opened the tall windows on every side to clear the smoke. But even as the vapors drifted out into the night, the wind had dropped to a standstill. Lanterns had been hung from the platforms, and a tall figure in a straight black dress had entered the chamber, hefting an aged weather vane in her hand, one shaped like a tall ship. "We've been looking for this," Mrs. Hudson had said, her heels coming together with a definite *clop* right in front of Jack. Her stern gray eyes, nearly crossed in her handheld spectacles, had shifted down to the severed fist at his feet. "And I believe we've been looking for that as well."

Then they had all been whisked away, back to the Keep, where Jack and Gwen were treated for minor burns and smoke inhalation and put to bed, though Jack had not slept at all.

"When is he going to wake up?" asked Jack, gazing at his father's bandaged face. John Buckles Twelve had not opened his eyes since the clock chamber—not once.

"I believe it's too early to tell." A doctor entered the room, the same gray-haired man Jack had seen in the hall outside Percy's room the night before. Jack's mom entered behind him, followed by Sadie and Mrs. Hudson.

The doctor lifted a chart from the end of the antique bed and made a note. "Your father has suffered much. We think the Clockmaker went to great lengths in his efforts to find the Ember. There are signs of torture, drugs as well, great volumes of them. They'll take time to flush out. Until then, he is unlikely to awaken."

"Drugs?" Jack didn't understand. "But he spoke to me last night."

The doctor gave him a pleasant but condescending smile as he returned the chart to its hook. "I'm afraid that's impossible, young man."

"Jack." Gwen sat forward in her chair, concern clouding her face. "Your dad never woke up. He never said a word to you. I was there."

Jack opened his mouth to argue, then closed it again, narrowing his eyes. He gave the clerk a silent *Really?*

She nodded gravely.

That didn't make sense. He knew what he saw. Or did he? Absentmindedly, Jack reached into the pocket of his leather jacket. The red sphere with the gold lattice inlay was still there. He was sorely tempted to draw it out, but he found that Mrs. Hudson was staring right at him, so he left it there and quickly withdrew his hand.

Sadie touched his arm. "Daddy will get better, Jack. You're going to help him. You'll see."

"I'll return in an hour to check on the patient," said the doctor, nodding to Jack's mom and Mrs. Hudson as he left the room.

Once he was gone, Mrs. Hudson closed the door and raised her spectacles. "Now that you're all together, I suppose it is time to explain what we're going to do with you."

"Am I going to jail?" Sadie marched forward, only to be pulled back by her mother.

If Mrs. Hudson was capable of a smile, Jack thought he saw it then, though it was exceedingly difficult to tell. "No, child. The ministry handles the enforcement of its own regulations. Besides, you're too young for jail, or for too many rules in general just yet. Your mother, however, is another story."

Jack's mom squared her shoulders, drawing herself up to her not-too-considerable height. "I am ready to face the consequences of my actions, madam."

"And so you shall." Mrs. Hudson lowered her spectacles to the end of her nose. You and your husband violated your oaths. More than once. However, as he is still recovering, the ministry believes a form of house arrest is preferable to the lock-up. We will consent to a period of convalescence at House Buckles, and decide what is to follow later."

"You mean we get to stay in that warm old house down-stairs?" Sadie beamed.

Her mother squeezed her shoulder. "Yes, dear. Now hush."

"And what about me?" asked Jack. "What does the ministry plan to do with me?"

"*That* is the primary question, isn't it, Mr. Buckles? A question both of philosophy and legality." Mrs. Hudson raised a thin, gray eyebrow. "There are *some* who would quarantine you down on Sublevel Twenty-five with the snakes and the sour grapes. You are, after all, a thirteen-year-old thirteen showing rather strong tracker capabilities, much earlier than normal"—she tightened her gaze—"not to mention certain roguish tendencies."

Jack gave her a thin smile. "You can't put a Buckles with the snakes. That's the *S* aisle."

Mrs. Hudson frowned. "Case in point." She let out a breath through her pointed nose, softening her expression, if only a little. "There are . . . others . . . who argued in your favor. Had you, a thirteen, not intervened, the Twelfth Buckles would have surely died. *And* you managed to recover the Ember from the Clockmaker—no small feat. Then again—"

"*Get* to the *point*." Gwen practically exploded from the

high-backed chair, arms flopping to her sides. "What are they going to *do* with him?"

Mrs. Hudson scowled, the force of the look pressing the clerk down into the chair again. "*You*, Miss Kincaid, displayed a *deplorable* disregard for Section Thirteen protocols yesterday. You overstepped the meager authorities of your office on *numerous* occasions. Sadly, the ministry believes you will continue to do so, and redirecting your energies seems an eminently easier task than suppressing them." Mrs. Hudson pursed her lips, pointedly clearing her throat before continuing. "Thus, contrary to reason and good sense, you are hereby promoted to journeyman clerk, with an immediate change of post." She lowered the spectacles and nodded toward Jack. "We are going to train him, Miss Kincaid. *That* is what we are going to do with him. And you will be his guide."

"You're . . . going to train me as a tracker?" Jack had a hard time spitting out the words. He had fully expected some type of brig or lab rat scenario. He had not expected a job.

"Don't restate the obvious, Mr. Buckles. That sort of thing is so terribly American. But, yes, the ministry thinks it best to mold you as we may, although you will not be a full tracker for some time—if ever." She shot another scowl at Gwen. "Among the *many* words that escaped Miss Kincaid's lips over the last twenty-four hours—most of them secrets—she may have failed to mention that all trackers begin their ministry service either as apprentice clerks or apprentice wardens." She raised the spectacles again, tracking them down to Jack's toes and back up to the tips of his hair. "And I think we can all agree you are far too small to be a warden."

Sadie left her mother's side and threw her arms around Jack. "Did you hear that? We all get to stay here together!"

Jack couldn't help but smile. There were worse outlooks for a thirteen-year-old than being moved into a manor house and inducted into a secret society of detectives. As he hugged his sister back, he noticed Mrs. Hudson reaching back to rap on the door. Immediately, an arm slipped through, handed her a clipboard, and slipped out again.

Mrs. Hudson crossed the room and pressed the clipboard into his hands. "No time like the present to get started, eh, Apprentice Clerk Buckles?"

Jack examined the papers. There were green pages on the top, pink on the bottom. The topmost page appeared to have been reconstructed from charred pieces. He could make out

Gwen's handwriting on a few of the lines, and he recognized the form number in the top left corner: 26-B-2.

Mrs. Hudson withdrew a pen from her sleeve and handed it over, showing that somewhat-possible smile again. "Welcome to the Ministry of Trackers, Mr. Buckles. All forms *must* be completed."

ACKNOWLEDGMENTS

The word "author" sounds lonely. I think it's the leading *A*. But there are dozens who walk with an author for one mile or another along the journey of a book. And some walk beside him the whole way. My wife is one of the latter. On top of all her love and support, she is a daily part of my writing process. She reads, critiques, and brainstorms. If not for her, there would be no calico cat. It was she who demanded that I finally man up and pitch Jack Buckles to my agent Harvey Klinger, who was expecting something else entirely. Harvey greeted the idea with all his usual encouragement and handed the thing over to Sara Crowe, the best children's literature agent ever. I am so grateful to all three of you. You gave Jack his first breaths.

Acknowledgments

And I am grateful to David Gale for his faith in this project, and to Liz Kossnar, Jen Strada, and all the others who placed their expertise, hard work, and enthusiasm behind this story through Simon & Schuster Books for Young Readers. You've made this process an absolute joy.

Others shaped this book through help, critique, and encouragement. John first, as always, James and Ashton, Rachel and Katie, Steve and Tawnya, Nancy and Dan, Randy and Hulda, the other Nancy, the Millers, Scott and Ethan, Seth and Gavin, and the Barons. Lastly, Adey Grummet of All Hallows by the Tower proved gracious and invaluable in aiding my research. Thank you all so much.

Turn the page
for a sneak peek at
The Fourth Ruby.

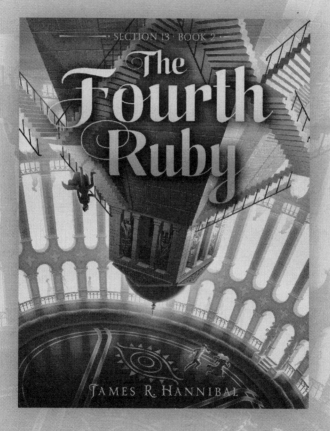

NIGHT HAD FALLEN on London's Baker Street. The orange glow of the streetlamps reflected off pavement that seemed perpetually wet. A good number of pedestrians still walked the sidewalks, mostly heading home from the cafés. Teatime had barely passed, and in London, tea was more than just hot drinks.

A little south of Regent's Park and a little north of the Baker Street Tube station—near 221B—one particular pedestrian opened his palm and let an etched gold cube drop to the ground. He kept on walking. No one shouted after the man to tell him he had dropped something. No one noticed at all.

The cube clinked and clacked like a metal die, only not quite the same, thanks to tiny gems at each of the eight corners. It paused once, balancing on a single jewel for an unnatural space of time, then rolled on for another meter or so before coming to a complete stop. There it sat in the grime, glittering and anonymous, as a group of twenty-somethings strolled by. Their scarves and their laughing faces were reflected in a darkened shop window, amid lettering that read LOST PROPERTY OFFICE.

Once the laughing pedestrians were safely past, the cube shook and bobbled. Its sides split open, unfolding into eight spindly legs, each crowned with one of the tiny gems. The spider pushed itself up. It lifted a bulbous glass abdomen filled with sickly green syrup and then skittered across the pavement to climb a rainspout, utterly oblivious to the irony of its actions. Reaching the top unscathed, it raced across the roof, spiraled its way up a steaming vent pipe, and disappeared inside.

The creature descended for what seemed like ages, spiked feet clicking all the way. It took several branches, making lefts and rights into joining pipes, but always it continued downward, deep into a massive, secret underground tower known as the Keep.

Finally, the spider came within view of a blazing fire and

slowed. It crept, inch by inch, to the underside of a great mahogany hearth, training its tiny cameras on a pair of children seated in high-backed velvet chairs in an otherwise dark room. The boy, a teenager, sat staring into the blaze. The girl, younger, her tiny form dwarfed by the Victorian chair, gazed at him with an expression of concern. After a moment, the boy stood to inspect the hearth, and the spider scrambled back out of sight.

Then again, there might never have been a spider in the first place. Maybe the gold flashes the boy saw in his mind's eye had nothing to do with a metal cube or tiny gems clacking on pavement. Maybe the silvery spikes had not been the clickety-clicks of a clockwork spider skittering down a pipe. Maybe the glittering confetti he saw had not been pedestrian laughter at all. Maybe the boy had imagined the whole thing.

Jack Buckles, a tracker by birth, had been struggling with his unusually keen senses. A year before, he had defeated a grown man in a smoky bell tower using only sound and feel to guide his actions. But these days, even the noisy Quantum Electrodynamic Drones—better known as QEDs—that hummed around the Ministry of Trackers could sneak up on him. Jack's senses had been failing him for months.

Of course, on the off chance Jack's senses had been correct, if a clockwork spider had really crawled down into the Keep to look for him, then that would be very, very bad.

JACK RETURNED TO HIS CHAIR, keeping his eyes on the fireplace. He could feel the weight of the inverted underground tower above him, with its black stone walls and unending levels filled with wood-paneled corridors. The Keep had become his prison. The Ministry of Trackers, the youngest of England's secretive Elder Ministries—behind the Ministry of Guilds, the Ministry of Secrets, and the Ministry of Dragons—had become home for his whole family, whether they liked it or not.

"You don't look so good," said Sadie, watching as he eased himself down in the chair again.

"I'm nervous. That's all."

Sadie pulled her ankles up into a cross-legged position

beneath her dress and leaned her elbows on her knees, auburn hair flopping forward. She stared at Jack as if she could see right through his skull and into his messed-up tracker brain. "No. That's not it."

Jack shot her a frown. "I've asked you not to do that."

His sister ignored the protest and shifted her eyes to an ornately carved mahogany door looming in the darkness behind his chair. "Is it time for you to go yet?"

"Yes." Jack did not stir.

Sadie seemed unperturbed by the contradiction between his answer and his actions. Her face remained as placid as ever. "Is the professor coming?" she asked, referring to Edward Tanner, the only remaining tracker of the eleventh generation. He wasn't known as *the professor* simply because he was Jack's teacher and mentor. Long retired from the usual ministry work, the elderly tracker now maintained tenure as a history professor up at Cambridge.

"He's molding young minds tonight."

"What about Gwen?"

Jack had known that question was coming. He sighed. "I don't think so."

"Because she's mad at you?"

"No."

"Because you're working with Ash now?"

"No." He gave a little shrug. "Maybe."

"Because Ash is a journeyman quartermaster, and Gwen is only a clerk?"

Jack said nothing.

"But you're only a clerk."

"Sadie." He gave her a *that's-enough* glare and the room fell silent for several seconds. It wouldn't last. It never did.

"Soooo, *why* can't she go with you?"

Jack rubbed his head. It hurt. Gwen hadn't shown up to see him off—twice in a row now. It wasn't his fault that he'd been assigned to a real quartermaster. And it wasn't his fault he couldn't study with her every day, or eat with her, or do whatever Gwen wanted to do whenever Gwen wanted to do it. His dad needed him. Couldn't she see that?

Jack slipped a hand into the pocket of his dad's leather jacket, the one he had taken as his own when he first found the armory and equipment locker in his dad's study. He wrapped his palm around a little red sphere with gold lattice-work, letting the silky pink coolness of the stone seep into his fingers. Feelings, sounds, smells—they all had color and texture to him, a side effect of his crisscrossed tracker senses.

He closed his eyes and released a long breath through

his nose. That same sphere had given him a brief connection to his dad the year before, on the night he had rescued him and confronted the Clockmaker at the top of Big Ben. On his return to the Keep, Jack had found a tiny scrap of packing paper folded up on the sphere's place in the armory, marked with a curvy Z. So he had named it the *zed*. After that night, no matter how hard he tried, he had never been able to reproduce the connection with his dad. He kept the zed with him at all times anyway. It calmed him, helped him think, helped him be the tracker everyone expected him to be. He couldn't say why. Maybe it gave him power. Maybe it gave him a little bit of his dad's tracker mojo. There were stranger artifacts with stranger abilities everywhere within the Keep.

The pain in Jack's head subsided, and he realized Sadie was standing over him. With the zed to settle him, he could see her without opening his eyes—by the blue-gray whisper of her breathing and the tan, sandpapery shuffle of her feet. He looked up anyway, because he wanted her to see the annoyance in his expression. "*What*, Sadie?"

"They're waiting for you." She glanced over at the big shadowed door. "All of them."

It was Sadie who finally opened the mahogany door,

leaning her little body back into the pull, with Jack standing reluctantly behind her. He winced as a thrumming white light assaulted his mixed-up senses, along with the bronze hum of the QEDs, and a black murmur of whispers. It was noise, all of it. But Jack could still make out some of the words.

Tracker.

Section Thirteen.

Freak.

Didn't they know he could hear them?

Jack left his sister in the little room and walked out onto a cobblestone lane. There were quaint cottage facades on either side. French, maybe. He couldn't tell yet. He crossed over to a broad semicircular platform set between two houses, and stepped up to a bronze rail to get a better look at what he was up against. Below him, level after level of arching bridges, steep stairways, and narrow streets were interwoven to form a village stacked upon itself. *English,* he thought, scanning the flats and storefronts that formed the circular periphery of every level. *Definitely English. What else?* Every home and store on the periphery was a mere facade—elaborate set dressings—but the eyes in the windows were real enough.

Section Thirteen.

Freak.

He shook his head, pushing back a creeping pain that shouldn't have been there—not after a year of training. Gray mist swirled in the light above him and in the darkness of the bottom level far below. The arena was so huge that it had its own weather system, gathering moisture in its upper and lower extremes. Sometimes, according to Gwen at least, it rained. Jack had never seen it. Then again, this was only his second time to enter the crucible. The bronze hum rolling across his brain intensified and two quad-style QEDs descended out of the clouds. Blue light glowed within round engine housings. Their cameras shifted to keep him in focus. Mrs. Hudson's voice, stern and cold, echoed from an unseen loudspeaker.

"Attention. The tracker has entered the arena. The Hunt is on."

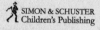

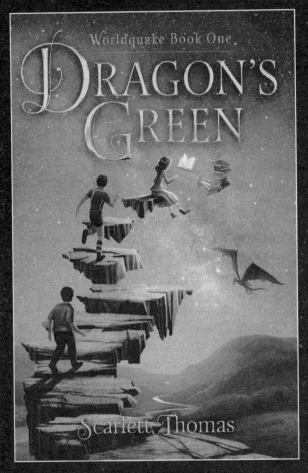

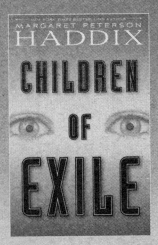

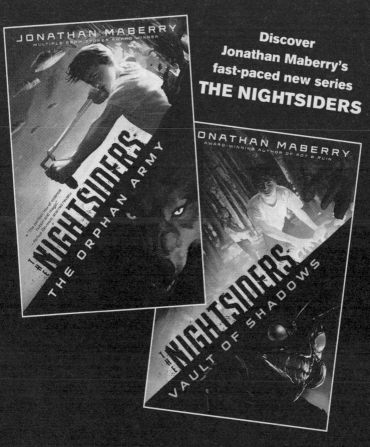